The Prince of Warwood
and
The Sword of
the Chosen

J. Noel Clinton

ISBN: 978-0-9773115-2-1

LCCN: 2013902927

The Prince of Warwood
and

The Sword of the Chosen

J. Noel Clinton

Chapter 1

The Trek

Dublin Minnows was dead! He was dead, and it was all Xavier's fault. It didn't matter how many times his father tried to reassure him that there was nothing he could have done. The fact of the matter was that his father and the prophet had lied to him. He knew without a doubt that he could have saved Mr. Minnows. Surely somewhere deep inside him he possessed an ability that could have prevented his murder. After all, with the prophet's help, he called upon such a power to save his uncle. His ability to heal Mike when no healer could only confirmed Xavier's suspicions. Dublin Minnows had died for nothing.

Xavier Wells stumbled up the mountainside as his gaze flickered repeatedly toward Robbie walking solemnly next to her mother. Robbie had been his best friend since kindergarten. She had always been there and stood by him, but now that he was responsible for her father's death, she despised him and hadn't spoken to him in over two weeks. Heck, she wouldn't even look at him. She hated him. God! Robbie hated him.

At this thought, his chest tightened as regret clamped its cold, clammy hand around his lungs, leaving him shivering and gasping for his next breath. Tears flooded his eyes, and as he hastily swiped them away, his foot snagged on a root. His body pitched forward, and he nearly landed face-first into the trunk of a large beech. His father's strong hands caught him inches from the tree.

"Whoa! Easy now. Take it slow." His smooth, deep voice steadied Xavier's reeling emotions.

He looked up at his father's rugged, stubble-covered face and nodded.

"How're you holding up, son?" he asked.

He shrugged. He couldn't very well tell his father that he still felt responsible for...well, everything. His father wouldn't understand. He would only talk and talk and talk, trying to convince him that he wasn't responsible and that it wasn't his fault when everything in Xavier's gut told him differently.

Dublin Minnows wasn't the only death on his conscience. His mother had been killed by the same sick psychopath. Julia Wells had been searching for him when William LeMasters took her. LeMasters was hell-bent on causing misery for his father through any means necessary, and when he hadn't succeeded in doing that through Xavier, he kidnapped and butchered Julia. But, it never would have happened if Xavier hadn't run away from home following an argument with his grandparents.

From the moment he was born, his grandparents had loathed him. For years, he never understood why. Then, about ten months ago, he learned the truth. He was an empowered human with supernatural, magical powers. But even in this amazing world, he was still quite extraordinary. First, he possessed an unusual number of abilities for a boy his age. Most twelve year old children had one or two abilities whereas he had five, well six if you counted the dream premonitions. Furthermore, Xavier Wells was the future ruler of Warwood, a kingdom full of these special humans. He'd never known popularity and fame like he found in his father's world. In Warwood, he was a celebrity, and since he was the spitting image of his father, his white curly hair was a constant beacon of his status. He received little relief from the constant stares, revered whispers, and general attention that being the Prince of Warwood brought with it.

"Are you sure you're all right?" his father questioned, interrupting his thoughts.

"Yes, sir. How much farther to the next campsite?" he muttered, trying to change the subject.

"Another mile, two at the most," he answered.

"Sire?" A tall, muscular man with blond hair jogged up to move into step next to the king. "Have you heard from Henrick and the men gathering supplies in Bern?"

"Yes, Loren. I contacted them yesterday. They've gotten the supplies and are already on their way to King's Mountain. We should expect them in a few days," Jeremiah responded.

As the men's conversation drifted to setting up and running their new home at King's Mountain, Xavier looked at the group of thirty silently following them. It was sad to think how they had ended up here. Just three weeks before, they were all nestled happily in their own homes, safe and warm. Now they were refugees, and LeMasters had control of their kingdom. With a heavy sigh, his eyes fell on Lana Applegate, and his guilt rose to new heights as his thoughts drifted to her daughter, Maggie.

Mr. Minnows and his mother had both died protecting Xavier whereas Maggie Applegate had died senselessly. A faithful servant of William LeMasters had released a deadly virus, killing Maggie and nine other children of mixed lineage, children who had both a common and an empowered parent. Of the eleven children infected, Xavier had been the only survivor, and he felt guilty for that. If it hadn't been for his father, he would have died as well. In order to save him, his father had broken the law and used the King's Key, to provide himself with healing powers. Afterwards, he had been arrested and endured a royal caning for misusing the magical staff. This brutal punishment was just one more thing to add to the growing list of things he felt guilty about.

He looked at Mrs. Applegate again. She walked apart from the others, and to Xavier, she looked lonely and depressed. Leaving the men to their conversation, he drifted back into the crowd until he fell into step beside her. She looked down at him with surprise before smiling. His gut fluttered madly.

"Hi," he muttered. "I just thought that maybe you'd like to have someone to walk with."

"That would be nice, Your Highness. Thank you," she replied, draping an arm over his shoulders. "How are you doing, Xavier?"

He shrugged. "Okay, I guess. How are you?"

"Well...it's hard sometimes. I don't have any family left now," she answered softly, tears swelling in her eyes.

Xavier took her hand and whispered, "You're not alone...you have me...I'll be your family. I know it's not the same, but without you, Dad would have faced a lot more than a caning. He could have gone to prison or...worse."

"The boy's right," Jeremiah added smoothly as he stepped into stride with them. "I owe you my undying allegiance, Lana."

Her cheeks deepened in color as she responded softly, "I only did what I thought was right and just, my king."

Near sunset, the group finally reached the last

campsite on their journey to King's Mountain. Most of the group simply collapsed on the spot, exhausted.

"Come on, son. Let's help with gathering firewood," Jeremiah suggested hoarsely, patting Xavier's shoulder.

Once the campfire was ablaze, the group began unrolling their sleeping bags around its warmth. Rations of trail-mix, beef jerky, and water were distributed among the group as they settled around the fire. Other than a few soft conversations, the group was extraordinarily quiet.

It didn't escape Xavier's attention that Robbie settled on the opposite side of the fire with her mother and the Jeffersons. She was still doing her best to avoid him, and he couldn't blame her. He deserved everything she dished out and more, but he wasn't sure how much more of her silent treatment he could handle.

"Son?" his father coaxed gently from beside him. "Try and get some rest; you look exhausted."

"Yes, sir," he mumbled, snuggling down into his sleeping bag.

Lana's sleeping bag was next to his where she sat motionless, staring into the fire as if in a trance. In many ways, Lana reminded him of his mother. Her hair was long and dark like his mother's had been, and she had an easy smile that made him feel special and that nothing mattered to her more than to be in his company. But, also like his mother, her eyes were terribly sad, and whenever she smiled, he didn't know whether to smile back or cry.

Unable to tolerate the haunting despair on her face any longer, he grasped her hand and whispered, "Goodnight, Mrs. Applegate."

She dragged her gaze from the fire and stared blankly down at him. For a moment, she didn't seem to recognize him. Finally, she smiled her sad smile, leaned toward him, and kissed his cheek.

"Goodnight, sweetheart."

Xavier slept fitfully. Nightmares continued to plague him. Long gone were the nightmares of his mother's torturous death. The nightmares he had now were usually of his father's caning or Dublin Minnows' assassination. However, this night, he dreamt of Robbie.

He found himself in a damp cell, chained to the wall with lead shackles. Even though he was drenched in sweat, he shivered, and his entire body throbbed as though he had been beaten by a metal pipe. Then, the cell door swung open with a groan, and Robbie entered the room, smiling.

"Oh! Thank God! Robbie! Robbie, please, help me!" he pleaded.

But Robbie didn't move and didn't answer. She continued to stare at him with the same peculiar smile.

Befuddled, he questioned. "Why are you smiling, Robbie? Look, you need to hurry; they'll be back any minute. Please, unchain me!"

Finally, she moved forward but stopped just feet from him. The strange grin fell from her face as anger and malice shadowed over her delicate features.

He shivered again and stammered, "R...Robbie?"

"Murderer!" she hissed.

"No, Robbie! It wasn't my fault. I tried to..."

"MURDERER!" she screeched, pulling a long gleaming sword out from under her cloak and lunging at him.

Xavier's eyes snapped open, and for an instant, he forgot where he was; then he remembered—the campsite. It was still dark and the fire was low. His father sat next to the fire stoking it and placing more kindling on the glowing coals.

"Sire, you really should get some sleep," Lana

whispered.

"I'm fine," he replied quietly.

She studied him in silence for a moment before rising from her sleeping bag and moving to sit next to him.

"King Wells, you won't be of any use to anyone if you pass out from exhaustion," she told him, lightly touching his arm.

He looked at her then, and the couple sat in silence, simply staring at one another. Finally, he whispered, "I'll be fine, Lana. How are you holding up?"

She blinked and responded hoarsely, "I...I'm managing."

The king turned and grasped her shoulders gently. "Only managing?"

Lana turned away, and Xavier watched as her fire-illuminated face twisted into grief and her chin quivered. A single tear rolled down her cheek as she whispered, "It's just that...when Peter died, I had Maggie to think about...I didn't have time to grieve, you know?"

"Yes, I know," his father cooed as he pulled her into his arms.

Her body shook as she fought to keep the sobs at bay, and she groaned, "But, now...now...I have nothing...they're both g...gone!" Her valiant struggle over her grief was lost, and she simply broke down.

Jeremiah held her close as she cried. "Oh, Lana. I'm so, so sorry. I wish it all could have been prevented."

The next day, the trek to King's Mountain became more treacherous and difficult. The group made slow progress as they scrambled and climbed up the steep mountainside. At sunset, Jeremiah led them to a sheer wall of rock. The weary crowd gathered around him and watched in silence as he ran his hand over the rough surface. After a moment, the king stepped back and raised his hand. Suddenly, a loud crack pierced the air and a low rumble began to build deep inside the mountain, shaking the earth beneath their feet. There was a moment of alarm and the group huddled together like frightened deer. Then, slowly, the great mountainside opened, revealing a wide passage lit by torches. Jeremiah turned to the group with a wide grin.

"Welcome to King's Mountain," he announced cheerfully.

The group instantly relaxed and smiled.

"Come. Let's take a look at our new home," he called, ushering the group inside the mountain.

Once inside, King Wells waved his hand, and the mountain closed up behind them. The group made their way down the long, seemingly endless passage. Xavier wasn't sure how long they walked, but at long last, they came upon a pair of towering metal doors, made of lead no less.

Again, with a wave of the king's hand, the massive doors creaked and squealed open. The doors revealed a spectacular sight! An enormous corridor made of the strangest stone Xavier had ever seen stretched out before them. There was no need for torches in this chamber as the silvery-gold, granite-like stone emitted a soft light of its own. The unusual stone was polished smooth and jutting out from the walls stood a dozen or more towering stone figures, each wearing a cloak and a royalty sash with initials carved into it. The passage held a silent yet powerful energy that tugged and whispered at Xavier's consciousness. The immense force of the room vibrated through him and burrowed its way into his soul, and he shivered.

His father's hand grasped his shoulder with a gentle,

reassuring squeeze as he announced, "Welcome to the Cavern of Kings, the entrance into King's Mountain. These statues are replicas of all the past kings of Warwood. At one time, they stood at the entrance to the ruins, but when the ruins fell into disarray, the kings were moved here. Legend has it that in times of danger, the kings of old would light the way to safety for those loyal to Warwood. And, it appears that the legend is true." He paused as the group responded in awe before adding sardonically, "Legend also says that when called upon by the king, the statues would rise up and smite the enemy."

The group snickered.

"Have you ever tried it?" Xavier asked, staring up at the ominous figures.

"No son," he snickered. "It's only a story. The statues don't really come to life to do the king's bidding. But, if you open your mind and listen, they can talk."

"Really? Have they ever talked to you? What did they say?" he questioned.

His father smiled secretively down at him. "Ah, my dear prince, what the kings of the past have to say to the rightful reigning king must never be repeated, but their message to me was invaluable. When you're king, you will come and speak to them."

Xavier looked up at the statues that looked more like real men frozen and held captive in time and shuddered. As the group continued down the corridor and drew closer to the figures, the energy filling the corridor intensified, leaving Xavier panting for breath. Anxiously, he peered up at the colossal men and staggered into his father. Jeremiah steadied him and peered down at him with fretful, questioning eyes. Xavier could only answer with a befuddled look and a weak shrug. Finally, they came upon a pair of doors made of the same strange stone as the cavern.

With a wave of his hand, Jeremiah muttered, "As King, I command you to open."

The doors opened soundlessly, and Xavier found that his awe didn't end at the Cavern of Kings. The doors led into the largest open chamber Xavier had ever seen. It was as broad as the Governing Hall and easily as high, but even more magnificent than the chamber's dwarfing size was its detail. Columns as broad as twenty men jutted toward the ceiling, and the highly polished limestone walls glittered like the night sky.

In the center of the spacious room sat a gigantic crystal arboretum. Lush trees and plant life strained against the transparent walls, and he could even hear birds chirping happily inside. But, what amazed him most was the sunlight flooding over the arboretum like a great spotlight.

"Dad? How can there be sunlight in here when we're in the heart of a mountain?" Xavier asked, squinting up at the light.

"The sunlight is redirected through a type of ventilation pipe that uses special crystals to magnify and intensify the light," Jeremiah answered.

"Cool. I didn't know crystals could do that," Xavier muttered, taking in the sight once more.

The king chuckled. "Yes, it's quite ingenious. The entire level above us uses this lighting system to cultivate a series of gardens that will provide us with fresh produce. The mountain is very nearly self-sufficient. With the exception of meat and a few other odds and ends, the mountain has everything we could possibly need. Come, our people are waiting for us in the Grand Hall. We will celebrate our arrival with a hot meal," Jeremiah announced, leading them through the chamber and into a broad corridor.

Chapter 2

Arrival

As the group approached the large oak doors to the Grand Hall, muffled voices and laughter grew louder, and a delicious aroma battered their senses. With a brief glance at the group, King Wells opened the door and entered the chamber, his back straight and his head held high. Instantly, the chattering stopped and hundreds of heads turned in their direction. In unison, everyone stood and began applauding and cheering.

Jeremiah reached for Xavier's hand and led him past row after row of tables to where Ephraim and his family sat at the head table, elevated on a platform a couple of feet above the others. As they made their way to the front of the hall, a wave of bows followed them. Once they stood behind their seats at the head table, Jeremiah waved at the crowd, and slowly they grew quiet.

"Wow, thank you, but I'm not sure I deserve all of that! We have a lot to discuss, but first, let's eat a good hot meal that, as I understand, Lieutenant Blake's group has prepared," Jeremiah announced, and again the crowd burst into cheers and applause.

Once the hall grew quiet again, he continued, "Ladies and gentlemen, let's have a moment of silence and prayer before the meal is served."

Everyone bowed their heads, many kneeling to the floor, including the king. Xavier quickly did the same. Then he said a quick prayer of thanks, crossed himself, and stood, eager to eat something hot for a change. His father was one of the last to finish praying, but he guessed that being king gave him a lot more to pray about. Finally, Jeremiah crossed himself, stood, and took his seat.

The first meal at King's Mountain was a modest one: hot rolls and a vegetarian soup since Henrick's group hadn't arrived yet with meats and other supplies. At least, it was hot and filling. As the group finished their meals, kitchen volunteers began collecting the dishes.

"Did you get enough to eat, son?" Jeremiah asked, rubbing Xavier's back.

"Yes, sir! The soup was great! I'm so sick of beef jerky! If I never eat it again, I'll die happy," he responded, leaning back in his chair and rubbing his stomach.

His father smiled. "I understand what you mean. A man can live only so long on leathery, dried out meat," he remarked, still grinning. "Well, we better get on with the meeting so we can settle in and get a good night's sleep. It will be nice to sleep on something other than the cold, hard ground for a change. Which, I must admit, I was getting pretty sick of," he replied, winking at Xavier as he stood.

The crowd in the Hall grew quiet almost instantly.

"Ladies and gentlemen! I would like to extend another thanks to Lieutenant Blake and his group for choosing to be the first arrivals and preparing this magnificent meal." The people erupted loudly, and it was several minutes before the king could continue. "Now, the mountain is very capable of housing and supporting our needs, but we must work together to keep it running smoothly. No one is excluded from contributing to the good of the group. At the back table, there are sheets to sign up for jobs and chores. We will need cooks, custodians, gardeners, laundresses, tailors, teachers, miners, and much, much more." He smirked at the indignant expressions on the children's faces and watched as a few mouthed "teachers" in disbelief. "Yes, children. I did say teachers. There will be schooling."

There was a loud collective groan from the children followed by light laughter from their parents.

"Now, some jobs are very demanding, whereas others are not. If you choose a less demanding job from the yellow sign up lists, then I ask you to choose a chore from the white pages. I repeat, no citizen over the age of five is excluded from choosing a chore or job, your king least of all. Aside from overseeing and maintaining defenses and security, I will also instruct all men ages sixteen and older in military strategies in the Grand Hall from one to three. Also, I will be supervising the boys' dormitory once a week and teaching a Latin class. Aside from your studies, children, you too will assist in the upkeep of this facility. For two hours every evening, every child over the age of five will complete a chore of their choosing from the list on the back table. Your prince has already been assigned his chore. Xavier will be helping to sweep and mop the Grand Hall after dinner. So, as you can see, no one is excluded, and everyone will pitch in to help."

Xavier's head whipped up, and he felt his temper rising. *"Father? How come I don't get to choose my own chore?"* he asked heatedly, using his telepathic ability. He would have preferred something else, and from the looks of it, it would take him all evening to mop the Grand Hall. But the only indication he received that his father heard his grievance was a brief pause and a sideways glance at him.

He stared indignantly up at his father as he continued with the announcements. It appeared that he wasn't going to answer him. "Geez!" Xavier grumbled, throwing himself back into his seat and muttering a string of curses. When a few citizens near the head table stared at him, he crossed his arms moodily and sulked.

Ephraim was at his side in an instant, firmly taking him by the arm. "Young sire, please stand and follow me," he whispered.

"Why?" he hissed indignantly.

Ephraim squatted to eye level with the boy and pinned him with an angry glare. "Because I told you to, Prince Wells. Now get to your feet before I throw you over my shoulder and carry you out," he growled quietly.

Huffing bitterly, he stood, shoved in his chair with a bang, and stomped out of the hall with his father's general on his heels. Once outside the hall, Ephraim grabbed him and spun him around, his face unmasked with fury.

"Master Wells, this isn't an easy situation for any of us...leaving our homes...our city...we must ALL make sacrifices. But most of all, this has been phenomenally difficult for your father! As king, he is responsible for Warwood and its people, and the taking of his city and the lives lost as a result has taken a piece of him. He is responsible and therefore his guilt is beyond anything I could imagine, and I hope beyond anything you'll ever endure. Now, stop acting like a spoiled brat and making things tougher than they need to be, or I'll bare your bottom and spank you myself!"

Xavier ducked his head against Ephraim's onslaught of reprimands. Finally, he whispered, "I...I'm sorry. I didn't mean to...make things worse and act like...I...I'm sorry, sir. I just wanted the chance to choose my chore like everyone else, that's all."

Ephraim's face relaxed. "I'm sure your dad has a good reason for choosing it for you. So, instead of throwing a tantrum, maybe you should ask him about it when the time is right."

"Yes, sir," he muttered, not meeting the general's eyes.

"Now, I think your dad deserves to hear an apology. Why don't we go back in and you tell him?"

"Yes, sir," he responded.

When they entered the Grand Hall, Jeremiah was wrapping up the last of the announcements. "Now, I think it's time for the adults to have a more detailed, serious discussion. Would the children please go with the adults standing at the back of the hall? They'll show you the classrooms, gymnasium, and game room."

"Xavier? Come here," his father's voice thronged firmly into his thoughts.

He tore his eyes away from the streams of children following Loren, Rebecca, and half a dozen other adults and looked instead at his father's displeased, hard face.

"Father...I...I'm sorry. Ephraim's already talked with me. Can't I go with the kids?" he questioned silently.

"No, do as you're told and come here," he responded.

"Come on, X!" Court hollered, waving at him.

"Xavier, now!" the king warned aloud, his voice impatient.

"I'll catch up," he told Court and slumped over to his father.

The moment Xavier was within his reach, Jeremiah grabbed him and pulled him to stand in front of him. The king stood with his back to the crowd, but Xavier wasn't spared from the crowd's prying eyes. Many were watching as much as they could of the exchange between their king and prince.

"I do not appreciate your pompous, indignant attitude,

young man. Your chore is necessary to ensure that our citizens view you as a humble, hard-working prince. They must see that even their king and prince are willing to pull their own weight without favoritism. That is why your chore was chosen for you. Now, I need to start this meeting. We'll finish this discussion later. Please go with Loren and join the other children while I finish up here," Jeremiah ordered, sending Xavier towards the door with a sharp smack to his bottom. To the casual observer, the act looked like nothing more than a fatherly playful smack, but to Xavier, it stung like a warning. He rubbed his backside, listening to the light snickers from the group in the hall as he approached Loren, waiting in the doorway.

When he stepped into stride with Loren, he held up his hand to block yet another round of reprimands. "Please, Loren, don't lecture me too. I've had an earful already."

Loren smiled as he led him down the hall toward the gymnasium. "Yeah, I imagine so. Things will be a little different here, little sire. With everyone in such close quarters, every adult will be watching out for you kids and disciplining you as well."

Xavier muttered, "Yeah, I'm figuring that out."

Chapter 3

King's Mountain

Xavier followed Loren into a busy corridor. Sir Blaire stood rigidly in the middle of the walkway, supervising the hall between the library and the gymnasium. A group of boys ran out of the gym and nearly collided with him.

"Oi! No running in the corridors! If you want to run around like ninnies, stay in the gym," he chastised. One of the boys shot Blaire a dirty look, and he nearly came unglued. "Are you eyeballing me, boy? Don't test me, or you'll find your backside sore!"

"Xavier! Come on! You're missing all the fun!" Beck called, grabbing his arm and hauling him into the games room where his friends surrounded a foosball table watching Court and Garrett's heated game.

"Bloody hell!" Court shouted when Garrett scored and took the lead.

"Courtney Aaron!" his mother snapped. "Watch your language! There are small children present!"

"Sorry, Mum," he groaned, rolling his eyes.

"Don't roll your eyes at me, young man!" she bellowed, grabbing him by the ear and hauling him away from the game.

"Ow! Mum, I'm in the middle of ...Ow...a game. Ow!"

he protested.

"Hardcastle forfeits! I won! Who's next?" Garrett bellowed.

"Me!" Beck announced. "Come on, little man. Let's see what you've got!"

As his friends exploded with laughter and banters, Xavier saw Mackenzie Clarke standing off to the side and watching them. Mac's father had aided Governor Yaman in his conspiracy and unwittingly helped William LeMasters invade and capture the kingdom. As a result, Timmins Clarke had fallen from grace and had been caned and demoted for his crimes. He was no longer an elite member of the prestigious Premier Royal Guard. Now, he held the rank of private in the regular Royal Guard. Even Mac's best friend, Ken Calhoun, was gone. Ken and his family were traitors and had remained behind in the kingdom with LeMasters. Mac was alone. He couldn't help but feel sorry for him. So, he approached the other boy.

"Hey, Mac," he greeted quietly.

Mac went rigid as though he expected Xavier to thrash him.

"Relax, mate," he soothed. "I just came over to see if you wanted to hang out with us."

"I...I don't think...*they* want me to," he replied, nodding towards Beck and Garrett, who had paused in their game to glare at him.

"Yo! X! What'cha doing?" Beck asked.

Xavier didn't answer, but turned back to Mackenzie. "Naw, if you're with me, they'll be okay with it. Come on."

Slowly, Mac nodded and followed him back to the group.

"What do you think you're doing, Clarke?" Beck challenged, stepping toward the other boy.

"Back off, Beck. I invited him," Xavier interrupted.

"What? Why would you do something like that? Mac and Ken did nothing but make your life miserable!"

"That may be true, but he's one of us now, an exile. He's loyal to my dad and for that, I'm willing to give him another chance!"

Beck glared at Mac as though he could think of several other things he would rather do, but finally he nodded.

"Hey, you guys! Did you know they actually have a rugby pitch in this place?" Court announced, returning from his mother's lecture.

"No way!" Garrett gasped with disbelief. "A rugby pitch? In here? You're mental, Hardcastle. How is that even possible?"

"I'm serious! I heard Dad and Sir Blaire talking about it. It's located on the garden level. Sir Blaire said that the facility custodian...Oi, did you know that four families have been living in this mountain for the past ten years taking care of the crops and keeping things in order just in case we'd ever need to live here? How weird is that? Can you imagine living your entire life in a mountain?"

"Court!" Beck spat. "The rugby pitch?"

"Oh, yeah. Right. The rugby pitch. Well, I guess it was supposed to be another garden, but the head custodian discovered that he didn't need it. So he planted grass and made it into a rugby pitch," he told them.

"Whoa! Let's go see it!" Beck exclaimed, and the mob of boys raced out into the corridor.

"Ah, guys. How do we get to the garden level?" Garrett asked.

"Maybe there's a stairwell or something," Xavier suggested.

"Oi! What are you ankle biters up to?" Loren called.

"We were going to go and check out the rugby pitch on the garden level," Court answered.

"Sorry, boys. Not tonight. The meeting should be over any minute, and then ..." Loren stopped mid-sentence when the Grand Hall doors banged open and throngs of adults spilled out into the corridor.

"Okay, boys, into the gym," he ordered, shooing them toward the door and following them inside.

"Okay, listen up, boys and girls," Loren called over the laughter and ruckus. "First, you'll need to put away the equipment you've dragged out. Then, I need all of you to find a seat on the gym floor. Girls on the left. Boys on the right. King Wells will be here shortly to speak with you."

The children immediately swept into action. Xavier made his way with his friends toward the right side of the gymnasium. Robbie was several feet from him, sitting between Erica and a curly, blonde-headed girl. She sat silently, staring off at nothing in particular. She looked so sad. Her large, dark eyes mirrored the grief in her soul. Guilt swept through him like a frigid wind, and he struggled to push back the strong impulse to cry. As he rubbed his eyes irritably, he collided with a hard, unforgiving barrier and fell to the floor. An explosion of laughter surrounded him, and he looked up into Drew Hardcastle's smirking face.

"You really should watch where you're going, *Your Highness*. You could get hurt," he teased.

He scrambled to his feet and glared at the older boy while rubbing his backside.

"Lay off, Drew!" Court growled, grabbing Xavier and pulling him away. "Forget him, Xavier. He's a complete waste of space. He always does that to me, usually in front of Erica so that I look like a complete git," he said quietly as they found seats next to Beck and Garrett.

When King Wells entered the room, there was a brief rustling as every child in the gym sat up taller and straighter. He whispered briefly to Mrs. Applegate before approaching the silently waiting children.

"Hello, children. I hear you've been enjoying the games room and gymnasium. I'm glad that it meets with your approval. However, it's been a very long day, and it's now time for bed. In order to maximize space in King's Mountain, all children above the age of five will share common sleeping quarters or dormitories. There will always be an adult supervising the area; so if you need something in the middle of the night, the grown up on duty can help you. Now, the living situation in the mountain will be very different than what you were accustomed to in Warwood. Besides the obvious, one major difference is that if you choose to misbehave or cause *mayhem*..." the king emphasized the last word and looked pointedly at his son, "you could find yourself being punished by someone other than your parents. There's a popular saying that it takes a village to raise a child. This will be our motto during our stay at the mountain. Every adult is responsible for you, therefore, every adult is to be obeyed and respected. If you do not do this, you will face my wrath. Do I make myself clear?"

"Yes, sire," the children chanted together.

"Good. Now, I will be in charge of the boys' dormitory tonight, and Mrs. Applegate will be in charge of the girls. Would the girls please rise and follow Mrs. Applegate? She will show you to your dormitory so that you can prepare for bed."

As the girls got to their feet and followed Lana, Loren shuffled up next to the king, whispered something in his ear, and nodded toward the exiting group. Voices gushed out around Xavier as the boys shifted in their seats on the floor and waited for further instructions from the king.

"It'll be really weird living here, huh, Xavier?" Frankie

whispered from behind him.

"Yeah. It'll definitely be different."

"Well, I think it'll be awesome!" Garrett announced. "Like a permanent sleep over."

"Yeah, right, Bracus. As long as you don't mind having an extra two hundred boys in that sleep over," Beck muttered. "There won't be any privacy. Sounds like a nightmare to me."

Sleeping in a dormitory didn't bother Xavier. He agreed with Garrett. It would be a blast hanging out with his friends and being just one of the guys.

His father's laugh drew his attention back to where he stood with Loren. From the looks of things, Loren was ribbing the king mercilessly, and Xavier found himself smiling along with the men. Then, his father laughed again, shook his head, and approached the waiting boys.

"Think that all you want, Jer, but I know what those looks mean! Besides, I think you're *glowing* just a bit," Loren called after him.

The king's step hesitated, and his face reddened as he turned back to his general. "Glowing?" he choked out.

He nodded, his smile widening into an enormous smirk. "Yep. Glowing."

"Don't you have somewhere to be, Jefferson?" he spat playfully.

Loren's laughter echoed off the gym walls. "Yep. Bed. Goodnight, sire," he responded.

"Night, Loren," he called, as his general exited the gymnasium.

King Wells turned back to the group of boys now chattering excitedly.

"All right, gentlemen. Let's get you settled. Come with me," he announced, waving the boys to follow him as he led them out of the gym and down the hall to a wide stairwell. "The level we're on now is known as the hall level or level two. The level above us is the garden level. Vegetables of every imaginable variety can be found growing there, not to mention a full-sized rugby pitch," Jeremiah announced, grinning at the sudden outburst of excited whispers. "The children's dormitories can be found one level down on level three, and below that on the fourth and fifth levels are the adult chambers and residences. The infirmary and laundry facility can be found on level six, and all the levels below that are strictly off limits. You are not to venture anywhere near the lower levels. Understand?"

"Yes, sire," the boys chanted together.

"Good. Let's go," he ordered, leading the boys into the stairwell and down one flight of stairs to the children's level.

Girls were scattered about at the foot of the stairs in pajamas, and at the sight of the boys, many squealed and raced into a room on the right.

"The lavatories are here on the right. The first door is the girls' lavatory; the second is the boys'. Across the hall is a small library and study area.

The room next to the library is a small clothes closet. There are a few clothing items stored in the closet for emergencies. So if you need an extra shirt, underclothes, or socks, you can check there. It's also equipped with a dumbwaiter to lower laundry directly into the laundry facility on the sixth level. Back to your right and next to the boys' lavatory is a broom closet. Toilet paper, extra towels, soap, and other cleaning supplies can be found there if you should have the need for them."

Halfway down the corridor, the walls ballooned out in the center and several squashy chairs and sofas cluttered around a great hearth containing a roaring fire.

"This is the commons area for both dormitories. If you need anything in the night, the guardians can be found here. The girls' chambers are across the hall on the left, and your chambers are here on the right. You will find two chests at the foot of each bunk. Inside, you will find toiletries and other items you might need. After you pick your bunk, see Madam Applegate or me to register your bunk number and obtain clean pajamas and underclothes. Go on in and get settled, gentlemen."

Immediately, the boys shoved their way into the dorm, each eager to choose the best bunk.

"Xavier?" his father called, beckoning him with a finger and an arched brow.

Xavier's face turned red. The other boys jostled and bumped into him as he made his way toward the king. He knew his father wanted to finish the discussion on his attitude over his chore assignment, and judging by his expression, it wasn't going to be pleasant.

Jeremiah took him by the arm and led him to the commons area next to the fire before speaking. "Son, Ephraim informed me that the only reason he pulled you from the Grand Hall was because your disgruntlement with me grew so obnoxiously apparent that you gained the attention of the citizens around you."

He slumped under his father's relentless stare. A hard lump wedged itself in his throat and he nodded.

The king knelt so that the boy was forced to meet his hard stare. "If you, ever, and I mean *ever*, embarrass me in public again, you'll find yourself over my knee with an audience looking on. Do you understand?"

He gulped before muttering, "Yes, sir. I'm sorry, Dad, really I am."

With a slow exhale, the king stood. "I appreciate that, son. Thank you. You can go and find a bed now."

Xavier turned and nearly ran into Lana.

"Oh! Sorry, Mrs. Applegate."

"It's all right, sweetie. Here's a pajama set for you," she told him softly, handing him a small pile of flannel.

"Thanks," he muttered before hurrying around her and slipping into the boys' chambers.

"Hey, X! Back here!" Court called, waving at him.

Xavier sauntered toward the back corner of the room where his friends were already settled. Court had saved him the lower bed of his bunk, and he plopped his things down and sank onto the mattress.

"What's up?" Court asked.

"Nothing," he grumbled just as his father entered the room.

"Okay, boys, if you've got your beds picked out, register your bunk number with me, and then I suggest that you visit the lavatory. You've got fifteen minutes before lights out."

Most of the boys left for the bathroom, leaving Xavier to make his bed and unpack his things into his assigned chest. The room reminded him of boot camp, or at least, the images of boot camps he had seen on TV. Idly, he wondered if there would be weekly inspections.

"Did you get in trouble or something?" Mac asked quietly.

Xavier looked up with a start at the other boy; he hadn't realized Mac was still there. "What makes you ask that?" he questioned stiffly.

He shrugged passively. "I dunno. Just a guess," he replied softly.

Suddenly, the act of smoothing out linens on the bed became intensely interesting for both boys.

"Ah, well, it's not that big of a deal. He's not too happy with me right now is all. I kinda messed up," Xavier muttered as he continued to straighten his top sheet until not a single crease remained.

Mac shifted uncomfortably from behind him. "Oh, well, I just thought...well, if there's anything I can do to help... I mean...oh, I don't know." He shrugged awkwardly and turned to leave.

Xavier stared after him. It was weird to see Mackenzie Clarke acting...nice.

"Hey, Mac?"

The other boy turned but didn't quite meet his eyes.

"Ah, thanks. But, Dad will get over it; he always does." Xavier stood and grabbed his toiletry bag and pajamas. "Come on. I want to wash off and brush my teeth. After three weeks without a toothbrush, I wouldn't be surprised if a new species of fungus was found growing on them."

Mac snickered, and feeling more relaxed in each other's company, the two boys headed to the lavatory.

Chapter 4

Nightmares Continue

Xavier jerked upright and slammed his head on Court's bed above him. Court moaned nonsense but didn't wake. The dorm was shrouded in darkness except for the soft glow flickering into the room from the corridor. Although his entire body was drenched in sweat, he shivered deeper into his covers as the dream came crashing into his thoughts like a tidal wave.

Dublin Minnows had been kneeling at the foot of the royal staircase like he had moments before William LeMasters had beheaded him. But it wasn't LeMasters who held the sword in the dream; it was him.

"Please, Xavier. You're the only one who can stop this. Please don't let me die. Don't let my girls grow up without a father. I beg you! Please, Xavier, please!" he implored.

Xavier felt a strange sense of euphoria at hearing the man's sobs, and he chuckled wickedly. What was wrong with him? He didn't want Mr. Minnows to die! But these thoughts didn't seem to matter in the dream; the feelings of excitement and bloodlust ruled his actions. In horror, he raised his sword, swung it in a full, wide arc, and watched as it sliced through the kneeling man. As Dublin's head hit the stone floor with a soft thud, he felt like throwing up. He had killed Mr. Minnows! The man who had been like a father to him was dead, and it was all his fault!

Overwhelmed by the lingering images of the dream, Xavier buried his face into his pillow, desperately trying to muffle his sobs, but like waves during a hurricane, the sobs continued to roll through him, gaining in strength and intensity. He couldn't stop. Fearful of waking one of the other boys, he stumbled out of bed and into the hall. His father and Lana sat on a couch next to the fire, facing one another.

"Believe me, it took everything I had not to burst out laughing at the sight of his egged face and robe..." Jeremiah's words dropped off as he caught sight of his son.

Lana followed his gaze, her smile fading.

"Xavier? What is it, son? What's wrong?" his father asked, getting to his feet.

His valiant battle against the racking sobs was lost, and he simply broke down. Jeremiah swept to him, lifted him into his arms, and hugged him close.

"Was it another dream?" he asked softly.

Xavier nodded, and his father carried him back to the sofa and held him. With his father's arms around him, he felt a surge of strength and was finally able to stop crying. Feeling a bit embarrassed for having bawled in front of Lana, he peered up at her shyly.

"Feeling better?" she asked, smiling and stroking his head.

He nodded.

"Do you feel like talking about it?" his father asked quietly.

He shook his head fanatically.

"Okay. Do you think you could return to bed now?" his father asked.

"C...can I stay up with you?" he implored, looking up at his father with large, pitiful eyes.

"Xavier, you need your rest," he told him.

"Please, Dad! I couldn't fall asleep right now even if I wanted to. I... please...please, let me stay," he begged.

"All right. You can stay, but I want you to lie down. Okay?" his father compromised, stroking the boy's cheek.

Xavier smiled gratefully. "Okay. Thanks, Dad."

He stretched out on the couch between Lana and his father. With Lana's gentle hand stroking his hair and his father rubbing his feet, Xavier felt his entire body go limp. His racing, busy mind relaxed instantly, and soon he drifted into a deep slumber.

"He looks like an angel," Lana noted, smiling and stroking Xavier's soft jaw.

Jeremiah chuckled. "Yeah, well, looks can be deceiving. You haven't seen his mischievous side, not to mention that temper of his."

"Well, I wonder where on Earth he got *those* qualities," she teased with a grin.

The king laughed. "Yeah, yeah, yeah. I've heard this before, and you're right. He's definitely his father's son. Poor kid."

The couple sat for several minutes in silence watching and listening to the boy's even breathing as he slept calmly.

"Does he have nightmares often?" Lana whispered.

Jeremiah nodded, staring at his sleeping son and rubbing his legs soothingly.

"What are they about, Jeremiah?" she asked.

He gave her a haunted look before answering. "Lately, they've been about Dublin's death," he muttered.

"Dublin's death?" she hissed. "You mean he saw Dublin Minnows die?"

Jeremiah's face turned to stone. He stood abruptly and scooped the sleeping prince into his arms as though he weighed nothing at all. He carried the boy back into the dormitory and gently laid him on his bed. He stepped back and watched as Lana covered his son with a blanket and brushed a lock of hair from his face. Then, he turned and treaded heavily from the room.

After a final stroke to Xavier's cheek, Lana left the dormitory and found Jeremiah leaning against the hearth, poking at the blazing logs. His broodiness sent the friendly, relaxed atmosphere they had created just moments before retreating into the cold, dark shadows of the corridor. Staring at his tall, large frame, Lana felt his authority, his supremacy vibrating across the space between them.

"Sire Wells?" she whispered, resorting back to his formal title.

Jeremiah didn't respond, but she saw his shoulders hunch forward slightly. Timidly, Lana moved toward him, studying his tense body language.

But, before she could offer any words of solace, he whispered hoarsely, "You must think that I'm a horrible father. He's been through Hell: the kidnapping, his mother's death, watching Dublin die." He turned to face her, the shadows playing hauntingly on his strong features. "And Maggie's death. All of it happened because of me, because he is my son, and I couldn't even protect him from it. What kind of father does that make me?" The anguish in his voice was raw and harsh.

"Jeremiah! You're a wonderful father! You are! Anyone who questions that would only need to see you with Xavier to know it to be true," Lana whispered as she touched his arm consolingly, and he visibly slouched at her touch. "As for everything he's been through, how exactly could you have prevented it? How could you possibly protect him from death? No one can be protected from that! It's unfortunate that some people must face that fact of life earlier than others. Xavier is the wonderful, sweet boy he is because of your guidance and love. You are a terrific father, Jeremiah Wells."

He stared at her for a long moment as her words sank into his soul. Then, blinking heavily, he took her hand and whispered, "Thank you, Lana. I really needed to hear that."

Chapter 5

Rejected

The first week at King's Mountain was marked with a lot of hard, muscle-aching work. The entire community worked together to tend to and harvest crops from the gardens, unload and store the supplies Henrick's group brought back from Bern, and prepare the facility for long-term habitation.

Xavier and his friends had been assigned to help with the harvesting in the gardens. Though he was happy that he had his friends with him to help break up the monotony of the mundane task assigned to them, he had hoped that he could be with his father. As it was, he hardly saw him, and his absence made him unsteady and a bit angry. But, he did his best not to think about it. His father had a lot to worry about without worrying about him. He'd just have to man-up and focus on the back breaking job of picking crops.

He had never known such hard work before, and when he went to bed at night, he was so exhausted that he fell into a deep, dreamless sleep the moment his head hit the pillow.

Finally, on the morning of the seventh day, with the facility ready and running smoothly, King Wells surprised the community with a special treat.

"Ladies and gentlemen," he announced grandly after

the breakfast dishes had been cleared away. "I am so very proud to call myself your king. You have worked hard to get the mountain prepared, and you have done everything I've asked of you and then some! Thank you. So, as a special treat for all your hard work, tonight we shall have a brilliant celebration with food and dancing."

The crowd murmured excitedly.

"But, of course," he continued with a grin, "it will need to be casual since I don't seem to have my tux with me." The crowd chuckled. "Tomorrow the school will open and we will begin our assigned jobs and chores. So, all school-aged children are asked to remain behind for a few minutes so that your class schedules can be distributed. That is all for now. Everyone have a pleasant and relaxing day."

The crowd began to disperse, leaving children in its wake. A group of adults lingered at the back of the hall, sorting through a stack of index cards. Once the hall was cleared, Jeremiah spoke again. "Okay, boys and girls. I need you to separate yourselves by your year. All children under the age of twelve who attended Warwood Grammar School please move to the first row of tables where you see Madam Jefferson and Governor Bracus." The king paused long enough to allow the younger children to move toward their assigned adults.

"All year one students move to Sir Spencer standing at the second row, please," Jeremiah announced.

Xavier stood and, falling into step with Beck and Court, made his way toward his uncle.

"You know, the only good thing about fleeing Warwood is that we don't have formal clothes to wear to the celebration tonight. I swear, I thought my bow tie had a mission to strangle me at the Old Christmas Dance." The boys around Beck snickered. "I'm serious," he protested. "Those things should be outlawed!"

"Mr. Wilcox! I could do without your usual commentary right now. Sit down and be quiet!" Sir Spencer reprimanded.

"Yes, sir," Beck replied, sinking into the seat next to Xavier.

Once all the children had been sorted into their years, Spencer cleared his throat and addressed the year one group. "Boys and girls, I have your class schedules, but before I hand them out, you should be aware of some changes. History has been cancelled until further notice. In its place, you will learn defense strategies and techniques. Your physical education class will be modified into calisthenics to help you build stamina and strength, and you'll begin fencing lessons."

"Cool!" Beck exclaimed. "Who teaches that?"

An ambush of comments and questions bombarded Spencer. He raised his hand against the sudden chaos of voices. "That's enough. All the information you need is printed on your schedule. Now, you still have empowerment classes, however, the classes will now focus on using your abilities offensively not just defensively."

Another outburst of excited chatter resulted in a warning glare from Spencer, and the chatter was cut humorously short as though he had used a mute button.

"Usually," he continued testily, "offensive techniques are not taught until year three, but King Wells believes it's necessary in the present circumstances. I want to remind all of you that learning offensive techniques is a huge responsibility. It is NOT to be done outside of classes. Any students found doing so will be caned by the king."

The children grew still and silent.

Spencer paused a moment longer, letting his threat sink in. "Attacking someone through the use of empowerments is not only dangerous, it can be deadly.

Does everyone understand?"

The group nodded.

"Sir?" Court piped up timidly. "What if we need to practice? How are we going to practice things if we can only do it in classes?"

"Luckily, Mr. Hardcastle, every teacher has a time in their schedule each evening where students can practice skills under supervision. So if you need to practice a technique, you'll need to make arrangements with that teacher during their allotted time. Any other questions?"

The children were silent.

"All right then, I'll pass out your schedules."

As Spencer hobbled up and down the tables distributing the schedule cards, Beck leaned in and snickered, "Caned by the king? Been there, done that."

"Ditto." Garrett laughed nervously. "And I sure don't want seconds of that! That's for damn sure!"

The other boys nodded in agreement.

"I feel for you, Xavier," Frankie observed and then whistled. "Man, I bet you've been whipped a lot!"

He looked at the other boy dumbfounded. "Geez, Frankie. What are you saying? That I always get in trouble?"

Frankie blushed. "Well, no, I mean. Well, you live with him and the odds are he's whipped you before...and..." Frankie gave up his explanation and hunched his shoulders.

Beck, however, burst out laughing. "God, Frankie! Talk about putting your foot in your mouth."

Xavier was the last to receive his schedule. When Spencer finally handed it to him, Court eagerly craned his neck to peer at the card in his hands.

"What's your schedule like, Xavier?"

"They're all the same except for empowerment classes,

Hardcastle," Beck chastised, but he too strained to see Xavier's schedule.

"Whoa! I think they've made some kind of mistake, X," Beck exclaimed, snatching the card out of his grasp and peering down at it. "They have you down for *both* introduction to fencing and advanced fencing techniques. And, oi! You have two electro force classes too! And look..."

"Sire Wells?" Spencer called from the head of the table. "I need to see you a moment, the rest of you are dismissed to enjoy your day off."

As the group scrambled out of the hall, Xavier approached his uncle.

"You may have noticed that your schedule has two teachers for fencing, electro force strategies, and your empowerment block," he told him quietly.

Xavier nodded.

"Your father has requested that you be placed in advanced classes as soon as possible. So you may find yourself in the introductory classes for only a few short weeks," Spencer explained.

"But why? Why is he in such a hurry to get me in advanced classes?" he sputtered indignantly.

"That is a question for your father, Xavier," his uncle concluded, looking at Jeremiah, who had just finished giving instructions to a group of older students and was now dismissing them.

He followed his uncle's gaze with a nod. "Ok. Thanks, Uncle Mike."

Spencer patted his shoulder affectionately, and with a weary smile, he whispered, "Good luck," before limping from the room.

The king moved to the head table and began straightening his notes and gathering file folders and booklets. Xavier shuffled over to him and waited.

"Do you have a question about your class schedule, son?" he asked, without looking up from his task.

God! Xavier hated it when he did that, and it never seemed to cease to amaze him either. Many times, he wondered, *'How did he know I was thinking that?'* Then, he would remember stupidly, *'Oh, yeah, telepathy.'*

"Yes, sir," he replied, unable to keep the irritation from his voice. "Why do you want me in advanced classes so fast? Why can't I stay in the same classes with my friends and kids my age? I don't want to be in advance classes with older, bigger kids. No one else has to! It's not fair!"

His father didn't answer him immediately, which only irritated him further. Instead, he finished gathering his papers and stacked them on top of the booklets and folders. Then, with a deep breath, he looked at Xavier, leaving him with little doubt that no matter what the reason, there would be no negotiating.

"Son, let's forget for a moment that you're the future king and that these courses will help you to develop the skills you'll need as king. Instead, let's remember that in the past ten months, you've been at risk of serious bodily harm not once, not twice, but four separate times. You will take the advance courses so you can learn how to protect and defend yourself. You will take the courses to help you develop the skills you need to be a powerful, competent king. You will take the courses because, quite simply, I'm telling you to!" he finished flatly.

"Oh, well, when you put it like *that*," Xavier muttered sarcastically as he stomped away from his father.

"Xavier Wells!" Jeremiah spat, slamming his stack of papers and booklets on the table with a loud thud. "Do not sass me, boy!"

Father and son glared at one another for several

seconds. Until, finally, Xavier's will broke, and he glanced away.

"Yes, sir," he mumbled meekly and quickly scurried from the room.

Beck and Court were waiting for him outside the Grand Hall. In an awkward silence, the boys traveled down the hall, down the stairway, and onto the children's level before Beck cleared his throat.

"Ah, X?" he muttered as they entered the dormitory.

"Yeah?" he responded moodily, not meeting his friend's eyes.

"Ah, w...whatever you said to your dad up there, well, mate, it didn't seem to work," Beck replied earnestly.

Xavier burst into laughter. He wasn't sure why he found Beck's grasp of the obvious so funny, but he did. Then, meeting the other boy's eye for the first time since they left the Grand Hall, he retorted sarcastically, "Thanks for the hint, Beck. I hadn't noticed."

As the morning wore on, the mountain's atmosphere became more and more excitable and playful. Children and adults alike were enjoying the day off and, for the moment at least, they forgot their troubles and grief.

Xavier and his friends spent most of the morning in the games room playing foosball and pinball. For the first time in a long time, he was having fun and enjoying himself. He was beginning to feel normal again until Robbie entered the room with a small group of girls, and the reprieve he had from his guilt and sorrow was ripped away.

Robbie was smiling for the first time in weeks. It wasn't an elated smile, but a smile nonetheless.

He wasn't the only one who noticed it. Beck blurted out from beside him, "Hey, Robbie. It's good to see you smiling again."

"Yeah, it is," Xavier piped up feebly, turning from his pinball game and losing his last ball.

But when Robbie's eyes fluttered to Xavier, her smile slipped, and she gave him a dark glare before turning back to Beck. "Thanks, Beck. I'll save you a dance tonight if you'd like," she told him, smiling sweetly.

"Ah...yeah. Sure," he stammered.

Her smile broadened. "Good. See you tonight." Then, she moved toward the ping-pong table where Erica was thoroughly pounding Harry in a match.

Her complete dismissal and coolness toward Xavier had the boys around him shifting uncomfortably, and a thick silence was left in her wake. Xavier watched as Robbie joined in with the other girls, teasing Harry about losing to a girl.

"So, who's next? Xavier's in the lead with two hundred sixty-five thousand points," Beck called tightly, pretending as though nothing had happened.

Xavier wasn't sure which emotion pulsating through him was the strongest: guilt, hurt, or jealousy. However, all the emotions wheeling through him came to a screaming halt in the next instant, and the only thing he felt was complete, utter fury.

Drew Hardcastle entered the game room with his cronies, Jonas McKnight and Seth Brown. As they walked past, Drew shouldered into Xavier, elbowing him hard in the gut, sending him unceremoniously to the stone floor.

"Oops!" Drew sang with laughter.

"Hey! Watch where you're bloody going, Drew!" Xavier growled, struggling to his feet and rubbing his left hip.

"Excuse me?" the older boy bellowed, stepping close to Xavier so that he towered over him. "What did you say to me, squirt?"

"You heard me!" he hissed, shoving the older boy away from him.

Drew lunged at him and shoved him roughly against the nearest wall. Xavier's head bounced painfully off the stone surface. "You don't get it, do you? You may be the son of a king, but here in King's Mountain, you're just another pipsqueak!" he snarled.

"Yeah," Jonas growled, pressing in from beside Drew. "And we eat pipsqueaks like you for snacks."

Drew gave a snorting laugh before releasing Xavier and giving his cheek a hard pinch.

"Lay off, Drew, and call off your thugs or I'm telling Dad!" Court spat, pushing himself between his brother and Xavier.

"Thugs?" Jonas spat, lifting Court into the air. "Did you just call me a thug?"

"I mean it, Drew!" Court yelled at his brother.

Drew gave a quick nod to Jonas, who dropped Court back to the floor. Then he sneered down at his brother and smacked him playfully on the cheek. "Now, now, *baby* brother. There's no need to get your panties in a twist."

Jonas snorted.

After surveying the group of younger boys smugly, he motioned for Jonas and Seth to follow him, and they moved toward the door. But, before exiting the room, Drew paused, turned, and with a cocky, taunting smirk bowed to Xavier.

"All hail, the Prince of Pipsqueaks!" he jeered.

Then, the older boys left the room, leaving a giggling group in their wake.

Among the laughing children, he saw Robbie. The girl who had always stood up for him and fought against bullies was now one of them. It was too much! Feeling betrayed and hurt, Xavier wanted nothing more than to hide.

"Catch you guys later," he mumbled, skulking from the room.

With tears pooling in his eyes, he stumbled down the stairs to the fourth floor in search of his father. Unsure of where to go, he shuffled down the hall until muffled, urgent voices brought him to a halt next to a door on his right. He couldn't hear exactly what was being said, but his father's name erupted from the room.

He moved toward the door, straining to hear the insistent muffled voices, but when he reached the door, it flew open, and Michael Spencer stood in the doorway, his hand on the doorknob. He was looking back into the room, so he hadn't yet noticed Xavier.

"I'm telling you, Jer. He'll buck everything if you don't tell him the truth about what's going on!" Spencer yelled angrily. He turned and nearly plowed straight into Xavier. His face lifted with surprise, and for a moment, he simply stared down at the boy. Finally, he called over his shoulder, "Sire, your son is here."

A chair squealed from inside the room, and a second later, Loren and Jeremiah were in the doorway. A chill passed over Xavier's body, and he realized that he had interrupted a conversation none of the men had wanted him to hear. The men shifted uneasily.

"Son? Is there something you need? I don't have a lot of time; Loren and I are meeting with the Royal Guard in five minutes," his father inquired.

"Ah," Xavier looked at each man in turn, and suddenly felt stupid for coming. "Ah, I just wanted to see your chamber. That's all."

"Oh, well, you can go and have a look if you'd like. It's the last chamber on the left. I need to get going. I'll see you later, okay?" he responded, patting his head as he brushed past him with Loren and Spencer. Xavier

41

watched as the men disappeared into the stairwell at the end of the corridor.

Chapter 6

Exploring Trouble

Xavier didn't go to his father's chamber. Instead, he returned to the empty boys' dormitory. He flopped irritably onto his bunk before conjuring a small electro force and spinning it inches above him. He wished he knew how to transform his force into shapes of animals like Court could. It would be cool to have a glowing, golden horse galloping in circles around his head. He closed his eyes and pictured the image clearly in his head, smiling at the thought.

"Cool horse," Garrett remarked suddenly.

Xavier's eyes snapped open and saw the remnants of a golden stallion above his head before it vanished completely.

"Where'd you run off to, mate?" Beck asked.

"Uh, nowhere special," Xavier muttered.

"Well, we're going up to the Grand Hall for lunch. The cooks have set up a huge table of sandwiches and stuff so that people can go and eat whenever they feel like it," Court told him.

"Oh, well...I think I should wait on my dad," he responded, but Court shook his head.

"Sorry, mate. Both our dads are having a lunch meeting with the Premier Royal Guard," he explained.

"Oh," he muttered. How had Court known about the lunch meeting and not him? He wouldn't have even known about the meeting with the Premier Guard if he hadn't gone looking for his father. It was obvious Court saw more of his father than Xavier saw of his! Or, at least his dad told him stuff. Resentment expanded inside him until he felt its bitter taste in his mouth.

After the boys devoured sandwiches, chips, and a large slice of chocolate cake, they sauntered out of the Grand Hall, belching.

"I don't think I could look at another sandwich again," Garrett moaned, rubbing his stomach.

"Yeah, I think we overdid it with that slice of cake," Beck agreed, releasing a deep, throaty belch, and the other boys snickered appreciatively.

"Now what?" Frankie asked the group.

The boys shrugged and frowned in thought.

"Let's go exploring!" Mac suggested. "There's loads of stuff we haven't seen or done here."

Beck looked at the other boy with a mixture of surprise and subtle respect. "Not a bad idea, Clarke," he replied, and Mac grinned at him. Beck turned to the group. "Well? What do you say?"

Beck needn't have asked for the group gave a roaring "Yes!"

Moments later, the group of boys, in one loud boisterous mob made their way down the stairs, past the children's and the infirmary floors until they spilled out onto the seventh level. This level was still under construction and posted in the middle of the main corridor stood a sign stating,

Warning!

Danger!

No unauthorized persons!

Frankie froze in front of the sign, reading and rereading it as the other boys barreled past, talking excitedly.

"Hey, wait a minute, guys!" Frankie hollered after them. "Didn't you see this sign?"

Beck gave him an impatient look. "Yeah, we saw it, *Francine*. What about it?"

Frankie's face went red as he blared, "It says danger!"

"Very good," Beck mocked. "Now, can you read the other big words, Mama's boy?"

Frankie glared at Beck with a don't-mess-with-me expression. "I'm just saying...it says no unauthorized persons."

"God, Frankie! If you're going to be like this, just go back to the dorm!" Beck bellowed, advancing aggressively towards the other boy.

"Cool it, guys," Xavier called, stepping between them. Then he turned to Frankie. "Look, Frankie. I'm your prince, right?"

He nodded.

"And, that means that I'm your future king, right?" he asked, and again, he nodded. "Then as future king, I give everyone here the authority to enter the restricted areas of King's Mountain."

Frankie stared at him dumbfounded, but after a brief glance at Beck, he grinned. "Okay. That's good enough for me!"

The group behind them exploded into cheers as the tense moment passed. The group continued down the hall, and Beck moved to walk next to Xavier.

"Sorry about that, X. It's just that you have to push Frankie to do anything normal. His dad split when he was a baby, and his mother keeps a tight hold on him. If we didn't make him act normal, he'd be some nerdy kid that nobody likes."

"Sure, I understand." And, he did, more than his friend knew. Beck's words reminded Xavier of something Loren had once said about Dublin, "Just think, if we hadn't loosened him up with our adventures, he would've squeaked when he walked."

"Come on. Let's go this way," Xavier declared brusquely, leading the boys down a passage that resembled a tunnel more than it did a hall.

The tunnel broadened into a crudely cut chamber that looked as though it had simply been created with a few sticks of dynamite. Mining carts were scattered about the room; many filled with debris and rock ready to be cleared from the chamber. On the other side of the room, a narrow, low tunnel extended into the darkness.

"I wonder where that goes," Beck muttered.

"I bet it goes outside," Court suggested, and all the boys gave him doubtful looks. "Well? Where else are they going to take all the rubbish they clear out of here?"

"Hey," Xavier started, an idea forming in his thoughts. "Have you guys ever ridden in bumper cars before?"

"I have," Garrett piped up. "My parents dragged me off to New York to visit some of their old college friends, and we went to this carnival. It's where people get into little cars and ram into one another, right?"

"Yeah! You have telekinesis now, right?" Xavier asked Garrett.

"Yeah, but I'm not all that great at it, yet," Garrett protested.

"Well, neither am I! Didn't you hear about the tornado I created in my room?" Xavier snickered.

"I heard about that!" Mac joined in. "That really happened?"

Xavier nodded but continued looking at Garrett. "Well,

what do you say, Garrett. Are you game?"

Garrett flashed him a grin and raced to one of the empty carts.

"Wait!" Beck yelled, following Garrett. "I want to ride with you."

"Court? Wanna ride with me?" Xavier asked.

"You bet," he agreed, following Xavier to another empty cart.

"Hey! What about us? We want rides too!" Frankie called.

"Don't worry. You'll get one," Xavier promised.

It wasn't long before the boys had several carts dented so badly, they could no longer sit inside them. So Xavier and Garrett entertained the others with a game of crash-cart-derby. In this game, each boy raised a cart into the air and attempted to knock the other boy's cart to the ground. Their friends cheered them on and kept score, awarding five points to the boy who succeeded in achieving the goal.

At one point, Garrett caught Xavier off guard, and his cart made solid contact with Xavier's, sending it pummeling toward the chamber floor. Xavier managed to catch it inches from the ground and lifted it back into the air. The boys around him cheered.

"Nice catch, Xavier!" Court yelled.

"Yeah, that was awesome!" Mac cheered.

"Nice try, Bracus, but Xavier's still in the lead, thirty-five to twenty-five," Beck announced.

"What in the bloody hell are you boys doing?" a deep voice boomed from the chamber's entrance.

Instantly, the carts hovering in the air dropped to the stone floor with a loud, thunderous crash. Xavier winced.

"Ah...we...we were..."

"Destroying property is what it looks like to me. All right, all of you come with me! The guardian can deal with you. Who's on duty tonight?" the man growled.

The boys looked at one another, filled with uncertainty. The shift always changed after breakfast each morning and before lights out each evening, so none of the boys knew for sure who was on duty. But, the moment they stepped onto the children's level, they saw their answer.

Michael Spencer sat in the commons area reading a newspaper. The boys groaned.

"Why couldn't it have been Loren?" Court whined softly to the others.

"Because we have rotten luck," Beck muttered. As former headmaster of Wells Academy, Spencer was a no-nonsense kind of man and could usually stop trouble and mischief before it ever got started; most likely due to his telepathy ability. Although Spencer could be stern and harsh at times, Xavier had grown close to his uncle in the past couple of months. Plus, he had saved his uncle's life.

When Warwood had been taken over by William LeMasters and the Dark Army, Spencer had been caught up in the thick of the battle. In order to provide families living in his area more time to flee, he had taken up arms and fought against two dozen Dark soldiers. He had managed to keep them at bay, but he paid a steep price for his valor. The wounds he had sustained in battle had been so severe that he nearly lost his life. If it hadn't been for Xavier, he most certainly would have died. Xavier had used his rejuvenation ability on his uncle, and Spencer had survived with two vicious scars and a limp. But, still, saving his life had to account for something! Right?

"Hey, Mike! Are you on kid watch tonight?" the man beside Xavier asked.

Spencer's gaze flickered from the man to the boys and back again. "Yes, Richard, I am," he answered slowly.

"You might want to involve the king with this since the

prince here was involved, but I found these boys in a restricted chamber. They've smashed four mining carts beyond repair, and badly damaged several others."

"Okay, Rich. I'll take it from here," Spencer announced, glaring down at the boys. "All of you, in the dormitory, now!"

The boys brushed silently past the other children moving about in the corridor. They entered the boys' dormitory, shuffled down the rows of bunks, and dropped onto their beds, waiting for the verdict to be handed down. When Spencer entered the room, Xavier was amazed by how quickly his uncle could move with a bum leg.

"All right, boys!" he spat angrily. "Let me see if I understand this correctly. First, you disobeyed your king and endangered your lives by venturing into restricted areas of the mountain. And, as if that weren't enough, you vandalized and destroyed much-needed mining equipment, making it difficult if not impossible for the miners to do their jobs properly. Is that it? Did I miss anything?"

Solemnly, the boys shook their heads. A burst of barely contained laughter sputtered from behind Spencer, and he turned on Drew and Jonas.

"Andrew, Jonas, unless you want to find yourselves caught in my crosshairs, I highly suggest you keep your comments to yourselves and leave us," Spencer growled.

The smiles dropped from the older boys' faces, and they muttered, "Yes, sir."

Spencer waited for the older boys to exit the room before continuing. "So? Who's responsible for the damaged carts?"

Xavier and Garrett eyed one another before whispering together, "We are, sir."

"All right, the two of you have a seat out in the commons area. I'll be there shortly," Spencer ordered.

Xavier and Garrett left the dormitory and fell into the couch closest to the fire. There were a few children still milling about, but for the most part, the hall was empty.

"Xavier, Garrett, come on! Dinner will be served in five minutes," Erica called.

"Can't. Thanks." Xavier exhaled shakily.

"Miss Jefferson? Please, leave us," Spencer called sharply, approaching Xavier and Garrett. The other boys scurried out of the dorm and down the hall, throwing fretful glances their way.

However, Erica didn't budge and stared down at them questioningly.

"Now, Miss Jefferson. I need to speak to the boys privately," he insisted.

Finally she nodded and followed the other boys up to the Grand Hall for dinner.

"Okay, boys," Spencer began, settling himself into an armchair beside them. "Your friends will be too busy for the next week to rally up to your idiotic ideas. They have all received extra chores, as will the two of you. But in addition to this, for the next two weeks, both of you will serve as assistants to the miners on the construction levels. You will help clear out and construct new passages and chambers. You will be given the dirtiest grunt work they can find so that you can learn to appreciate the extremely difficult job the miners have."

"But you said it's too dangerous to be down there..." Xavier complained.

"It is," Spencer told him. "You will be working in secure sections of the mines. Your fathers have already agreed to this punishment."

"How does my..." Garrett began, but Spencer cut him

off with an impatient wave of his hand.

"Mr. Bracus! Use your *head!*"

"Oh...yeah. I forgot," Garrett muttered.

"Is Dad coming down to see me?" Xavier whispered.

Spencer looked at him, bemused. "No, he's left me to handle this situation."

He should have been relieved that his father wasn't coming to punish him, but he wasn't. He was angry and hurt.

"Now," Spencer continued, "you will report to the entrance of level seven as mining helpers immediately after classes at three thirty. After dinner, you will do your assigned chores, and then, at seven o'clock you will complete your extra chore. The pair of you will clean and mop the main level lavatories until they shine!"

"What if I say no?" Xavier asked.

Garrett's mouth gaped open, and his uncle looked at him in surprise.

"Excuse me?" he challenged.

"What if I said no, I'm not doing any of it?" he asked again, his voice quivering.

Spencer's eyes narrowed. "You're not challenging my authority are you, boy?" he asked, standing.

"Maybe," he mumbled.

His uncle's eyes flashed thunderously down at him before darting towards the other boy. "Garrett, do you understand your punishment?" he snapped.

"Yes, sir," he squeaked uneasily.

"Good. Then go to dinner."

"Yes, sir." Garrett nearly ran into Mrs. Minnows as he raced to the steps.

Spencer turned to Mrs. Minnows. "Tamarah, will you make sure that the rest of the children have gone to the Grand Hall? Xavier and I will follow when we're through here."

"Sure, Michael," Tamarah answered, turning to gather the few remaining children.

"On your feet, boy!" Spencer hissed.

When he didn't act immediately, Michael pulled him to his feet and hauled him down the corridor toward the boys' dormitory. Three older boys had lingered and were huddled around a bunk, snickering.

"Gentlemen, give me that magazine and get to dinner," Spencer ordered.

The boys jumped into action, handing Spencer the naughty magazine and exiting the room. Spencer plopped the magazine and his coat onto a bunk and propped his cane against its frame before advancing on Xavier.

"U...Uncle Mike..." he stammered, backing away. "Wh...What are you doing?"

But Spencer didn't answer as he continued toward him and grabbed his arm. With a firm tug, he had Xavier pinned against his left hip.

Heat burned over his cheeks as he realized his uncle's intentions. "Uncle Mike, please don't! I'm sorry. I'm sorry! Please, don't spank me!"

Suddenly, he pulled him upright and glared down at him. "Give me one good reason why I shouldn't, Xavier. You crossed the line and you know it. If your father had heard you speak that way to an adult, he would do the same," he growled, his voice oozing with fury.

"I...I know, sir. You're right. I crossed the line, but it will never happen again. I promise! Just...please...don't whip me...I saved your life, Uncle!" he pleaded.

Spencer froze and if anything, it appeared Xavier's words only enraged him more, but after a moment, he faltered.

"Sit," Spencer commanded, pointing to the nearest

bunk, and the boy immediately complied with the order. Spencer studied him a moment before he whispered, "Xavier, I am very grateful to you for what you did...but you can only use this card, this guilt-trip on me once. After tonight, if you so much as give me a cross-eyed look, I'll leave welts on your backside. Got it?"

"Yes, sir. I'm sorry, Uncle Mike. I'll never do it again," he muttered, relief pouring through him.

His uncle gave him a curt nod. "All right then. Let's get ourselves up to the Grand Hall for dinner."

Chapter 7

Jealousy

As Xavier entered the Grand Hall, everyone in King's Mountain was already present, seated, and eating. He felt the crowd's eyes following him as he trudged to the head table, and judging by the whispers, the news of his involvement in damaging the mining equipment was now widely known.

"Hello, son," Jeremiah whispered as he sank into the seat next to him. "Do we need to discuss the mining incident further, or did Mike cover it thoroughly enough with you?"

"No, sir. Uncle Mike covered it all," he grumbled and reached for his plate of hot food.

After dinner, a handful of telekinetic citizens removed several tables to create a dance area. A man Xavier recognized as a Royal Guard member set up a stereo and sound system. Soon, the lights dimmed and music filled the hall. Jeremiah was the first on the floor with a pretty petite blond.

"Excuse me? Prince Wells? Would you dance with me?" asked a red-headed girl Xavier recognized on sight but not by name.

"Ah...sure," he responded.

As he took the girl's hand and led her to the dance

floor, his friends shouted out taunts and hoots from behind him. He grinned haughtily at the other boys before pulling the girl close and swaying to the slow rhythm.

Several dances later, Xavier finally got a break and made his way back to where his friends sat, drinking sodas.

"Hey, where did you get the soda?" he asked, plopping down next to Court.

"By the kitchen. Here, we got you one," Court told him, shoving an orange soda toward him.

"Thanks," he blurted and gulped down half the cold drink in a matter of seconds before belching loudly. The boys around him snickered, and a belching contest ensued until Rebecca Hardcastle walked past.

"Oh for heaven's sake, boys! Where are your manners? This is a dance, not the boys' dormitory! Keep the crude noises to yourselves!" she chastised before continuing toward the dance floor.

The boys stifled snickers but stopped belching.

Then, pointing, Frankie piped up, "Hey, guys! Check out King Wells!"

Jeremiah was still on the dance floor, but now he had a slender brunette in his arms. Lana? His father was dancing with Lana Applegate. Xavier's stomach somersaulted with renewed interest as he watched his father and Lana dance. The tune was sultry and lively, and the pair moved well together. The king's body swayed silkily with the beat of the music, and Lana responded gracefully to every step in perfect rhythm. The couple seemed to float across the floor, their bodies in complete harmony. His father's eyes held fast to the woman in his arms as he dipped her, swept her upright, and glided her across the floor again. Heat rushed up Xavier's neck and over his head and face as every person in the Hall stopped to watch the mesmerizing dance. He didn't know why his father's dance embarrassed him, but it did. Maybe it was the way the crowd stared at him and Lana. Or, maybe it was the memory of his father dancing with that evil witch, Catherine Stokes. But, as uncomfortable as it was seeing his father dance so...close with Lana, he found, like the rest of the crowd, he couldn't look away. Finally the song ended and the room burst into applause and a few catcalls. Jeremiah grinned at his audience, and he and Lana curtsied to the cheering crowd.

"Man! If I could move like that, girls would be lining up to date me," Beck groaned, closing his eyes to daydream.

"Well, you can't, and they're most definitely not..." Court teased.

"Beckley?" Robbie's voice came from behind Xavier, and every boy whipped around to look at her. "Will you dance with me now?"

Beck's eyes were still a bit glassy from daydreaming, and he blinked heavily as if trying to determine whether or not he was still dreaming. Finally, he grinned and looked smugly at Court before answering, "Sure, Robbie. I'd love to dance with you."

Xavier watched, overwhelmed with jealousy as Beck took Robbie's hand, walked her to the dance floor, and pulled her into his arms.

Trying to distract Xavier from Beck and Robbie, Court nudged him and said, "Hey, your dad's still dancing with Lana Applegate. Do you reckon he's sweet on her or something?"

It worked. He looked to the other end of the dance floor and studied his father and Lana. They didn't seem to be talking much. They were simply looking at one another and dancing. But, he was confident in his answer. His father had promised to tell him if he ever got serious about anyone again.

"Naw, if he was sweet on anyone, he'd tell me," he responded with certainty. He turned back to where Beck and Robbie were dancing and his breath caught painfully in his chest. Beck was holding her so tightly that a piece of paper couldn't have fit between them. Then, she whispered something in his ear, and he kissed her.

Xavier's entire body flushed with anger, and he jumped to his feet, sending his chair to the floor with a bang.

"Xavier! Xavier, don't," Court warned, trying to grab his arm, but he was too late. Xavier, consumed with jealousy, barreled onto the dance floor, shoved Beck, and knocked him to the floor.

"What the...Xavier? What'cha' do that for?" he questioned angrily, getting to his feet.

"Of all the girls here, why do you have to go after Robbie?" Xavier growled.

"I didn't go after her, mate, she came after me!" he spat.

"I don't care, Beck! Keep your hands and lips off of her or else!" he yelled.

"Boys!" Loren called, fighting his way through the dancing crowd.

"Or else what, *sire*? You know what? That "I'm your future king" bit may work on Frankie, but it doesn't on me!" Beck bellowed, bumping aggressively into Xavier. "And I'll touch, kiss, and dance with anyone I want!"

"Oh, yeah?" he challenged.

"Xavier! Beck! Stop, now!" Loren shouted, drawing the king's attention to the confrontation.

"Xavier?" his father barked, shuffling towards the boys as well.

"Yeah! So, if you don't like it, you can just kiss my..."

Beck never finished his sentence.

Xavier swung his fist as hard as he could, punching the other boy in the mouth. Beck's head snapped back, and he staggered backwards, but it didn't take long for him to recover and lunge at Xavier, tackling him to the floor. In the next moment, Loren and Jeremiah had reached them, and each grabbed a boy by the scruff of the neck and hauled him to his feet.

"That's enough, boys!" the king's voice boomed and vibrated throughout the hall. The music screeched to a stop, and the lights flickered on to full power. Every person in the hall stared disapprovingly at them, and Xavier felt like he was two inches tall. Once he was sure the boys had calmed and weren't after each other's blood any longer, Jeremiah turned to the crowd. "Sorry, folks. Please excuse us and resume the dance."

The men dragged the boys from the hall and into the nearest classroom.

"Okay, boys. Who wants to tell me what that was all about?" Jeremiah growled, trying to keep his voice even.

Both boys stared at their feet, shifting uneasily, but neither answered.

"I asked you a question! I expect an answer!" Jeremiah demanded, his voice no longer calm.

Beck jumped and quietly answered, "I was dancing with Robbie... and ...Xavier came out of nowhere and plowed into me."

Jeremiah turned to his son. "Is this true? Did you start this fight, Xavier?"

"Yeah! So?" he blared, angrily.

The smack came so quickly that its sting didn't immediately register on his butt until after his father had released him and stood glaring down at him.

"You'd better watch that attitude, son," Jeremiah spat.

Then, after a few deep breaths, he continued, "Why? Why did you attack Beck? I thought he was your friend."

"He is. He...he just...he made me mad," Xavier muttered.

"That's it? That's your reason?" Jeremiah asked, dumbfounded.

He shrugged, not daring to meet his father's furious glare.

"Fine. If that's your reasoning, I think you should spend the rest of the celebration in the dormitory," he told him.

"What? Why? Why do I have to leave the party? Why doesn't Beck have to leave too?" he spat.

Jeremiah pinned him with a heated glare until the boy's eyes dropped and he squirmed uncomfortably in front of him. Finally, he looked at Loren. "Who's on duty tonight?"

"I am," he responded. "I'll take him down. Tell Lucy, will you?"

Jeremiah nodded before looking back at Xavier again. "Goodnight, son."

"Yeah, right," he mumbled angrily, stomping out of the room.

Xavier lay in his bunk pouting for nearly thirty minutes before Beck and Court entered. He rolled over, turning his back to them.

"Ah, come on Xavier! Don't be like that! I don't want some girl to come between our friendship," Beck pleaded.

"Robbie isn't just some girl," he mumbled, sitting up and looking at the boys standing at the foot of his bunk. "She...she was always there for me, and now she's treating me like I'm a disease."

"I know it, X, but I know my cousin. She's really

hurting, and you're just a convenient punching bag. She'll come around...someday," Court finished quietly.

"I wouldn't count on it, Court. She's never been this mad at me...I mean...would you be able to forgive me if it had been your dad who sacrificed his life so I could live? Would you be able to just forgive and forget?" Xavier asked, meeting Courtney's eyes.

Courtney blinked, and Xavier knew his answer before he could spout his comforting lies.

"No. What happened wasn't your fault. She'll figure that out too, in time."

"But, the weird thing is, Court, I have this feeling that it was my fault. I can't shake the feeling that I could have done something..." he told him, his voice breaking at the thought.

Court didn't respond, and when Xavier looked at his friend, he found him staring down at him with a strange, worried expression.

Chapter 8

New Classes

The next morning, Loren barged into the boys' dormitory singing at the top of his lungs. "Gooooood moooornning! Let's get a move on, gentlemen. Come on, come on! Get up!"

Xavier groaned and pulled the covers over his head, but Loren was unrelenting.

"Let's go! Let's go! Classes begin in an hour! You don't want to be late for class on your first day!" he called as he strolled down the aisle between the rows of bunks. When he reached Xavier's bunk, he grinned and yanked off his blankets. "Come, Your Highness! Get a move on!"

Xavier sat up and glared grumpily at the general, who simply laughed as he continued moving about the room rousing the still-sleeping boys. The boys slowly got out of bed, stretching and yawning. As Loren exited the room to supervise the hall, Xavier pulled clean clothes from his trunk and began stripping off his pajamas.

"Aw, look at that blokes. Isn't the Prince of Pipsqueaks just as cute as a button?" Drew chastised from his bunk a few feet away. Snickers erupted around them.

"Yeah, he is! He's so cute and...*little*," Jonas agreed in a high-pitched squeal, eying Xavier's boxers. Several older boys burst into laughter. Jonas and Drew weren't just referring to his height but to more embarrassing, private things as well.

Xavier's face ignited, and he blurted angrily, "At least my face doesn't look like road kill!"

"What did you say, squirt?" Jonas bellowed, stomping toward him.

For an instant, he thought Jonas was going to punch him, but he didn't. Instead, the older boy snatched his tennis shoes from his bunk and tossed them to Drew.

"Hey! Give those back!" Xavier yelled, running toward Drew, but Jonas tripped him and he slammed to the stone floor, biting his lip.

"Give those back!" Jonas mocked, leaning down and pinching his cheek.

He swatted the boy's hand away.

Drew cackled cruelly. "Do you want your shoes, Prince Pipsqueak? Well, you'll have to swim for them." Then the older boys ran from the room, laughing.

"Hey! Stop!" Xavier called and scrambled after them.

"Xavier, wait! You don't want to run out there in just your underwear!" Court hollered and tossed him his corduroys.

He yanked on his pants and ran into the hall, but Drew and Jonas were nowhere in sight.

"Did you find them?" Court asked, running to Xavier's side. Then, they spotted them coming out of the bathroom, and Court swore under his breath.

"Drew? Where're Xavier's shoes?" he yelled, attracting several curious glances.

His brother didn't answer. He simply flashed the younger boys a wicked smile and shrugged before disappearing up the stairs with Jonas.

"Come on. Let's find them." Xavier sighed.

The boys searched the bathroom for several minutes

until they finally found the shoes floating in one of the toilets.

"Yuk! I can't wear these to class! What am I going to do?" he exclaimed, holding the dripping wet shoes at arm's length.

"Maybe one of the launderettes will have another pair you can borrow while they clean these," Court suggested.

By the time they were dressed and went to the laundry room for a spare pair of shoes, they had completely missed breakfast and were running ten minutes late for Latin class.

Xavier groaned, "God! Of all the classes I could be late for, why does it have to be Dad's Latin class?"

"Yeah, I'm beginning to think that Beck's right. If it weren't for bad luck, we wouldn't have any luck at all!" Court laughed dryly. "Come on. We'd better get going. All classes are held on level two. We've got four flights of stairs to climb!"

As the boys ran down the sixth level corridor past the infirmary, Xavier desperately wished they could simply teleport to class and save themselves from being any later. Suddenly, a strange tingling sensation exploded inside him and quickly radiated over every inch of his body. Then, he felt a harsh yank in his chest and abdomen like he was being jerked up and out of his own body. Everything around him blurred into blackness, and he collided into something solid and unforgiving, knocking him to the stone floor. As his vision returned and his surroundings came into focus, a tidal wave of laughter surrounded him. He blinked and found himself in a classroom full of laughing students staring down at him. Slowly, he looked up at the tall, unyielding man standing in front of him and met his father's stunned face. He had teleported! Xavier had teleported straight into his father!

"Ow!" he muttered feebly. God that hurt!

"All right! That's enough. Everyone settle down," Jeremiah called over the giggles and laughter, and the class instantly fell silent.

"Hello, son. You're a bit late for class, aren't you?" he remarked quietly.

"Ah, yeah. Sorry, Dad. My shoes got wet, and I had to go to the laundry room and get another pair," he responded wincing as he rubbed his head and found a knot there.

The king's stern face softened, and he lifted the boy to sit on the edge of the desk to examine the contusion. His fingers gingerly brushed over the bump, and Xavier hissed and winced. The entire class was staring at them. He felt heat rush over his face, and he batted his father's hand away.

"Geesh, Dad. It's okay."

He hopped down from the desk. Dizziness spun the room, and he had to cling to the table until it passed.

"How did your shoes get wet, son?" his father questioned.

He hesitated, not sure what to tell him. Then, Court crashed into the room, out of breath. "Sire! Sire, X...Xavier...he just...vanished! He disappeared, sir!"

"It's all right, Courtney. Xavier found his way to class, safe and sound," Jeremiah commented, stepping aside so Court could see Xavier.

Court's eyes widened, and he grinned broadly. "Crikey! You can teleport!""Yeah, it appears so," he murmured, brushing off his pants.

"All right, boys, take your seats. You've disrupted this class long enough," the king ordered softly.

"Yes, sir," they muttered and scurried to a pair of seats at the back of the room.

Whatever Xavier had expected in having his father as a

teacher, the reality turned out to be much worse. Quite simply it was a nightmare! He couldn't get away with anything! Anytime his attention wandered, his father would ask him a question for which he had to answer in Latin. Then, as soon as he leaned toward Beck to whisper a joke, his father stopped him, made him stand in front of the class, and translate the entire joke. And finally, when the king was busy writing the class's assignment on the board, he tried to pass a note to Court, but it failed miserably.

"Xavier? Bring me that note," his father demanded without turning or hesitating in his task.

He froze comically in mid-action and stared incredulously at the king's back. Finally, he straightened and slid the note under his book and asked angelically, "What note, sir?"

He turned and pinned him with an unyielding stare. "Don't play games with me, young man," he uttered with such quiet authority it caused the entire class to stiffen and watch the exchange with bated breath.

He stared boldly back at his father for several long seconds. Finally, with a bitter huff, he stood and took the note to his father. The king took the note and pulled him close until they were merely inches from one another.

"Son, have you not determined that any shenanigan you attempt in my class won't be successful? If you continue these games, you'll find yourself with extra chores and loss of privileges," Jeremiah hissed.

He swallowed and muttered, "Yes, sir. Sorry, Father."

In Xavier's opinion, Latin couldn't end soon enough. He needed a break from the intense concentration that his father demanded from him in class. Finally, an hour later the class was dismissed with a list of twenty words to memorize that night.

As the class exited the room, Court muttered, "Crikey! Having King Wells as a Latin teacher is going to be rough. No one can get away with so much as a sneeze without his knowing!"

"No? Really? I hadn't noticed," he spat sarcastically to his friend.

The class that Xavier and his friends looked forward to the most was fencing. Finally, an hour before lunch, all year one and year two students entered the fencing hall. The large chamber was elaborately adorned with ancient armor, weapons, and swords of all shapes and sizes ranging from daggers to magnificent sabers and even javelins. As the children peered around in awe, Henrick Davies strolled into the room.

"Hello, students!" he bellowed happily with a broad smile.

"Hello, Lieutenant Davies," the children chanted.

"Sir Davies? Do you know where all this stuff came from?" Harry asked eagerly, inspecting a set of armor that looked to be in immaculate condition.

"Well, most of it, I do," he answered with an easy grin. "The armor you see there, young Harry, belonged to King Michael. The bow and sheath of arrows there," Henrick pointed to the items mounted on an opposite wall, "belonged to a great general, Craig Cameron. Sir Cameron became famous for defending the kingdom against 100 armed men with only what you see posted there on the wall."

There was a moan of appreciation.

"Many of these pieces go back centuries and had at one time been stored in the castle at Warwood. When King Michael Abraham Wells, known simply as King Michael, had King's Mountain constructed, the articles were brought here for safe keeping."

"Sir Davies?" Court began, standing tensely next to Xavier and staring into a case a few feet from him. "What about that sword? Does it have magical properties or something?"

"What makes you ask that, Mr. Hardcastle?" Sir Davies questioned.

"Well, I thought…" Court shook his head. "I thought I saw it… glowing a little."

Henrick looked at Court with shock. "You saw it glowing? That's not possible, Mr. Hardcastle. I'm sure it was just a trick of the light. You see, that sword is known as the Sword of the Chosen. Legend says that over a hundred years ago, a time bender visited King Wells' great grandfather and gave him that very sword. This man claimed that he was the Chosen and had come back in time to leave the sword for himself for when he came of age." The class burst into chatter and whispers, and Henrick smiled. "Yes, I'm sure that's how the people living in the kingdom at the time reacted too. You can imagine the uproar it caused. When other kingdoms around the world learned of the sword and the prophecy, parents with young children poured into Warwood, each claiming that their child was the Chosen. But, of course, the king dispelled each claim."

"How could he tell? How did he know that one of those kids wasn't really the Chosen?" Xavier asked.

Henrick grinned and winked secretly down at him. "Well, young sire, legend states that the sword will emit a fantastic light in the presence of the true Chosen One. The king would only need to present the sword to each child to see if it would glow."

Collective sounds of awe and excitement filled the room.

Henrick looked back at Court. "So you see, Courtney, it's not possible that you saw the sword glowing," he stated before adding jovially, "unless the Chosen is secretly hiding among us."

Court laughed with the rest of the class. "Yeah, you're right. I'm sure I just imagined it."

"Now, as fascinating as the legend of the Chosen is, we have a lot of work to do this morning. So, let's get started. I need everyone to set their books on the floor along the wall and then stand here in a line facing me," he announced, gesturing toward the center of the room.

The children quickly dumped their books out of the way, took their places in the middle of the room, and waited anxiously for the lesson to begin. Henrick picked up a sword from a table at the side of the room and held it up.

"This is a foil. Foils are special swords designed for training. And this," Henrick continued as he laid down the foil and picked up a second sword, "is a saber. This is a deadly weapon and can cause severe injury. Therefore, you will not be studying or using this sword until you've mastered the basics with the foil. However, it doesn't matter whether your weapon is a foil or a saber; you will respect it. There will be NO horse playing with your weapon and absolutely NO bouts until you've learned and mastered the fundamentals. Do I make myself clear?" Henrick finished firmly.

"Yes, sir," the children responded.

"Good," Henrick replied with a small smile as he strolled up and down the line of children. "Now, the fundamentals can be summarized into one word. Balance! You must achieve balance of the body, the mind, and the soul. Achieving this could mean the difference between life and death."

The children exchanged nervous glances before Henrick continued. "Okay, show me how you would stand if you were being attacked," he announced. The children glanced uneasily at one another. "Oh, come on, come on! How would you stand if you were going to fight someone?"

Slowly, the children shuffled into various postures as Sir Davies roamed along the line inspecting the children's positions. Finally, he stopped in front of Xavier, who stood in a boxing stance with his feet pointing forward and his legs slightly apart. Every eye watched with bated breath when, without warning, the lieutenant shoved the prince and sent him stumbling backwards before toppling to the floor.

"If I were your enemy, Your Highness, you would be dead," he noted quietly with his saber pressed lightly over Xavier's heart. Then, with a rueful smile, he lowered the sword and helped the boy to his feet before turning to the rest of the class. "What happened here?"

"I was off balance, sir," Xavier answered.

"Exactly! Now, the correct stance for sword fighting is this," Sir Henrick stated and shuffled into the correct position. "Your sword foot should be extended, pointing toward your opponent, and the opposite foot should be perpendicular to your sword foot," Henrick explained before easing out of position and looking back at the class. "Okay? Now you try."

The group immediately shifted into the position as Henrick walked up and down the line of children, inspecting and making slight adjustments to their stances. When he reached Xavier, he studied the boy's stance before shoving him again, but this time Xavier didn't stumble. He simply stepped backwards and grinned.

Henrick beamed back at him and announced with an

approving nod, "Superb balance, Your Highness."

Chapter 9

Another Fight

Following fencing class, the group entered the Grand Hall buzzing over what they had just learned.

"Jeez, did you see that move Henrick put on X?" Beck remarked in awe. "That was wicked! I sure wouldn't want to sword fight against Henrick; he'd chop me down and never even work up a sweat!"

"Yeah, he sure seems to know his stuff," Xavier agreed as the boys shuffled toward a large buffet of food on a long table next to the kitchens. Xavier looked around the hall at the children settling at tables to eat their lunches. "Where are all the adults?"

"Dad said that they staggered lunch times to ease the burden on the kitchen staff. The grown-ups eat after us, I think," Court responded.

"Oh," he muttered and picked up a plate from the end of the table and began filling it. As he weaved through the tables behind Court and Beck to where the rest of the group was already seated, he saw Robbie sitting at a table to his right, laughing and talking quietly, and he stopped.

"Hi, Robbie," he greeted timidly, and she looked up at him. Encouraged by this brief connection between them, he rambled on. "How was your first day of classes? Wasn't fencing the best class so far? Sir Davies sure knows his stuff, huh? Latin is going to suck with Dad as the teacher though. No one will be able to get away with anything in there! So, how were your classes?"

She stared at him, looking astounded that he dared to talk to her. Then, she turned to a redheaded girl sitting next to her and asked loudly, "Do you hear something, Rene? It sounds like a buzzing fly found its way into the mountain. What are the odds?"

Rene looked uncomfortably between Xavier and Robbie before answering timidly, "Ah...yeah...it must be a fly."

His throat became dry and tight as he stared grievously at the back of Robbie's head. Finally, without another word, he scurried away from the table of giggling girls.

"Ouch! That had to hurt!" a voice chastised from behind him.

He turned and glared into Drew's sneering face.

"Shut it, Drew!" he muttered, turning to walk away.

"Are you sure you're King Wells' son? I mean, last night that man had to fight the women off with a stick! Whereas you...*you* have to beg them to even look at you!" Drew continued mercilessly, nudging Xavier in the back.

"I said shut up, Drew!" he bellowed, but Drew wasn't stopping.

"Hey! I've got a suggestion for you, Prince Pipsqueak! Maybe you should ask Beck for pointers. It took him less than two minutes of dancing with Robbie before she started snogging him." Drew cackled wickedly.

Xavier's face burned with anger and before he knew what he was doing, he turned and smashed his chocolate pudding into his tormentor's face. The crowd of children around them burst into hysterical laughter, and he felt a brief wave of triumph before Drew's rampage. After smearing the pudding away from his eyes, Drew grabbed him, sending his tray clattering to the floor.

"You little..." he growled as he slammed Xavier onto a table and punched him.

Pain exploded across Xavier's jaw and a kaleidoscope of color clouded his vision. He cowered and tried to cover his face as Drew delivered a second punch, knocking his own hand into his nose, bloodying it.

"Andrew! What in God's name are you doing?" Henrick exclaimed, lifting the older boy off Xavier and restraining him.

Xavier sprang from the table and lunged at the older boy, tackling him and knocking Henrick off balance. He was only able to get in a single punch before Drew flipped him hard onto the stone floor and began pummeling him again. Finally, Henrick managed to pull the snarling boy away as another pair of hands hauled Xavier to his feet and held him firmly.

"Andrew Hardcastle!" the man holding Xavier roared. Although he couldn't see clearly through his blood-smeared eyes, he recognized Loren Jefferson's voice. "What in the hell are you doing?"

"He started it! Just look at me, Loren! He smashed pudding in my face!" Drew protested.

"Look at you!" Henrick roared. "Look at the prince! Do you..."

"What's going on?" King Wells' voice called as he and Ephraim Hardcastle advanced toward the confrontation.

"Andrew?" Ephraim started slowly, anger seething in his voice. "What happened?"

"I didn't start it, Dad. I was only talking to Xavier when he just turned around and threw pudding in my face! So I..."

"Andrew?" King Wells interrupted as he lifted Xavier onto the table and began cleaning up his face with napkins. "Are you sure you want to stick to that story?" he questioned, pinning the older boy with a fierce stare.

Drew met the king's eyes briefly and blushed. "No, sire. I...I was teasing him about being dismissed by Robbie when he tried to talk to her. I guess that's why he smashed pudding in my face..."

"Sire? I'm so sorry about Andrew's behavior. I don't know what has gotten into him lately, but I can assure you he will be properly dealt with," Ephraim apologized.

"It's not an apology for us to make, Ephraim. I think this is between the boys. They both had a responsibility in what happened," Jeremiah noted, peering down at his son.

"What?" Xavier rebuked grumpily. "You want *me* to apologize? I won't! He deserved it!"

"Xavier," Jeremiah warned quietly. "Your behavior was inappropriate!"

"Inappropriate? What was I supposed to do? Continue to let him harass me and give me a hard time?" he blared.

"As future king, you cannot go around attacking your citizens," Jeremiah insisted, his voice raising.

"That's bull!" he spat. "He deserved it, and I won't apologize!"

His father's eyes went fiery and burrowed into him, as he stubbornly glared back. Finally, the king looked back at the group. "Will you excuse us? Xavier and I have a couple of things we need to discuss," he concluded, lifting him from the table and setting him on his feet. "Andrew, he'll be ready to apologize to you at dinner."

Then, with his hand clamped painfully on Xavier's shoulder, he steered him from the room and down the stairwell to the fourth level corridor. Rebecca Hardcastle appeared from a room on the left and stopped short at the sight of Xavier's face.

"My word! Prince Wells, what happened?" she asked, inspecting his face.

"He had the worst end of a fist fight, I'm afraid," Jeremiah answered.

"Oh, Xavier! Fighting? Again? What has gotten into you?" Rebecca responded, looking down at him in disappointment.

He felt guilt and embarrassment rush over him, and he tucked his head shamefully. "Well, Drew started it," he muttered.

"Drew? My Drew did this?" she hissed. When Xavier nodded, Rebecca's face went rock hard, and she mumbled to herself, "Just wait until I get my hands on that boy."

"I think Ephraim's got his hands on him right, now, Becky," Jeremiah reassured her, winking.

"Oh, I'm sure he does, but Drew will still face me when his dad's through with him. See you both tonight at dinner," Rebecca finished quickly before hurrying up the stairs, undoubtedly to find Drew.

His father prodded him down the corridor and through the last door on the left. He didn't need to ask where they were; one look at the chamber, and he knew he was standing in his father's room. The chamber was modestly furnished with beautiful, ornate antiques in mint condition. The walls were a highly polished stone washed in gold from the sleepy flame flickering in the hearth.

"Sit and let's heal those wounds," Jeremiah announced, steering him to a wooden chair next to a small table.

Xavier sat as his father dragged another chair toward him and sat facing him.

"Close your eyes. This might sting a little," his father warned, lifting a hand so that it hovered inches from his face.

A radiating heat slowly sank into his wounds. It was quite soothing and relaxing at first, but as the empowerment intensified and began the bulk of the healing process, his face burned and stung like it was on fire!

"Ow! Dad!" he complained, moving his head, but his father grabbed him, keeping him still.

"Ow! God, Dad! Stop it! I'll keep the wounds!"

Finally, Jeremiah pulled the empowerment away and released him. "Wash your face off," he instructed, pushing a small basin of water toward him and handing him a towel.

Xavier splashed water over his face and dried it gingerly. Then, his father grasped his chin and examined him. "You'll still have a black eye and a bit of a fat lip, but the rest seems healed."

"Sire?" Court called timidly from the doorway. "I brought some food down for Xavier."

"Thank you, Courtney. You can set it on the table here," the king replied.

Court carried the tray over to the table where father and son sat and set the food down before hurrying from the room. Xavier dove hungrily into the turkey sandwich and had it half-eaten in just three bites.

His father snickered. "Boy, slow down before you choke!"

"Yes, sir," he mumbled past the mouthful of food.

"How's the face feeling? Better?" he asked.

"Yeah. It's better," he responded.

"Son? Who is the most powerful man in our society?" his father asked quietly, leaning back in his chair.

He swallowed and looked up at him. "Well, you, Dad."

"Why is that?"

"Because..." he was confused. "Because you're the

king!"

"Exactly. And being the most powerful man, what image would I give others if I physically attacked one of my subjects?"

He knew where this conversation was headed, and he defiantly slouched and crossed his arms. "I don't know," he muttered contrarily.

Jeremiah sighed. "Don't you see that your conduct was not appropriate for a prince?" he asked.

Xavier groaned inwardly. He knew what his father wanted to hear from him, but he disagreed. Andrew Hardcastle deserved to be humiliated. After all, how many times had Drew embarrassed him? How many times had he taunted and teased him? In his opinion, he had shown the patience of a saint up until now, and Drew deserved much more than a punch and pudding smashed in his face. However, that wasn't what his father wanted to hear. It was best to agree with him and get through the lecture as quickly and as painlessly as possible.

Slowly, he nodded and muttered, "Yes, Father. I'm sorry."

"You need to apologize to Drew, son. Then, tonight the two of you will wash the dinner dishes together," Jeremiah told him.

"Wash the dinner dishes? But, Dad, there'll be hundreds, and I already have two extra chores as it is. I won't have any free time! Can't..." his complaints buckled after one look at his father's face, and he sank deeper in his chair with a huff and sulked moodily.

His father stood glaring down at him. "If you're through eating, then I suggest that you get moving. Your electro force class started ten minutes ago," he ordered tightly.

Xavier stood abruptly and shoved his chair noisily into

the table before stomping from the room.

Chapter 10

No Joke

Xavier didn't see much of his father over the next couple of weeks and if Jeremiah hadn't been teaching Latin, he wouldn't have seen him at all. Not that seeing him in Latin was much comfort. The king was all business, and Xavier grew increasingly disgruntled by his father's aloofness.

A few weeks following the fight with Drew, he sat in his father's Latin class feeling particularly ignored and neglected. His father hadn't even said his usual, "Good morning, son." In fact, he hardly acknowledged his presence at all. Even when he threw a note folded into a paper airplane across the room to Beck, the king had barely reacted. He simply paused in his lesson, took the note from Beck, and placed it on the corner of his desk.

Near the end of the period, he was thoroughly annoyed by his father and scowled at his back as he finished writing the new vocabulary list on the board before settling behind the teacher's desk to grade the quiz they had taken at the start of the class which Xavier was pretty sure he had failed.

That was when the idea came to him and before he could talk himself out of it, he flicked a finger at the chalk board. Instantly, the vocabulary words squiggled and moved around the board to form the words: "Knock, knock."

Xavier looked around at the class and found that nearly every student was watching the board with puzzlement. With a small grin, he flicked his finger at the board again and spelled the words: "Who's there?"

Then, came: "Latin."

"Latin who?"

Finally, big letters appeared: "EXACTLY! WHO SPEAKS LATIN ANYMORE?"

A burst of muffled snickers erupted, and the king's head snapped up. With a quick flick from Xavier's finger, the words on the board returned to normal, and not a moment too soon. Jeremiah turned toward the board, but finding it as he had written it, he looked back at the class. Xavier felt his father's gaze rake over him, and he desperately concentrated on studying the terms in front of him.

Once his father's attention returned to the quizzes, he looked back to the board and flicked his finger again. This time, cartoon images filled the board: a dog, a boy, and a character that looked remarkably like Sir Blaire. With a swirl from his finger, the characters came to life. Sir Blaire was shaking a finger at the boy, and a conversation bubble with the words: "Gripe, gripe, gripe. Blah, blah, blah," appeared over his head. The dog kept tugging on Sir Blaire's pant leg, and whenever he turned to shoo it away, the boy would make obnoxious faces behind his back. Finally, with cartoon Blaire's attention back on the boy, the dog hiked up its leg and peed on Sir Blaire's shoes.

The class burst into laughter, and before Xavier could hide the cartoon display, his father turned and saw it. With a smooth wave of his hand, the images disappeared and the vocabulary terms returned. Then, he turned and pinned Xavier with a furious glare. The class's laughter was cut into silence.

"Finish your work," he told the class before turning to his son. "Xavier Wells? You will stay after class."

"Yes, sir," he responded with a quiver and stared unseeingly at the vocabulary words in front of him.

At the end of class, Xavier remained seated with nothing to do but wait and try to ignore the sensation fluttering in his gut.

"Good luck, Xavier," Garrett whispered.

"Thanks, I'm gonna need it, I think." he groaned.

"Well, if it's any consolation, X, that cartoon was a scream!" Beck grinned and followed Garrett out of the room.

For the first couple of minutes, his father didn't say a word and didn't even look at him. He simply continued grading papers, and judging by his deepening frown, the current paper was not a good one. Finally, he looked up and fixed him with a cold stare for several long seconds before he spoke.

"Well? What do you have to say for yourself?" he asked so quietly Xavier could hardly hear him.

"I...ah, nothing I guess, sir," he muttered, unable to meet his father's intense gaze any longer.

"How about this? Can you explain this?" his father asked rigidly, holding up Xavier's quiz with a large crimson "F" written on it.

He gulped. "I...I forgot to study. I'm sorry, Father. Really! I just forgot!"

"I have half a mind to pull you from the boys' dormitory and move you into my chambers," he announced stonily.

"Jeez, it was just one quiz, Father!" he rebutted bitterly, but a small part of him rejoiced. If his father made him stay in the royal chambers, at least then he would see him more often.

"Don't sass me, boy!" he growled, standing and sending Xavier sinking deeper in his seat.

"Jeremiah, I was wondering if we could meet..." Lana Applegate's words evaporated, and her broad grin dropped slightly as her eyes settled on Xavier's huddled figure. She gave him a small smile. "Oh hello, Xavier. How are you doing, sweetheart?"

He shrugged and looked anxiously at his father.

She turned toward the formidable king and smiled at the exasperation she saw there. "Excuse me, sire. I hadn't realized you were busy. I'll talk to you later about my ideas for the new chambers on the fifth level."

She turned to leave, but the king's voice stopped her. "Lana, please wait a moment. I need to have a word with you in the hall if I could."

"Of course," she replied, leading the way out of the classroom.

Before he exited, his father pinned him with a stern glare. "Don't move. I'm not finished with you."

"But, dad? I have..."

The king's sharp glare killed the rest of his complaint, and sighing indignantly, he dropped his head despondently onto his desk with a thud.

A minute or two later, the king returned looking less irritable and angry and approached the sulking boy. "Son," he prompted, handing him his failing quiz. "First, I want this corrected. Then, you will write each missed vocabulary word along with its definition fifty times and have it on my desk by tomorrow morning."

"Fifty times!" he complained indignantly. "That'll take me all night!"

"It just might, but when you're through, you will know

those words," his father replied, unfazed by his outburst. "As a result of your little pranks today, you will sit in the front of the room next to the teacher's desk until you learn that your purpose in class is to learn, not visit with friends, pass notes, or be a jokester. However, if you ever try pulling stunts like you did today, you will face more severe consequences than a simple seating change. Understood?"

"Yes, sir," he whispered meekly.

Jeremiah nodded with satisfaction as he straightened. "All right, then. You better get yourself to your next class."

Xavier quickly scrambled from the room.

He arrived ten minutes late for his government class. Mrs. Applegate simply nodded toward an empty seat but didn't attract any more attention towards him than what was necessary. Thankful for her mercy, he quickly sat and tried to catch up with the lesson, but he was completely lost. In the end, he gave up and pulled out his notebook. After his fight with Beck during the celebration dance, he found that the events of that day wouldn't leave him alone, and at night, his mind was restless and wouldn't stop pondering ways to get back into Robbie's good graces. Finally, last night he formulated a plan to break through to her and make amends. He would have to share his feelings and lay his heart out for her to either accept or destroy. It started with a letter. So, he spent the rest of the class period writing Robbie a note. Then, he folded it in quarters, wrote Robbie's name on the outside, and tucked it in his government book.

At the end of class, Xavier strode into the corridor with his friends, feeling confident and relieved that his plan to get Robbie back would work. As he started down the hall towards math class, Drew tripped him for the fifth time that week. His books and notebook flew out in front of him, spilling papers everywhere. Drew's cronies, Jonas and Seth, cackled loudly.

"Jeez, Wells! How could someone be that clumsy? That's the fifth time you've tripped this week!" Drew chastised.

"Wow, Drew! I'm impressed," he retorted sarcastically, getting to his feet and doing his best to ignore the throbbing pain in his knee. "That tripping prank is definitely some of your *best* work, mate! Seriously! I know it's hard for you to come up with new material considering you're a thick git, but I'm sure all the kids in the pre-school wing would laugh their asses off. You should go try it out there because no one here seems to be laughing."

Drew's face went crimson, and he looked as though he was about to explode. And, just when Xavier thought he would punch him, a horrid grin slipped across his face, and he patted his shoulder. "That's cute, Wells. Really funny. Let's just see how everyone likes this."

Before Xavier could defend himself, Drew plowed into him and knocked him completely off his feet. There was nothing he could do. He had no control over his body as he collided with someone, and they fell into a heap onto the hard floor. Xavier took the worst of the landing for the kid he crashed into landed on top of him. His head slammed against the floor, and the room spun dangerously dark, and just as Drew had planned it, there was an explosion of laughter.

Consumed with pain, he blinked hard to clear his vision as the girl on top of him gingerly stood. Even through tear-filled eyes, he had no trouble recognizing Robbie climbing off of him. Her face flushed as she looked down at him horrified. Before Xavier could utter a word, she turned and ran down the hall.

"What's going on here?" Ephraim Hardcastle's voice

called over the dying laughter as he fought his way through the crowd.

Instantaneously, Drew's smirk disappeared, and he dropped to Xavier's side. "Say one word about this to Dad and this will all seem like a fond memory," he spat out quietly. Then he looked to Courtney. "That goes for you too, little brother." He turned just as Ephraim emerged from the crowd.

"Drew? What happened here?" his father asked suspiciously, his gaze darting between the prince and his son.

"Xavier had a bit of an accident, Dad. He was rushing about; I told him not to run in the hall. Anyways, he ran into Robbie, and they fell. I think he's a bit banged up," he explained. Xavier was mildly impressed by Drew's ability to sound sincere and concerned. It was an Oscar-worthy performance.

Ephraim knelt next to Xavier. "Are you all right, Your Highness?"

He nodded and tried to sit up, but the hallway spun and he fell against Ephraim.

The general steadied him and whispered, "Take it easy a moment, young sire. You must have hit your head." Then, he looked at the silently watching crowd. "All right! All right! The show's over. Get to class."

There was murmuring as the crowd dispersed, and Ephraim looked at his older son.

"Andrew? Would you please go and inform the king that the prince has been injured."

"Yes, sir," he responded importantly and hurried off past the Grand Hall, toward the offices and conference rooms at the other end of the corridor.

"Do you think you can stand so I can help you to the infirmary?" Ephraim asked.

Xavier nodded and tried to stand, only to stagger and collapse to the floor. So, General Hardcastle scooped the boy into his arms and carried him. When they entered the infirmary, Rebecca came bustling over to them.

"What happened?" she asked, fretting over Xavier like a mother hen.

"He fell and hit his head. He seems a bit woozy," her husband explained, setting the boy onto the examining table.

"Oh my, he may have a concussion," she exclaimed, peering down at him with concern.

Suddenly, Jeremiah barreled through the door. His face was flushed, and he was panting as though he had sprinted the entire way to the infirmary. His eyes darted manically around the room until finally settling on Xavier.

"Son? Are you all right? Drew said you were injured. What happened?" he rattled out, rushing over to him and taking his face into his hands.

"Ah, well...I fell," he muttered.

"Well, now that Jer's here, I'm going back to work," Ephraim interjected as he started toward the door but hesitated. "Oh, Xavier? Since I doubt you'll make it to fencing class, Henrick was supposed to tell you that you will begin your advanced classes tomorrow. You'll have advance fencing with me right after lunch, and your electro-force class will be scheduled before lunch. The rest of your courses will remain as they are. I'll see you tomorrow. Don't be late."

"Yes, sir," Xavier responded meekly.

By the time Xavier was thoroughly examined, scanned by a healer for signs of a concussion, and rested for an hour at Rebecca's insistence, it was just five minutes before lunchtime.

"Do you think you can make it on your own, son?"

Jeremiah asked, as Xavier slid off the examining table with a wince.

"Yeah. My head hurts a little, but I'll be fine," he answered as he moved slowly to the door, but his father continued to hover over him, which he had to admit that he secretly enjoyed. "Dad," he protested. "Really, I'll be okay. Go back to work."

With a hesitant face, he nodded. "All right, son, but if you need me, just find a Royal Guard. They'll know where I'll be."

"Okay. Thanks, Dad."

Chapter 11

The Love Letter

Xavier entered the Grand Hall and was happy to find that he was the first to arrive for lunch. Relieved that he could get his food and find a seat without being jostled about, he filled his plate and settled at a table moments before the doors banged open and throngs of children burst into the hall. Court and his friends led the group to the buffet tables, and they sauntered over to Xavier carrying their lunches.

"Hey, X," Court greeted as he slid into the seat next to him. "How're you doing, mate? What did the healers say?"

"I'm fine, but I don't want to talk about it. It's humiliating enough without going on and on about it."

"Sorry, mate, but it was kind of funny," Beck noted quietly, and Xavier glared at him.

"You try having a girl fall on you, slamming your head against solid rock, and listening to every citizen under the age of sixteen laugh at you. Then, you tell me how funny it is!"

"Ouch! Okay, okay, it's not funny at all. I get the picture. But you do realize that this requires less than gentlemanly tactics for retaliation," Beck interrupted.

"Yeah, I know. Believe me, I will get even with Drew," he growled with a scowl as Drew shot him a mocking smile from across the hall.

"Here, Xavier. I got your stuff from the floor," Garrett told him, shoving books at him.

Xavier muttered thanks and took the books from Garrett. Then remembering the note to Robbie, he sprang to his feet and grabbed his government book, ignoring the pain thumping behind his eyes. Frantically, he flipped through its pages. His Latin quiz was still there, but the note was missing! The room began to spin, and his stomach lurched into his throat; neither had anything to do with his concussion.

"Whatcha' looking for?" Court asked through a mouthful of fruit cocktail.

"A note! Garrett, did you see a folded up note lying around where I fell?" he asked, trying to swallow back the panic rising in him like a flood.

Garrett slowly shook his head.

"Are you sure? It was a piece of paper folded in half twice! You didn't see it anywhere?" he demanded, his voice spiking into near panic.

Garrett looked at him, horrified. "No, Xavier. I didn't see any note."

Realizing how loud he had become and feeling several pairs of eyes on him, he sat down and covered his face with his hands. The other boys simply stared at him.

"Ah, X? What's so important about the note?"

Beck's question was answered, but not by Xavier. For in that moment, Drew stood on top of his chair in the center of the Grand Hall, and with the broadest, most conniving grin Xavier had ever seen, he announced, "Hey everybody! Can I have your attention, please?"

Slowly the chattering children quieted and looked at Drew curiously.

With every eye on him, Drew's grin broadened, and he

continued, "I'd like to share something with you all today. You see, I found this note in the hall this morning, and I had every intention of returning it to its owner. However, when I opened it to see who wrote it, I couldn't help myself, and I read it. I'm not ashamed to admit it, but when I read these words, they brought tears to my eyes. Then, I thought, 'Why should something this beautiful be hidden away?' After all, I believe it's important for royalty to connect with their common citizens so they don't appear to be more than human. I'm sure that Prince Wells would agree with me, which is why I am sure he'll be strongly... *moved* by this note."

The color drained from Xavier's face as Drew paused, withdrew a folded note, unfolded it, and cleared his throat. He didn't need to hear a word of the note. He knew exactly what it said; he had written it. Xavier looked at Court pleadingly, and Court, suddenly realizing what was about to happen, jumped to his feet.

"Drew! Don't! I'll tell..."

The older boy's grin grew enormous. "You know something, baby brother? Go ahead and tell. It'd be worth it." Then, he turned back to the note in his hand and began reading in an exaggerated high-pitched voice.

"My Dearest Robbie,

I just wanted to let you know how much I really miss you. I understand why you're mad at me. I'm mad at myself. Everyone, my dad, Loren, Ephraim, even the prophet has told me repeatedly that what happened to your dad wasn't my fault, and there was nothing I could have done to prevent it. But I know they're wrong. I can feel it in my gut, but more importantly, you told me that I could have stopped it and that I could have saved your dad. You have never lied to me. There have been things you couldn't tell me, but you've never outright lied to me.

So I know it must be true. I could have saved your dad and I didn't. For that, you have every right to hate me for the rest of my life, but I hope you won't. Please forgive me; don't hate me.

The guys don't understand why I care so much, but they don't know all that we've been through together. They don't know how you were always there for me. They don't know that seeing you and talking with you is the best part of my day. They just don't understand that I love you. It's true and that won't ever change, no matter what.

Love,

Xavier

Whatever reaction Drew had anticipated, it wasn't what he got. At first, there were snickers, but as soon as the note mentioned Dublin, the snickers fell away. A few older girls were even crying and muttering comments like, "Oh, how sweet," and, "That was beautiful."

Although the reaction fell well short of Drew's expectations and he looked thoroughly put out, Xavier was humiliated nonetheless.

"What do you mean; you love her?" Beck whispered, staring at him with something between surprise and anger. Oh, yeah, Beck was jealous all right.

But Xavier didn't answer; he had had enough. As quickly as he could, he stood and left the Grand Hall.

The other boys found him thirty minutes later in the boys' dormitory, laying face down, his face buried in his pillow.

"I don't want to talk about it," he mumbled into his pillow before any of them could say a word.

Most of the boys stopped abruptly in mid-stride, prepared to honor his request. Beck, on the other hand, ignored it completely and moved to the foot of his bunk. "Why didn't you tell me that you were...well, that you *liked* her? I mean, you said it when you had the flu, but I didn't take that seriously. I thought it was the fever talking. Does she know? Have you ever told her?" Beck asked, trying to sound supportive, but Xavier could feel jealousy oozing from him.

"God, Beck! You're an idiot! Duh! Of course she knows! After what Drew did, EVERYONE knows!" Garrett bellowed.

"Oh, yeah. Right," Beck grumbled.

"Look, it doesn't matter if she knows or not! She hates me! Now, can we stop talking about this! I DON'T WANT TO TALK ABOUT IT!" he yelled, standing and walking toward the door.

"Xavier! You're forgetting your books!" Garrett called.

"I don't care! I'm not going to classes," Xavier announced and stormed out of the dormitory.

Moments later, Court caught up with him and fell into step beside him. "Ah, X? You can't just skive off classes. Your dad will kill you. Maybe you should talk to him about this..."

"He's never around and when he is, he doesn't have any time for me..."

"God, Xavier! He's reorganizing a city. Of course he's been busy. So has my dad! I can count on one hand the number of conversations I've had with him over the past month and half," Court told him.

"Okay, okay. I'll go and see him," Xavier groaned.

The boys wordlessly made their way to the Royal Chambers, and as Xavier reached for the door and pulled, soft music poured from the room. He started into the room but froze at the sight in front of him. His father was on the sofa with a woman in his arms. But as shocking as it was to see his father in this intimate situation, it was nothing compared to what he felt seeing him engulfed in a bright, pink light.

"Whoa," Court whispered in awe.

Court's voice jolted Xavier from his initial shock, and he felt the temperature rise in his face. The image of his father kissing another woman branded in his brain, and a sudden fury exploded from him.

"No! Stop! Stop it! You...you jerk. You lying jerk! I hate you!" he screamed, startling Jeremiah and the woman, and the pink glow immediately disappeared.

Xavier ran for it. He had no plans of where to go, he simply ran. Soon, he found himself outside his electro force class. Even though he was five minutes late, Loren didn't say a word to him as he stomped into the room and found his seat. The class was busily copying notes describing how to use electro forces to deflect attacks from the enemy.

He didn't have anything to copy the notes with, so he nudged the girl sitting next to him and borrowed paper and a pencil. It took all his concentration to fight his father's insistent pounding on his mental defenses. So, when Loren spoke, standing right next to him he jumped with a start.

"Xavier? Your father is looking for you."

"I know," he responded flatly and began copying the notes from the board.

"He wants you back in the Royal Chambers," Loren continued.

"I'm not going," he retorted stonily and continued to write, but his penmanship was quickly growing erratic and sloppy.

The general sighed and shifted his feet. "If you don't go, he'll come and get you."

Xavier stopped writing with a soft curse and looked moodily up at Loren. "I don't care. I'm not going. Besides, I was just there, and he was...busy."

"Have it your way, then. But, I'm telling you, little sire, he's coming for you, and if you don't go with him, he'll carry you out," he concluded, returning to the teacher's desk at the front of the room.

Xavier could feel the students around him studying him, but he ignored them and continued with the notes. In a matter of minutes, Jeremiah appeared at the door nervously smoothing down his disheveled hair.

"Xavier?" he called softly, "we need to talk."

"Not now, Dad. I'm busy," he replied bitterly.

"Son, it wasn't a request or a question. Get to your feet and come with me," he ordered his backbone stiffening. It was a reaction he'd grown accustomed to seeing whenever his father's temper was sparked.

But Xavier didn't respond and simply continued copying notes. Fuming at the boy's refusal to comply, the king stomped across the room, grabbed him by the arm, and hauled him to his feet.

"Get off me!" he yelled and without thinking, he tried to hit his father.

Jeremiah deflected the punch lazily, lifted him, pinning his arms at his side, and carried him out of the room. He carried the squirming, disgruntled prince through the corridors and didn't release him until they were outside the Royal Chambers, when Xavier's heel made sharp contact with his knee.

"Ow! Damn it, Xavier! Settle down before I blister your backside," his father hissed, rubbing his knee and glaring down at him.

"No! You're just ticked off because I interrupted your little... love fest... with that... that FLOOSY!" he bellowed.

Jeremiah seized him roughly, and his voice exploded with fury. "LANA IS NOT..."

"Wait! What? You mean the woman you were kissing...*that* was Mrs. Applegate?" he blurted, no longer combative.

Xavier's reaction took the king aback, and he released the boy and stared down at him. "Yes," he answered slowly.

"Oh," he replied meekly.

His father shook his head, exasperated. "Come on. Lana is waiting for us in the chamber."

They entered the Royal Chambers and found Lana sitting anxiously on the sofa. She stood up when she saw them and smiled weakly at Xavier.

"Hello, Xavier," she greeted quietly.

He grinned sheepishly and muttered, "Hi."

"Sit down, son," Jeremiah ordered gently, and he immediately sank into an armchair as his father joined Lana on the sofa.

"Now, I can understand your... ah, embarrassment after walking in on us, but I don't understand the outburst..."

"Because you lied to me!" Xavier interrupted.

"I did not...," his father responded patiently.

"You did, too!" he insisted.

"Xavier," Jeremiah warned.

"Okay, okay. That's enough, boys," Lana intercepted, holding up her hands. "Quit interrupting one another and hear each other out."

Jeremiah and Xavier exchanged stunned looks.

"Now, Xavier, why do you think your father lied to you?" Lana asked.

"Well, because he told me... after that...that witch...Catherine, he told me that I'd be the first to know if he started a relationship again, and I wasn't. He lied to me," he explained adamantly.

"Xavier, I didn't..." his father began, but Lana stopped him.

"Jeremiah, did you say that to him?" Lana asked.

"Well..." he stammered.

Xavier had never seen his father at a loss for words, and he couldn't help but smirk at him.

His father glared playfully down at him. "Now, see what you've done? You've gotten me in trouble with her!"

Lana gave him a vicious glare, and the king laughed, hugging her close. "I'm sorry, son. You're right. I did tell you that you'd be the first to know, but in my defense, my feelings for Lana snuck up on me. I didn't go looking to start a relationship. But I should have told you before now, and for that, I'm sorry."

Xavier grinned and with a shrug, replied, "That's okay. I really like the idea of you and Mrs. Applegate dating. Do you think you'll get married?"

His father nearly choked as laughter erupted from him. "Xavier, that's a presumptuous thing to ask! This relationship is too new to make those kinds of predictions just yet."

He ducked his head bashfully and mumbled, "Oh. Sorry."

"Well, I think I'll leave you two to talk. See you both at dinner," Lana announced as she stood. His father quickly got to his feet and walked her to the door. After a quick, awkward kiss, Lana left the chambers. He turned back to his son, smiling like a fool.

"Lord, Dad! You've got it bad for her! Haven't you?" Xavier laughed.

Ignoring his son's comment, he returned to his business-as-usual demeanor. "Now...do you...are you sure you're all right with this?"

"Yeah," he answered.

He hesitated and eyed the boy skeptically.

"Really, Dad! I'm fine with it!"

Jeremiah nodded and smiled. "Good. I'm glad to hear that."

"But, I have a question. When I walked in on you and Mrs. Applegate earlier, I saw a light, a bright, pink light. Where did it come from?"

His father shifted uncomfortably, and his eyes fluttered away from Xavier's. "Ah," he started and stopped to clear his throat. "Well, the light...the light came from me, son."

"From you!" Xavier blurted with a snicker. "What was it?"

His face turned red. His father was actually blushing, and he continued to squirm uncomfortably under Xavier stare. "Well, I create...I've always created a pink force whenever I express certain feelings."

Xavier was confused. "Really? What does the light do?"

"Well, it's a...uh...well it's hard to explain what it does," he stammered, turning even redder. He took a deep breath and added, "It's a kind of pleasure empowerment; I can make people relaxed and happy."

"Oh. Well, how come you didn't glow when you kissed Catherine?" Xavier wondered aloud.

"I didn't love her, son," he replied simply, his eyes solemn and unwavering. "I only seem to lose control over the empowerment when I'm in love."

"Oh," Xavier muttered.

His father was in love with Lana! He could definitely live with that. She was super-nice and gorgeous! Plus, she was good for him. He didn't mind someone like Lana taking his mom's place.

"Dad? Did you glow with Mom?"

He straightened and murmured quietly, "Yes, I did."

Chapter 12

The Bat Attack

As Xavier made his way to anima-lingua class, happiness ballooned inside him, and he couldn't stop grinning. He loved the idea that his father and Lana Applegate were seeing one another. She was so beautiful, and she didn't seem intimidated at all by the king. The look on his father's face when she'd put him in his place for lying to him had been priceless! Xavier snickered at the memory. Oh yeah, with Lana in their lives, things were going to be very interesting and definitely a lot more fun!

Still smiling, he entered anima-lingua class and found his classmates stood in two lines facing stuffed figures that resembled crash-test dummies.

"Sire Wells! Why are you late?" Sir Blaire barked.

"Ah, I...my father had asked to see me, sir," he responded.

The teacher eyed him suspiciously before snapping, "Well, don't just stand there! Select an animal from the table there and get in line behind Mr. Hardcastle!"

With a grimace, he picked up a caged ferret and joined the line.

"Hey, pipsqueak!" Drew muttered. "Did you see Robbie's reaction to your love letter?"

He was still in such high spirits that at first Drew's jeer

didn't bother him. But he was relentless.

"She was...well, disgusted would be an understatement. I swear, it looked like she was going to hurl. And after you left, she was telling anyone who'd listen that she hated you and that she'd never forgive you. She said that you were the reason her father was dead. She said that you're nothing more than a murderer!"

Xavier's state of euphoria was lost. His entire body went numb as the older boy's words drummed into his mind. "You're nothing more than a murderer. You're nothing more than a murderer."

"Still, that letter of yours was priceless," Drew added. Then, batting his eyes dramatically, he squealed, "My Dearest Robbie, I miss you sooooo much..."

"All right, that's enough!" Sir Blaire called over the chatter, and instantly, everyone grew still and quiet.

Xavier was left fighting the rage mounting inside him. He wanted nothing more than to thump Drew, and he contemplated the idea as he glared at the back of his head.

"Now," Blaire continued, "over the past few weeks, you've learned how to use animals as distractions in battle. Today you will learn how to use animals as weapons. Watch as I demonstrate." Sir Blaire took a cage from a student in the first row, withdrew the cat inside, lifted the animal so they were eye-to-eye, and then simply released the cat.

The cat hit the ground in a sprint! It lunged toward the nearest stuffed dummy and attacked its head, hissing and clawing viciously. The group groaned appreciatively. Then, Sir Blaire gave a whistle, and the cat immediately ceased its attack and trotted over to him before rubbing affectionately against his legs.

"Now, your animals may not react this quickly with your first few attempts. So it's important for you to have patience and develop a close bond with your animal before you give it the suggestion to attack. If you attempt to give the suggestion before a bond is thoroughly established, your animal can become unpredictable, and it may even attack you!"

A soft mutter of alarm rippled through the students, but Xavier grinned. Sir Blaire had just given him a brilliant idea!

As Blaire continued to explain the details of accomplishing a solid bond, Drew busied himself with tormenting the girl in front of him by zapping her iguana with a small electro force. This gave Xavier the opportunity to connect and bond with his fruit bat. Agitated by Drew's shenanigans, the bat easily bonded with him and agreed to his suggestion.

"Does everyone understand? You must prove your trustworthiness to the animal before it will do your bidding. All right, who'd like to try it first?" Sir Blaire finished.

Drew, looking smug, pushed to the front of the line. "I will, sir. I've used this technique with my brother's hamster once."

"All right, Mr. Hardcastle. The floor is yours. Just remember that bonding with an animal you already have a relationship with is different than bonding with an animal who doesn't know you."

"Yes, sir," he responded automatically.

After a brief pause to connect with his animal, he opened the cage and withdrew a squirming, squeaking bat, but when he released the animal to attack the dummy, it made a wide sweeping arc and flew straight at his head. Drew ducked just in time to avoid the collision, but the animal circled back and this time clawed his face.

He stumbled backwards and fell to the floor. "Get it off

me! Get it off!" he yelled, his voice muffled from behind the bat's body. The entire class erupted with laughter.

Sir Blaire ran to help him, but Drew wasn't helping matters much. His body flailed across the floor like a fish out of water as he continued to scream, "Get this bloody thing off me!"

Finally, Blaire pinned the panicking boy to the floor and spat, "Stay still so I can get the animal to release you without doing any more damage."

But, Xavier's connection with the bat was quite strong, and it took several minutes to pry it from Drew's face.

With a struggling bat in his hands, Sir Blaire turned toward the class. Several were beside themselves with laughter that they had sunk to the floor holding their aching stomachs. "All right! That's enough," he snapped as he returned the bat to its cage.

The class slowly grew quiet, and Drew got to his feet, looking meek and humble. His cheeks had two small scratches where the bat had latched onto him. Then his eyes locked with Xavier's, and for an instant, Xavier thought he saw vulnerability there, but it was quickly swept aside and replaced with a smug glare. He returned the glare with a triumphant grin.

"Sire Wells!" Sir Blaire barked, his eyes flaring. "Can you tell me why this bat believes that the light boy suggested he attack his charge?"

Xavier's smile slipped and he stammered, "Ah...I...I don't know, sir."

"Really? You haven't the slightest clue?" Blaire questioned contrarily, his body straightening and swelling with rage. "What if I told you I know you gave this animal the suggestion to attack Mr. Hardcastle?"

Xavier held the man's piercing stare briefly before blinking and looking away. He stared at the professor's scuffed dull boots.

"Uh, I'd say that it's not true, sir," he muttered.

"Excuse me? What did you say? Did you just call me a liar, boy?" he blared, stomping toward him.

He stumbled backwards in retreat. "N...no, sir! I just meant...I mean, I'm just saying..."

"Careful, Sire Wells," he warned. "You're about to dishonor your father."

Xavier fell silent and looked up at the man's stony face, and he surrendered. "Yes, sir. I told the bat to attack Drew."

Sir Blaire nodded and pointed to a desk at the other end of the room. "Sit. You will remain there for the rest of the class period. We will discuss your punishment after class."

"Yes, sir," he whispered and skulked across the room to the desk.

Following class, Sir Blaire approached Xavier with an astringent stare. "Sire, did it even cross your mind that what you did could have been dangerous?" he whispered.

Slowly, he shook his head, staring fixedly at Sir Blaire's scruffy boots.

"Although we can suggest and coax animals into responding as we wish, ultimately, it is the animal's decision. That bat could have chosen to attack Mr. Hardcastle's eyes or his neck! How would you have felt if you'd been responsible for a serious injury like that?" he questioned sternly.

Xavier gulped. He hadn't thought of that as guilt clawed its way into the pit of his stomach. "I...I'd have felt horrible, sir. I'm sorry."

Sir Blaire nodded and continued stonily, "I'm not the one who needs to hear the apology, sire. But you can start making amends for your behavior by cleaning out the animal cages before dinner. Report back here at 4:30."

"Yes, sir," he whispered with a grimace, stood, and left the room.

After classes, Xavier only had thirty minutes to relax before he was scheduled to report to Sir Blaire for his punishment. So he sank onto his bunk and reluctantly pulled out his Latin quiz. With a begrudging sigh, he set to work on copying each missed term fifty times. He only managed to get through three words when Court burst into the dormitory.

"Hey, X! Is it true? Did you really make a bat attack my brother?"

"Yeah, sorry about that."

"Don't be! I think it's brilliant! I'll have a blast tormenting him!" Court sighed blissfully.

"Yeah, he's really pissed. Awesome pay back, X!" Beck chirped, collapsing onto the bed next to Xavier and hitting his head on the bunk above him. After a few choice curses, he grinned at Xavier and rubbed his head. "You've got to tell us about it and don't leave anything out, mate."

Grinning, he told the boys every detail of the bat attack. His friends were an eager audience and hung on his every word, laughing heartily in all the right places. But, when he told them about Sir Blaire's punishment, the group groaned in disgust.

"Yuk!" Frankie exclaimed. "That sucks!"

All the boys nodded in agreement.

"What are you working on?" Frankie asked, snatching Xavier's Latin book out of his hands. "I thought Sire Wells only gave us a few vocabulary words for homework!" Then he saw Xavier's quiz. "You got an F on today's quiz? Man, it was so easy, too!"

"Speak for yourself!" Xavier growled, grumpily seizing

his book and quiz back from Frankie. "I've got to write each missed word fifty times!"

"Fifty! Crikey! That'll take you all night!" Court exclaimed.

"Damn, X! I was hoping we could go exploring later," Beck complained.

"Exploring? Are you sure you want to do that? It didn't work out too great for us last time."

"But, Xavier, there's an underground river in the lower tunnels! I heard a couple of guys talking about it!" Beck exclaimed with fervor.

"A river?" Xavier gasped, his curiosity sparked.

"Yeah! I thought we'd go and check it out. Maybe we could even go swimming," he responded.

"Man, it sounds like a blast, but I... I can't," he concluded despondently, looking down at the Latin quiz in his lap. He had been working for over twenty minutes and only managed to complete three words. From the looks of things, it would take him well past bed curfew to complete it. With a bitter huff, Xavier slammed the book closed and threw it onto the floor beside his bunk. "All right. I'll meet you at the dormitory stairs at seven."

His friends let out a loud whoop, and Xavier stood, grinning.

"Well, I'd better go. If I'm late Sir Blaire will tell Father about the bat attack. If that happens, I won't be able to sit, let alone go exploring for an underground river," he muttered.

When Xavier arrived at the anima-lingua classroom, Sir Blaire was waiting for him.

"You're late, Your Highness!" he barked gruffly.

Xavier felt his temper rise. Geez, he was only two minutes late! What was the big deal? However, he swallowed the cheeky rebuttals bubbling inside him and muttered, "Sorry, Sir Blaire."

"Sorry doesn't solve the problem, young sire, but staying later does. You'll just have to explain to the king why you're late for dinner," he scolded.

"Oh, come on! I was only two minutes late!" he blared, the weak reign on his temper loosening.

"Hold your tongue, sire! You've just increased your punishment time by ten minutes, and if you sass me again, it'll be fifteen!" Blaire growled.

"I wasn't sassing you!" he sassed.

"Fifteen minutes it is, then," he announced.

"But I..."

"Sire? Do you really want to continue arguing and miss dinner completely?" he demanded.

"No, sir," Xavier grumbled, his gaze dropping to Blaire's boots.

After Xavier finally finished cleaning out the animals' cages and got cleaned up, he was nearly twenty minutes late for dinner. He raced up the stairs and down the Grand Hall corridor, frantically brainstorming for an excuse to give his father for being late. The only reason he could think of was that he had lost track of time while working on his Latin assignment. Anxiously, he approached the large wooden doors and paused to listen to the low hum of voices and the clatter of silverware. Then taking a deep breath, he opened the doors and entered the Grand Hall. He tried to move quickly and inconspicuously to the head table, but the citizens made this impossible. As soon as he entered, a hush fell over the crowd, and he felt his face go crimson from the attention. He looked to the head table and found his father watching his approach, with Lana sitting next to him. Once he was seated next to his father, the crowded hall returned to their meals and conversations.

Then the king turned toward him. "Son? Why are you late for dinner?" he asked, as a kitchen server hurried over with a plate of food.

"I...I lost track of time," he replied with a shrug, sinking his fork into the potatoes.

His father didn't respond and continued to stare at him, waiting for an explanation. Xavier shifted uncomfortably under his intense study. Then, trying to appear relaxed, he added offhandedly, "Yeah. I was doing my Latin assignment, and I lost track of time."

"Really, now?" the king remarked, his voice low and deep, the way it got when he was about to yell at him.

He didn't respond to his father's baiting. Instead, he continued to shovel food into his mouth until finally Jeremiah put a hand over his, stopping him.

"It's interesting that you'd say that, son, because Sir Blaire mentioned to me that he had assigned you an extra chore for an incident in class today and that you might be a little late," he whispered sternly.

Xavier sighed. "Yes, sir. I...I'm sorry, Father. I don't know why I lied. It's been a really bad day, and just when I think it couldn't get any worse, it does."

"Sorry about your day, son, but lying only creates more problems. If Sir Blaire had wanted, he could have reported the incident to the High Council," Jeremiah told him.

"What? You're kidding! It was just a joke!" he blurted.

"Joke or not, you used your empowerments to attack a fellow citizen without good reason," Jeremiah continued, visibly reigning in his anger.

"But there was a reason! Drew was being a complete and total git! And, technically, the bat attacked Drew. I...I just suggested it," he spat.

His father's hold on his temper slipped as he grabbed

him and spun him seat and all to face him. "Don't be a smart aleck with me, boy! You could be caned for your actions, damn it!" he growled threateningly.

"Your father is right, honey. As future king, the use of empowerments on citizens without provocation, without *acceptable* provocation, can invoke High Council action," Lana whispered in a calm voice.

He sank deeper in his chair wishing he could teleport away from this lecture. "I'm sorry...I...I didn't know..." he muttered.

"NO!" the king snapped. "You did know! You just didn't think! There's an enormous difference between the two. We've had this discussion before, son! You knew full well the consequences of your actions, but that didn't make a bloody difference! You *know* that using an empowerment against another person to humiliate him is simply wrong!"

He didn't like the direction his father's tirade was taking. Fearing that his exploration plans with the guys were in jeopardy, he quickly changed his strategy.

"Yes, sir. You're right. I knew all of that, but I did it anyway. Please, Dad, what can I do to make it right?"

It worked! Almost instantly, his father's face relaxed and the vein bulging in his forehead returned to normal. He released a heavy breath. "Well, Sir Blaire believes he's handled things properly. So, I'll let his punishment stand, but with one addition. You must apologize to Andrew."

Xavier grimaced inwardly, but nodded. "Yes, sir," he agreed, looking toward Drew sitting next to Court at the end of the head table. Eager to get it over with, he stood and moved toward him.

"Drew?" he whispered, waiting for the older boy to turn.

He glared up at him. "What do you want?" he spat.

"Ah, well, I wanted to say sorry. I'm sorry I made that bat attack you in class today," he stated biting his lip to keep from smiling. But, when Court snorted in his drink, he could no longer hold back the wide grin that snaked over his face.

"Your apology is not accepted, *Your Highness*, but don't worry. I'll get even, and when I do, you'll wish you had never been born!" he growled, his eyes flashing with fury.

Xavier's eyes jumped from Drew to Court who sat studying his brother suspiciously. Finally he looked at the older boy and shrugged.

"Well, I tried. Dad can't be mad at me just because you're being an ass about it," he muttered before turning and returning to his seat next to his father and Lana.

For the remainder of the meal, Xavier found himself watching his father with Lana. Jeremiah's eyes had a sparkle in them he hadn't seen before. His smile came readily and easily, giving him a boyish, youthful appearance. He was completely enchanted by the woman sitting next to him, and he went out of his way to find reasons to touch her.

Xavier wasn't alone in his study of the king and Lana Applegate. Nearly the entire hall kept a watchful eye on the couple who seemed oblivious to everything and everyone around them but each other.

"Did you know about this?" Loren questioned, nudging Xavier.

He shook his head and answered through a mouthful of food. "No, I just found out today."

"Well? What do you reckon? Is Lana on the level?" Loren asked.

He studied Lana for a moment before answering with a wide grin. "Yeah. She's perfect! Dad won't be able to get away with anything!"

Loren chuckled heartily. "Good! Your father has been getting away with too much for way too long. He needs a good woman to keep him in line."

Chapter 13

The River

After mopping the Grand Hall following dinner, Xavier raced down the stairwell to meet his friends on the dormitory level.

"About time, Wells! My haircut is going out of style!" Beck ribbed.

"Wilcox, your hair was always out of style!" he teased back.

The other boys groaned appreciatively as Beck seized Xavier and wrestled him into a headlock.

"You think you're so funny, don't you?" he jeered, playfully rubbing his knuckles over Xavier's scalp.

"Get off!" he spat, giving his friend a hard jab in the gut before spinning out of his grasp.

"Come on, guys! Stop messing about and let's go find that river," Garrett whined.

With a cheer of agreement, the group made their way down the stairs and emptied out onto the seventh level corridor. As they walked past the warning sign, once again Frankie hesitated.

"Remember Frankie," Xavier told him, "As future king, I give you permission to enter the restricted levels and chambers of the mountain."

With a nod, he joined the others as Beck announced, "I

think they said the river was down the tunnel on the left."

"Okay. Let's go then," Xavier ordered and led the group down the passage. Unlike most passages on this floor, this one was wide with a high ceiling and smooth, polished walls.

"Uh, guys? Don't take this the wrong way, but does anyone know who the guardian is tonight?" Mac asked quietly.

All the boys looked at him.

"What? I just like to know who's going to punish us if we get caught down here again."

"We're not going to get caught," Xavier muttered.

"I think it's Sir Blaire?" Beck responded.

"No, he had morning duty. The shift has changed," Court reminded them.

The boys stared at one another.

"We're not getting caught," Xavier repeated stoutly.

Then Harry whispered, "The king's on duty. It's his turn."

Every head turned in Harry's direction. Finally, Beck choked out, "The king?"

Harry nodded, and the boys' eyes darted to Xavier, who immediately felt a wave of irritation.

"What? Do you all want to back out now that you know we have to fool my dad?" he hissed impatiently.

The boys exchanged uneasy looks.

"God! You're a bunch of babies! You can all go back if you want, but I'm going on," he spat, turning and stomping down the corridor without looking back.

"Come on guys. If Xavier isn't worried about the king catching us, then we shouldn't be either," Court told them.

"But, Court..." Frankie whispered. "Don't you think Xavier has been a bit...*risky* lately?"

"What are you blubbering about, Frankie?" Court snarled.

"Well, he's..." he looked at the other boys for support, but the others were suddenly interested in the toes of their shoes. "Fine! They won't say anything, but we all think that since...everything that's happened...since Maggie's death... and especially after Mr. Minnows, Xavier seems...a bit... reckless. It's as if he wants to get in trouble or hurt or something."

Court hissed disbelievingly. "I can't believe it! Look, you know what he's been through! You all do! Of course Maggie and Uncle Dublin's deaths have him a little...off, but that's more of a reason to stick by him. If you want to turn your back on him now, if you won't support him when he needs us the most, then you're not the friend he needs!" His angry gaze flickered to the rest of the boys standing behind Frankie. "Does anyone else have something to say about Xavier? If you do, say it now and get the hell out of here!"

The group squirmed under his scrutinizing glare without a word.

Finally, Mac stepped forward and declared, "I'm with you, Court. I support Xavier."

"Me too," Beck and Garrett announced and moved to stand next to Mac and Court.

One by one, all the boys sided with Court until Frankie stood alone looking uneasy. "I wasn't turning my back on him! He's our prince! You know that I'm on his side. I was only saying...oh, forget it."

"Guys!" Xavier interrupted, peeking around the corner of a jagged rock. "I found it! I found the river! Come on! You've got to see it! You won't believe your eyes!"

They raced after him and entered an enormous cavern. A frigid, vicious wall of wind generated by the violent water battered their faces and bodies. The boys skidded to a halt and stared at the spectacular sight in front of them. There was more than just a river here. At the far end of this massive cavern a thirty-foot waterfall crashed thunderously into the churning, wild river. The sound was deafening! The river water moved swiftly, weaving and cutting through the cavern floor. Slowly the group inched closer to the river's edge. The water was crystal clear, and the rock bed was visible under the riotous surface. It was breathtaking and very ominous.

"Whoa!" Beck muttered, speaking every boy's thoughts.

"Well, I didn't come here just to stare at it," Xavier stated, tugging off his shirt and kicking off his sneakers.

"What are you doing, Xavier?" Court asked shrilly.

"What does it look like? I'm going to swim out to that rock," he answered, nodding to a large rock three meters from the hammering waterfall.

"Why in the hell would you do that, mate?"

"To see if I can. Why else?" he retorted, giving Court a devilish grin as he unfastened his jeans.

"You're completely mental! I can't let you do it, Xavier! I can't!" Court stated.

Xavier's spine straightened and met his friend's determined eyes with unwavering stubbornness. Idly, he wondered if Court knew how much he sounded like his dad.

"You can't *let* me?" he hissed softly. "You can't stop me! You're not my father."

"No!" Court spat grabbing his arm. "It's suicide!"

"Get your hands off me, Court," he growled. "Just because you're too chicken to try it doesn't mean I am. Now, back off." He shoved Court away and stripped off his jeans.

"Xavier, don't do it! It's...it's too dangerous," Mac

protested weakly.

He looked at Mac with wild eyes. "That's what makes it such a rush to try."

For a moment, the boys stared at him flabbergasted, but when he turned and approached the savage river, they charged at him and tackled him to the stone floor.

"We can't let you, X! You'll drown for sure! Don't do it! Please!" Garrett urged.

"Okay, okay!" he yelled. "I won't do it...just get off me! Harry's knee is crushing my spleen!"

Slowly, the boys piled off the prince. Beck paused long enough to give him a wet-willy before Court pulled him to his feet with a wide grin.

"It's good to see you haven't lost all your marbles. That river is too...XAVIER, NO!" Court bellowed as Xavier shoved past him and dove into the water.

The boys raced to the edge of the river and frantically searched for any signs of the prince. For several long seconds, he'd simply vanished.

"I'm going for help!" Frankie cried and raced from the chamber.

Finally, Xavier shot to the surface about five meters downstream, sputtering. He pounded at the water trying to reach the rock, but it didn't take long for him to realize that Court had been right. This was suicide! Why had he wanted to swim the river? It accomplished nothing! It changed nothing. Robbie still hated him. No, she not only hated him; she thought he was a murderer. Her father's murderer! There was no changing that.

The river was fighting back, pushing and pulling him around like a child's bath toy. The under current twisted its watery tendrils around his legs and pulled. He struggled to keep his head above water as he turned and fought to get back to shore. But the river was too strong, and Xavier was losing. Suddenly the current yanked him deep beneath the surface, and he clawed at the water in a panic.

"Xavier!" Court yelled, racing along the shore.

"Where is he?" Garrett cried, as he and the other boys followed.

"I don't know!" Court screamed, nearly in tears, as he ran farther down the riverside.

After several intense seconds, he emerged to the surface, coughing and wildly flailing his arms.

"There!" Mac bellowed, pointing another four meters downstream.

"Swim downstream at an angle to me, X! Don't try to fight against the current," Courtney hollered, but Xavier could barely keep his head above water, and he quickly disappeared again.

"Xavier!" Court screamed, tore off his shoes and shirt, and before any of the other boys could stop him, plunged into the icy water after the prince.

Meanwhile, Xavier fought to break free from the wicked undertow holding him prisoner. His lungs protested painfully, and his vision grew dim. He was on the brink of giving in to this watery grave when something amazing happened. As he inhaled the first lungful of water, his vision improved and the pain in his chest lessened. He exhaled the water and breathed in another lungful. His vision became sharper and clearer, and his mind more alert and aware.

Now confident he wouldn't drown, he had another concern. He didn't have the strength to fight the water to get to shore, and the river would sweep him away to God knows where. On the verge of complete panic, he felt a pair of hands rake his head, grab him by the hair, and yank him to the surface. Courtney held him above the water and pounded against the river, trying to get them to shore, but his head kept bobbing under. It took the boys nearly a minute to swim six feet. It grew less and less likely that they'd have the strength to make it to safety. Suddenly, the water beneath them changed into a swirling, powerful tidal pool, sweeping them apart and dragging them under the bubbling water. They hadn't traveled far when a pair of strong arms enveloped them and hauled them back to the surface. Then with a warm surge of energy, the boys collapsed onto the cold, stone floor at the river's edge.

Xavier coughed and spat water from his lungs as Ephraim Hardcastle dropped next to Courtney, who was a horrific shade of blue and deathly still. He watched in horror as Ephraim cleared his son's airway and began CPR.

After the second breath, Court choked and sputtered water. "D....Dad?" he coughed and began crying.

Ephraim looked as though a light breeze would blow him over as he pulled his son into his arms. "Jesus, boy. I...I thought..." He couldn't finish, and Xavier had to look away.

"Son?" his father's hoarse voice came from behind him. "Are you all right?"

He turned and found his father kneeling, soaking wet next to the river. Unsure his voice would work, he nodded and looked away.

"Ephraim, King Wells, we should get the boys to the infirmary," Loren suggested, standing next to the pale, terrified group of boys, his arm draped around a red-faced Garrett.

Xavier staggered to his feet, but his legs were too wobbly, and he collapsed. His father scooped him up and carried him from the river cavern.

Both boys were taken to the infirmary and relinquished under the watchful eye of Tamarah Minnows. The instant they entered the hospital chamber, Jeremiah was ushered from the room to dry off and change into dry clothes, and Xavier was given warm pajamas and told to strip off his wet undershorts.

Court, on the other hand, received immediate medical attention. While Ephraim stripped him of his wet clothes and dressed him in dry flannels, Tamarah busily listened to his chest with a stethoscope.

"He swallowed a lot of water, Ephraim. He's in danger of developing dilutional hyponatremia, more commonly known as water intoxication. And, being a near-drowning victim, there's a risk for acute respiratory distress if the surfactant in his lungs has been compromised. He must be watched closely over the next 48 hours for signs of swelling in his airways. I'll need to keep an eye on his sodium levels as well. He'll need to remain in the infirmary for a few days," she announced, gently brushing Court's wet hair from his eyes. Suddenly, there was a scream as Rebecca Hardcastle burst into the room.

"Ephraim?" she cried shakily, rushing toward him. "Ephraim? Is...is he okay? Where's my baby?"

Ephraim held up his hands to calm his wife. "Becky, he's going to be all right. Calm down. He's fine."

Rebecca burst into sobs as she went to Court's side and enveloped him in her arms.

"Mum, I'm okay. Please, don't cry," Court consoled hoarsely.

Xavier's chest grew tight and heavy, and his eyes stung with unwanted tears. His best friend nearly died today...no, correction, his best friend *had* died today, and once again, he had been at fault. Guilt mauled at him as he climbed into bed and buried himself under the covers and pillows.

"Xavier, sweetie?" Mrs. Minnows called gingerly, peeling away the blankets and pillows. "Oh, honey. Courtney is going to be okay. I promise. I'm just keeping him as a precaution. That's all."

He nodded and wiped his wet cheeks without a word.

She gave him a small encouraging smile and asked, "Do you think you could sit up? I need to examine you and listen to your lungs."

He sat up and shuddered as she placed the cold metal stethoscope on his chest. Mrs. Minnows listened for several long seconds, a frown burrowing into her brow.

"Hmm, that's strange," she murmured just as Jeremiah, in dry clothes, entered the room with Lana behind him.

"What's strange, Tamarah?" he asked, his voice spiking in alarm as Lana immediately went to Xavier's side and hugged him close to her.

"Well," she began, straightening and looking at the king with a befuddled expression, "as I understand it, Xavier was in the water for nearly two minutes before young Courtney jumped in after him, right?"

He nodded. "Yes, that's right."

"Well, I find it odd that there's no sign of the prince having fluid of any kind in his lungs when Courtney's lungs sound like gurgling radiators," she explained.

Jeremiah's brows shot up in surprise, and he looked down at Xavier with nothing short of shock.

"Xavier? Did something happen while you were in the water?" Lana asked quietly.

He didn't look at her but stared fixedly at his hands. "What do you mean?" he whispered.

"When you were underwater, did you discover you could breathe the water as if it was air?"

The boy's head jerked up and his eyes fastened on hers. Slowly he nodded.

His father whispered in disbelief, "An aqualung? He's an aqualung? But there hasn't been an aqualung since…"

"Since my grandfather," Lana finished. "Yes, it's a very rare ability, almost as rare as aeronautics, but I recognized the effect. He appears to be unscathed from an incident that by all accounts should have killed him."

The king grew rigid as the realization of what could have happened sank in. A muscle in his jaw rolled, and he blinked back the fear filling his eyes.

Lana looked at Tamarah Minnows. "If you'd take an x-ray of his lungs right now, you would see the book lung chambers still partially flared. In a couple of hours, the adaptation would no longer be visible."

"King Wells? Would you like me to perform the x-ray to substantiate the ability?" Tamarah asked.

Jeremiah nodded, staring down at Xavier with shock.

"Alright, I'll prep the x-ray room," she told them before turning and striding through a metal door at the far end of the room.

For several long minutes, the three sat in an uncomfortable, tense silence. Xavier glanced sideways at his father who sat looking at the ceiling and taking slow, deep cleansing breaths. He was angry.

Finally, his father's turbulent eyes bore into him as he growled quietly, "Son? Never mind that you had absolutely no business being in those passages and chambers to begin with, but can you tell me how in God's name you ended up in that river?"

"Jeremiah, not now…" Lana interjected, placing a hand on the king's arm. "The boy's worn out."

"Lana! He could have been killed, and he endangered the lives of his friends! I don't care how tired he is!" he blared.

"Jeremiah Wells, don't yell at me!" Lana retorted with quiet firmness. "I understand that his actions scared the life out of you tonight, and I'm sure Xavier realizes this as well. But, I think it's best to save this conversation for the morning."

Jeremiah deflated and simply stared at her. Then after a long intense silence, he nodded and looked at Xavier. "All right, we'll talk about it tomorrow."

Xavier gave a slight nod, and continued to stare fixedly at his hands. His eyes were burning with unshed tears, and he desperately wanted to curl up in bed and sleep forever.

"Okay, I'm ready for you now, young sire," Tamarah announced, returning with a wheelchair.

Jeremiah swept him out of bed and settled him in the chair in one quick motion. Then, Mrs. Minnows wheeled him from the room for the x-rays. They didn't take long, and twenty minutes later Mrs. Minnows returned with the results.

"Lana's suspicions were correct. Xavier is in fact a...an aqualung."

Jeremiah and Lana exchanged a quick glance before looking down at Xavier. He didn't need the x-ray results to tell him what he already knew to be true. He was some kind of freak.

"Son," his father's soft voice and gentle touch drew his eyes to him. "You are not a freak. It's a rare ability, but it doesn't make you a freak."

"Sire, I'd like to keep him overnight just to be on the safe side, but I see no reason why he couldn't return to the dormitory tomorrow. But, right now, he needs his rest," Tamarah ordered.

"Okay. Thank you, Tammie," he responded and turned

back to his son. "Looks as though we're being evicted."

Xavier gave his father's joke a feeble grin.

"Try to get some rest. We'll talk more tomorrow. I love you, son," he whispered, kissing his forehead.

"Goodnight, sweetie," Lana called softly and kissed his cheek. "Sleep well."

"Night," Xavier muttered and watched as they left the infirmary with his father's arm draped around Lana.

Chapter 14

The Caning

Early the next morning, Xavier was discharged from the infirmary and sent to the dormitory to shower before classes. When he reached the children's level, he found his uncle stretched out on the couch next to the fireplace.

Spencer stood the moment he saw him. "How are you feeling, Xavier?"

"Okay," he mumbled.

Spencer looked down at his nephew, skeptical. "Are you sure? Do you want to talk? We have a few minutes before the wake-up call."

Xavier looked up at his uncle. He wasn't sure which was his undoing, Spencer's gentle probing or the extreme silence of the passage, but his chin began to quiver, and he simply burst into tears. Spencer engulfed him in his arms, which only made him cry harder.

"He nearly died. He nearly died," he muttered. "Why did he jump in after me? He should have just let me drown! I'm not worth it. I don't even know why I did it! God, why do I do such stupid stuff? I hurt everyone around me! Everyone would be better off if I'd just off myself. Then maybe no one else would be killed because of me."

"Oh, Xavier...don't say that. It's not true," Spencer consoled.

"It *is* true! It is! Maggie died because LeMasters was trying to kill me...Catherine told me!"

"Xavier..."

"And Mr. Minnows! He died so I could have a father. He died so I wouldn't grow up without my dad! I could have saved Dublin! He didn't have to die!"

"Xavier, feeling guilty is normal, but, boy, none of this is true. It wasn't your fault. You couldn't have saved Dublin. There was nothing you could have done," Spencer told him savagely.

"You're wrong, Uncle Mike! I saved your life, didn't I? I saved your life with a power I never knew I had! Maybe I could have done the same for Dublin!" he spat feverishly.

"Xavier..."

"No! Oh, just forget it. I'm going to take a shower." Xavier wiped his face and tore himself from his uncle's grasp. Spencer watched him enter the dormitory, return a moment later with an armful of clean clothes, and walk heavily down the corridor to the boys' lavatory.

Xavier stood under the hot shower for quite some time, letting the steaming water run over his face and his body and wash away his tears. He hadn't meant to break down like that. He hadn't wanted anyone to know the guilt he carried with him because he knew they would tell his father, and he would want to talk about it. But the thing was, talking didn't seem to help; it only made those feelings stronger and closer to the surface. Well, it was too late now. Uncle Mike would most definitely tell his father everything. With a weighted sigh, he began scrubbing shampoo over his hair and face, but before he could rinse, two pairs of arms grabbed him and lifted him off his feet.

"Hey! Put me down," Xavier bellowed.

Although Xavier was blinded by the shampoo in his eyes, there was no mistaking the voice that hissed in his ear. "Now, now, Prince Pipsqueak, enough of that! I told you that I'd get even with you and that you'd regret ever crossing me. But now, it seems I have a lot more to collect payback for...you nearly killed my brother."

"Drew! No! Stop!" he yelled as he felt the cooler air of the corridor hit his naked, wet body. "Oh, God! Drew, please, don't!" he cried as squeals erupted around him.

But, he didn't stop, and the squeals and laughter grew louder and more numerous.

"Drew! Put Xavier down, or I'm telling," Garrett's voice yelled.

"Let me see if I understand you correctly, Bracus. You want me to put this little piece of crap down?" Drew asked slowly, as he continued walking.

"Don't call him that!" Mac yelled. "He's your prince!"

"Put him down, Hardcastle," Beck spat viciously. "Or, I'll knock the crap out of you!"

"Are you sure about that?" Drew challenged still parading Xavier down the hall. "Are you really sure you want me to put Prince Pipsqueak down?"

"Yes, damn it!" Beck spat savagely.

"Oh, well, okay. If you insist," he replied nonchalantly.

Suddenly, Drew threw him, and Xavier felt himself hurling through the air before smashing to the floor and slamming his face on the stone surface. With his arms no longer pinned at his sides, he wiped the soap from his eyes and peered up at the shocked faces of nearly every girl in the mountain. Even Robbie stood staring at him with her mouth gaped open. As the shock wore away, a few girls began giggling while others tried not to.

Xavier's entire body blushed, and concealing himself the best he could, he scrambled to his feet and ran from

125

the girls' dormitory to the safety of the boys' dorm.

Beside themselves with laughter Drew and Jonas staggered into the room as Xavier yanked on a pair of boxer shorts.

"Well, *Sire*, it's now official! Everyone in the girls' dormitory thinks you're the cutest *itty, bitty* prince they've ever seen," Drew chastised wickedly while Jonas burst into hysterics and looked dangerously close to falling to the floor.

It briefly crossed Xavier's mind that what he was about to do was wrong. It even crossed his mind that when his father found out, he would receive more than a harsh lecture. However, neither of these thoughts stopped him as he lifted his hand and slung an electro force at his tormentor. Drew's eyes widened in horror a nanosecond before the force struck him and sent him airborne across the room.

Jonas' laughter died instantly, and shouts burst out around him.

"Xavier! Don't!" Mac yelled, grabbing him as he stomped toward Drew.

"Get off me, Mac. I don't care!" he hissed and shoved the other boy away.

Drew stumbled to his feet. "I knew it!" he growled. "No wonder Robbie hates you. You're the reason her father's dead...and...you're not even worth it. I mean, there might be something noble in dying for your king if he's an honorable and just man, but YOU? You're nothing more than a bullying, murdering dictator!"

"Shut up!" Xavier screamed manically.

"What's the matter, Wells? Does the truth hurt? If your father hadn't come when he did yesterday, you would have added my brother to your list of victims! He nearly died because of you! You're no better than William LeMasters!"

Drew blared.

"I said SHUT UP!" he roared, lunging at Drew and wrapping his hands around his neck.

Drew punched him, and he staggered backwards and fell to the floor. The last of his control snapped, and he jumped to his feet and shot out his hand again.

"XAVIER, NO!" Garrett screamed.

But, Xavier didn't care. He propelled a stream of electricity into the older boy's body, and Drew sank to his knees with a moan. Before he could continue his torturous empowerment on the older boy, he was struck by another sharp, painful force that sent him stumbling backwards and falling on his butt. Heavy footsteps stomped toward him, and a pair of powerful hands seized him roughly and jerked him to his feet.

"Jeremiah Xavier Wells!"

He looked up into his father's furious face. He had never seen him this angry. His face was scarlet and a vein bulged and pulsated in his forehead. He looked dangerous and every bit of the powerful man he was. A chill of fear shivered through Xavier's body.

"Drew? What happened? Why was Prince Xavier attacking you?" Ephraim questioned, helping his son to his feet.

"No, Ephraim," Jeremiah interrupted. "It is not important at this time to know why...I only need to know if Andrew used his powers against Xavier to warrant this attack."

Drew looked meekly up at the king and shook his head. "No, sire. I didn't."

The general turned to the group of anxiously silent boys before zeroing in on Garrett Bracus. "Is this true, Garrett?" he questioned. "Did Xavier attack Drew without just cause?"

Garrett looked as though he would rather be asked to swim the river than to answer a question that would undoubtedly cause trouble for Xavier. He glanced at Mac and Beck before looking at Xavier with dread.

"Leave him out of it!" Xavier hissed. "I used an electro force on Drew, and I'd do it again. He may not have used his powers against me, but he still deserved what he got!"

Both men looked at him with something between shock and anger.

Then, the king erupted. "OUT! I want everyone out of here, now, except you, Drew!

The crowd of boys scrambled to comply, many running from the room.

Jeremiah stomped away from Xavier and paced the width of the room, his fury snapping and popping around him. His father's anger was so strong that it blasted its way into his mind, and he cowered against it. It took the king several minutes of pacing before he had control of his emotions again. Finally, he stopped and looked at the general.

"General Hardcastle, I will report this incident to the High Council if you wish, or we can resolve this indiscretion here and now."

Ephraim looked at his son. "Well? How do you wish to handle this?"

Drew looked smugly at Xavier. "I think King Wells will handle things right."

"I concur. I also have faith in King Wells," Ephraim agreed.

When the king glared down at him, Xavier shuddered and gulped.

"Well, son. The good news is that you won't be brought up on formal charges for your actions, but the bad news is that I will be your judge, jury, and executioner."

Xavier stepped backwards, his stomach reeling with fear.

"D...Dad?"

"Face the bunk, son," he ordered as he slid the leather belt from his waist and looped it in his hand.

His fear escalated into terror, and he groaned. "Dad...please...I... I..."

"Turn and face your bunk, son," he repeated pitilessly.

"Dad...Da...Daddy...please, I'm sorry!" He began crying.

But the king didn't waver. He spun the boy and whispered, "Hold onto the bunk."

Shaking and whimpering, Xavier placed his hands on the bunk's frame and waited for the worst punishment of his life to begin. With nothing on but his boxers, he had little protection from the vicious lashes, and there was no doubt in his mind that this was going to hurt.

Then, the whipping began. If his father was holding back in his swings, he couldn't tell as each stinging lash bit at his exposed flesh. However, remembering Dublin's words during his father's caning, he fought to remain upright and tried desperately not to cry out. He was successful with remaining on his feet, but he failed miserably with the second. Each time the belt struck his exposed flesh, he yelped. Finally, after ten lashes, the punishment ended, and he sank to the floor on gimpy legs.

With a shudder, he peered up at his father still holding the belt in a trembling hand. Regret filled the king's tear-soaked face, and he turned abruptly and strode to the far side of the room. He stood for several seconds staring at the ceiling and drawing in several slow, deep breaths. Finally, he wiped his face, looped the belt back around his waist, and turned to Ephraim and Drew.

"Andrew?" The king's voice was shaky, and he paused

before continuing more stoutly, "Are you satisfied with how things were handled?"

Drew's smug expression was long gone. He looked up at the king with wide, anxious eyes before glancing ruefully at Xavier. The vulnerability Xavier had seen after the bat attack was back, and as Drew's eyes swept back toward King Wells, he wrung his hands and stared at the king's feet. In that moment, he looked very little like the cocky, haughty teenager who had tormented him since the moment they met.

Finally he moaned, "No, sire. I'm...not. I...It wasn't completely Xavier's fault, sir. I...I provoked him."

The men looked at the older boy with alarm.

"Andrew! Please don't tell me that you lied to the king about using your empower..." Ephraim began.

"No, Dad! I didn't use empowerments, but I humiliated him. I was angry because Court was nearly killed saving his life...and because of what he did to me in anima-lingua class...so, I...I caught him in the showers and...I threw him in the girls' dormitory...naked."

"You did what?" Jeremiah hissed, stomping toward him.

"What? Andrew Hardcastle! He is your PRINCE! He will someday be your king! How could you be so disrespectful to the throne! I didn't raise you to be so insolent!" Ephraim spat heatedly.

Drew looked very close to tears, and his head dropped at his father's words.

Finally, Jeremiah declared quietly, "Andrew? I want you in my chambers at 12:30 sharp. We'll deal with this then!"

"Yes, sire," he sniveled.

"Until then, you will need to have a long talk with your mother and me. Let's go, son!" Ephraim insisted, steering

Drew from the room.

"Come, Xavier. Let's get that soap rinsed out of your hair."

Nodding, Xavier slowly got to his feet and followed his father to the boys' lavatory.

Chapter 15

A Friendship Begins

As painful as the whipping was, the belt never broke the skin, and even the redness began to fade as Xavier finished the shower that Drew had so rudely interrupted. Although he hadn't thought it at the time, his father had been merciful during the punishment. If he hadn't, he would have had a lot worse than a few fading red marks. What if his father had chosen to strike him like the Royal Guard had beaten him during the royal caning a couple of months ago? The thought was unsettling to say the least, and as they entered the Royal Chambers, Xavier decided he never wanted to find out what a real caning was like.

"Eat," his father instructed simply, pointing to the plate of food on the small table.

He obediently sat at the table but didn't eat. His stomach felt tied in knots, and he was guilt-ridden. His father had been embarrassed and ashamed of him today. He had felt it in his tone, he'd heard it in his thoughts, and worst of all, he'd seen it in his eyes. With a shaky sigh, he looked up at his father who was adding logs to the fireplace.

"Dad?" he whispered timidly. "Do...d...do you hate me now?"

Jeremiah's head whipped up from the fire, and his

piercing eyes met his. "What?" he questioned, bewildered.

He choked on a sob and moaned miserably, "Do you hate me after what I did?"

"Oh, Xavier!" he consoled, quickly moving to his side and pulling him into his arms. "Son, how could you ever think that? Nothing you could do would make me hate you! Nothing! I get angry at your choices because I love you. I love you more than I could ever describe."

"But I...I used my abilities to hurt another person. I knew it was wrong, but I didn't care. I was so angry. I just wanted to hurt Drew like he hurt me," he cried into his father's chest.

"Xavier," he began firmly, pushing the boy at arm's length to look at him. "I didn't imagine that you'd grow up without making a few mistakes. Lord knows, I made some major ones growing up."

"Did you ever use your abilities against someone?"

His father's face darkened, and his hands dropped from Xavier's shoulders. "Yes, as a matter of fact, I did. When your grandfather found out, he stormed into Wells Academy and whipped me in front of the entire school."

Xavier stared at him, stunned. "In front of everybody?"

The king nodded.

"Jeez, that must have been horrible! How old were you?"

"Fifteen."

Xavier tried to imagine what it would have been like if his father had done the same today. What if he had whipped him in front of the entire dormitory instead of ordering everyone out?

"Son, you need to eat," Jeremiah told him, nodding to the plate on the table.

He sank back into the chair to eat as Lana entered the chambers.

"Jeremy? Is everything okay?" she asked.

"We're still working it out," Jeremiah answered, nodding toward Xavier.

When Lana looked over at him with large, disappointed eyes, Xavier wanted to hide under the table, and what she said next made him want to swim the river again and this time never come back up.

"Oh, Xavier! I couldn't believe my ears when I heard you attacked Andrew Hardcastle! What has gotten into you? Didn't your father just talk to you about this recently? I...I don't know what else to say other than I'm very disappointed in you!"

He felt tears looming at the edges of his eyes, threatening to overflow when his father intervened. "Lana, I understand how you feel. Xavier knows what he did was wrong, but he was provoked. I probably would have reacted the same way at his age."

He peered up at his father, grateful and a bit taken aback. Of all the things he had expected his father to say, this wasn't even close.

"What do you mean?" she asked.

"Well..." Jeremiah looked at him, silently asking permission to tell Lana. Xavier blushed but nodded. "Well, it seems Andrew kidnapped him from the showers, paraded him through the hall, and threw him into the girls' dormitory."

"Oh, my! What a horrible thing to do!" she gasped.

"Yes, it was, and he will face consequences. But, Xavier realizes that Andrew's actions were not an excuse or *just cause* to use his powers against him. Don't you, son?" Jeremiah demanded sternly.

"Yes, sir," he answered dutifully and began eating his breakfast.

"Lana," Jeremiah began softly. "Since you're here, I

have something I need to talk to you both about." He inhaled deeply before continuing quickly, "Ephraim and I need to go on a short trip."

"A trip?" Xavier asked through a mouthful of oatmeal. "What kind of trip?"

Lana had already surmised the answer. "A trip to gain information about William LeMasters and the status of Warwood?"

The king nodded.

"What? You're going back to Warwood? What if he catches you?" Xavier gasped, standing.

"He won't, Xavier. That is why only Ephraim and I are going. We can teleport out of there the moment there's any sign of trouble," he explained, moving toward the boy and rubbing his head soothingly.

"When do you leave, Jeremy?" Lana asked steadily, but she couldn't completely mask the worry in her voice.

With an arm draped over Xavier's shoulders, he reached for Lana and pulled her to his side, giving her a light squeeze.

"Tomorrow morning," he whispered. "I need to see what strengths and weaknesses LeMasters' has in order to develop a plan to get our kingdom back. Please, don't worry. I'll be back in two days, three at most."

Lana and Xavier both nodded solemnly. Jeremiah gave them another light squeeze before releasing them.

"Son, after you've finished your breakfast, I want you to go to the dormitory, pack all your belongings, and move them here."

"Here? Why?" he rebuked.

"You attacked another boy today! You will no longer share the dormitory with the other boys. You will stay in the royal chambers from now on..."

Xavier interrupted, "But, Dad, I like it there."

"Xavier! This is a matter of consequences for your actions; it's not a debatable topic. Now, do as you're told!" he demanded firmly.

"Yes, sir," he grumbled. Then a thought came to him. "Dad? If you're going to be gone for a couple of nights, can't I stay in the dorm until you get back?"

"No, Mike will be staying in the Royal Chambers with you until I return." His father's answer squashed any remnants of hope he had left.

He sighed heavily. No more late-night storytelling and joking around until the guardian came into the room to yell at them. No more waking up with his friends all around him. No more feeling somewhat normal. "Fine, I might as well get started with moving my stuff then," he grumbled as he stomped from the room.

When Xavier entered the dorm, it was empty. Of course, everyone else was in class, and he was thankful for that. He didn't feel like facing a lot of questions from his friends at the moment. They would understand soon enough when they found his bed stripped and his trunk gone. He began throwing his books and tablets into the trunk along with his pillow, bed linens, and a week's worth of clean clothes.

Then, just as he began dragging his trunk out of the dormitory, Drew entered, with red, puffy eyes. The boys froze when they saw one another. Drew shifted his weight nervously.

Finally, he muttered, "Need some help with that?"

Xavier looked down at the heavy trunk he had been struggling to heave down the rows of bunks before looking back at the older boy. "Ah, yeah. Are you offering?"

Without a word, Drew moved toward him and lifted one end of the trunk while Xavier lifted the opposite side. "Where are we taking this thing?" he asked.

"Dad's chambers," Xavier grumbled, and Drew looked down at him guiltily as they walked out of the dormitory.

"Your dad's kicking you out of the dorm? For good?" he asked.

"Yeah," Xavier groaned.

"Sorry about that. Really, I am. I'm sorry about...well, everything, Your Highness," he finished, and it sounded as though he truly meant it.

"Don't," Xavier replied with a snicker. "Don't call me Your Highness; it might go to my head."

Drew laughed. "Okay, Xavier, then."

"Drew?" he began timidly as they descended the stairs to the level below. "Why have you been harassing me? It seems like you didn't like me from the first day we met. Why?"

Drew didn't answer right away, but finally he stopped and lowered the trunk before turning to him. "Your dad and I have always been tight, ever since I could walk and talk. He used to do stuff with me, and I always felt like I was something special because of it. You know? He had been giving me private tutoring lessons on justice and government. I want to be a judge, maybe even part of the High Council some day. But when you came to Warwood, all of that ended. He was too busy with you. I guess I was jealous. He had always treated me like a son, but now, he has you, his real son."

He looked at Drew's hurt-filled eyes. "I'm sorry, too. Dad sure is a bit dense sometimes. I should know; I live with the man!"

Drew smiled again, and the despair in his eyes disappeared.

"Maybe you should talk to him about it. When you go in at lunch, you should tell him what you told me," he suggested.

"I will, but I deserve a good beating for what I did this morning not to mention the way I've been treating you from the beginning. God! Looking back, I don't blame you for zapping me! In fact, if you want to do it some more, I'd let you and not tell a single soul," he stated.

Xavier laughed. "Well, I'll have to get back to you on that."

"Ok. Just let me know," he said with a shy grin as he lifted his end of the trunk and waited for Xavier to do the same.

As the boys entered the Royal Chambers, Drew staggered at the sight of the king kissing Lana Applegate. Xavier dragged his truck and the older boy across the room, elbowing his father playfully as he moved past him.

"Jeez! Get a room!" he teased.

"Get a room?" his father bellowed, releasing Lana, lunging at him, and tackling him to the floor. "You better watch your manners, boy, or I'll sic Lana on you!"

Jumping at the opportunity, Lana joined father and son on the floor and began delivering multiple wet kisses all over Xavier's face. "Oh, he's nearly as fun to kiss as his father!" she taunted, kissing him more as his father held him still.

"UGH! YUK! Get off me," he spat, laughing.

Chuckling, Jeremiah released him, stood, and helped Lana to her feet. Drew stood anxiously next to the trunk with a small grin. Xavier got to his feet and went to the other boy.

"Thanks, Drew. Thanks for helping me carry that thing down here."

"Not a problem," he responded, looking timidly at the king. "Sire, I will be in to see you at 12:30."

"All right, Andrew. I'll see you then," Jeremiah replied, nodding at the older boy.

"See you in fencing class, Xavier," he whispered and left the room.

Once Xavier unpacked his things and settled into the small bedroom in his father's chambers, it was nearly lunchtime. His father had left a couple hours before to supervise training and preparation sessions with the Royal Guard. So he wandered into the Grand Hall for lunch alone, but he was fine with that. He didn't feel up to being around the mountain's entire population of children after being chucked naked into the girls' dormitory. Plus, he was certain that the news of his caning would be wide spread by now. No, the last thing he wanted was to be subjected to giggles, ridicule, and taunts.

He quickly filled a plate with pasta noodles and salad. Then after grabbing a pint of milk, he rushed toward the door, but his luck of not being seen ended there. Just feet from the doors, they slammed opened, and loud, chattering children burst into the room. If he hadn't stepped to the side, they would have trampled over him. The line of children hiccupped then they saw Xavier standing next to the door with downcast eyes. Their thoughts rushed into him, and he suddenly wished he had the ability to become invisible.

"Xavier!" Erica blurted, scrambling through the crowd over to him. "You okay?"

"Yeah," he whispered, allowing her to pull him to the side, as the other children continued on their way toward the buffet.

"The boys are talking..." she started carefully. "They said that...you used an electro force against Drew and that your father...well, they're saying the king *caned* you! Is it true? Did you really zap Drew? Not that I blame you...in fact, I would have loved to have seen it, but it's illegal. Did you really do it?"

He simply shrugged in response, his eyes avoiding hers.

"Look, Xavier, I know it must have been really embarrassing...but it wasn't *that* bad!"

"Not that bad?" he hissed, looking at her for the first time since their conversation began. "Tell me that after someone chucks you naked in the *boys'* dormitory..."

"Okay, okay. You're right. I'm sorry. But, Xavier, the girls aren't dwelling on it or anything...well, maybe a few are, but they're silly airheads! The point is... are you just going to hide away forever?" she demanded.

A small group of giggling girls sauntered by him and looked him up and down.

"I was going to try to. Besides...I told Court that I'd have lunch with him. I better go. See ya," he gushed before rushing out.

Xavier arrived at the infirmary just as Courtney's lunch was being served.

"Hey, Court! Thought you might like some company for lunch," Xavier announced, entering the room.

"X!" he exclaimed at the sight of him. "Thank God! Mom won't let me get out of bed! I've been bored out of my mind!"

"Well, I'm sure that didn't take long, seeing how you're practically out of your mind to begin with," he ribbed.

"Ha, ha! You're a riot!" Court spat playfully.

The boys sat for several minutes eating in silence. Then Xavier asked, "Court? Why did you do it? Why did you jump in after me?"

He stared at him in disbelief. "I can't believe you need to ask that! You're my mate, my best friend, and my prince! I'd die for you..."

"Don't say that!" he spat. "I don't want anyone else to die for me! I can't take the guilt of someone else dying to protect me."

"Is that what all of this has been about?" he asked, straightening. "You feel guilty for Maggie's and Uncle Dublin's deaths? You still think that their deaths were your fault?"

And Mom, Xavier added silently, but he didn't say it aloud. Ignoring the questions, he demanded forcibly, "Don't ever risk your life for mine again! Okay?"

"Xavier..."

"Promise me, Court!" he hissed.

"NO! I won't!" he retorted, sitting up tall.

"I'm ordering you as your prince..."

"Order all you want, Xavier! I'm not doing it! I have a higher calling than your orders. It's my duty!" he blurted.

"What? Your duty? Your duty as a citizen? What do you mean, it's your duty?" he asked.

"What's going on in here? I can hear you boys arguing at the other end of the hall!" Ephraim blared, eying his son, and Court's rebuttals died away.

"It was nothing, sir," Xavier muttered.

Ephraim continued to study the boys skeptically. Then he finally moved to sit on the opposite side of Court. "Well, son, if there's no sign of water intoxication or swelling on your next scan, I imagine you'll be discharged."

"Oh, thank God!" he bellowed with relief.

"Yeah, we'll see, but until then, do as you're told and stay in bed! If another healer tells me you've been sneaking out of bed again, I'll tan your hide." Ephraim warned before looking at Xavier. "Young sire? Lunch break is about over. You might want to get a move on. I expect you in fencing class today, and you don't want to be late."

"Yes, sir," he responded.

Chapter 16

Farewell

As Xavier entered the advanced fencing classroom, Drew wasn't anywhere in sight. Assuming his meeting in the Royal Chambers must have run over, Xavier timidly drifted through the crowd of older students pulling on protective tunics, gloves, and helmets. Skimming the room, he saw a table in the back stacked with gear, and he weaved his way to it. It didn't take long for him to realize that the equipment was three sizes too big.

"What's the matter, Pipsqueak? Can't find anything in midget size?" Jonas remarked loudly and laughed at his own joke.

Red-faced, Xavier ducked away and stood off by himself, trying not to feel too out of place.

"Prince Wells?" a tall gangly girl whispered. "Sir Hardcastle wanted me to give you this." She held out a tunic, gloves, and helmet.

"Uh, thanks," he muttered, and the girl blushed.

"All right, you lot! Enough talking and let's get to work!" Ephraim announced as he walked into the room dressed in his own protective tunic and gear. "Partner up!"

As the class scrambled to form pairs, Jonas approached him with a smug smile.

"I'll be your partner, pipsqueak."

"Ah, no thanks," he muttered before turning away from the older boy, but Jonas grabbed his arm.

"I don't think you have a choice. With Drew absent, I don't have a partner, and everyone else has someone already."

One quick glance around the room confirmed that Jonas was right, and Xavier grimaced.

"Alright, everyone, listen up! Today you and your partner will bout and practice the techniques you've learn so far. I will be making my rounds from group to group to make adjustments and offer advice as needed. Tomorrow, I will introduce a couple of complex moves that you can add to your repertoire. If there aren't any questions you can begin."

Xavier quickly pulled on the tunic and helmet, but he didn't have time to properly strap his equipment in place for Jonas was at the ready.

"En guarde!" he bellowed as he lunged forward, thrusting his sword.

Xavier staggered backwards and was barely able to lift his arm to parry to defend himself from the attack. Forgetting every basic skill of stance, balance, and control that Henrick had taught him, he lost his footing and fell hard on his butt, and his helmet flew off and clattered across the floor. Jonas burst into laughter.

"Prince Wells! I know Sir Davies taught you better than that. Concentrate on your fundamentals, young sire," Ephraim called.

"Yes, sir," he responded meekly as he slowly got to his feet. He scrambled to pick up his helmet, slid it back onto his head, and took his stance across from his smirking opponent.

Then, without warning, Jonas attacked again. He managed to parry the first two strikes, but beyond that, the bigger boy's brute force pulverized his defense maneuvers, and he served more as a piñata than an opponent. Although protective gear would usually prevent lacerations and pad the body from most blows, Xavier's unfastened tunic was less effective, and by the end of the class period, his body felt like one big bruise.

That night, Xavier awoke to soft music drifting into his room. Rubbing sleep from his eyes, he climbed from bed and tiptoed toward the door. Standing in the middle of the common room with firelight licking their bodies in a golden glow, his father and Lana swayed slightly with the music, but they seemed more interested in holding and staring at one another.

"Jeremy...must you go? Can't you send someone else with Ephraim?" she asked quietly.

"Oh, Lana, I can't do that. I must go; it's my duty, sweetheart. I promise you, I will be back," he whispered, stroking her cheek.

"I...I just have this horrible feeling that if you go, something...terrible will happen. I...I don't think I could bear...to lose another person I love," she choked out.

"Please, Lana, don't cry. You're not going to lose me!" he reassured her, holding her close. "I'll be back before you know it. You can't get rid of me that easily."

They clung to one another for a long moment before Jeremiah finally pulled away. "Come. I'll walk you back to your chamber." Lana nodded and the couple moved toward the door. His father paused and called over his shoulder, "Son? You'd better be in that bed asleep when I return!"

Xavier stiffened before slumping with an exasperated sigh. "Yes, sir."

Early the next morning, Jeremiah entered Xavier's bedchamber fully dressed.

"Son?" he whispered, shaking him awake.

He blinked sleepily up at his father and moaned, "Is it time to get up?"

"No, it's only five. You have another couple of hours to sleep yet. I just wanted to say goodbye," he answered.

Xavier sat up quickly. "Goodbye? You're leaving now?"

He nodded. "Yes, son. Ephraim and I need to get to Warwood before sunrise. It'll make it easier to get into the kingdom undetected."

"Oh," Xavier muttered, biting his lip with worry.

His father cupped his face in his large hands and drew Xavier's gaze to his. "Don't worry, kiddo. I'll be fine. Any sign of trouble, Ephraim and I will teleport out of there."

"Promise?" he pleaded.

Jeremiah kissed his forehead and hugged him close. "Yes, I promise. I love you, son. Mike is out in the common room. He'll stay with you until I return. Be good and mind your uncle."

"I'll try," he replied with a faint, coy smile.

The king laughed softly. "You'd better do more than try, boy. Mike's temper is shorter than mine!"

"I seriously doubt that," he teased.

"Hey! Watch it, boy!" he laughed, tickling him.

After another kiss, his father patted his knee and stood. "All right. I need to get going. I love you."

"I love you, too, Dad. Be careful!" he called as the king left the room with a reassuring smile.

Xavier couldn't get back to sleep after his father's visit and simply lay in bed staring at the ceiling. Finally, he stood, gathered clean clothes, and padded into the common room. He found Spencer sitting on the couch, staring into the flickering flames, drinking tea. He turned the moment Xavier entered the room.

"You're up early," he noted simply.

"Yeah. I couldn't get back to sleep. So, I figured I might as well take a shower and get dressed. Where's the bathroom?"

"Come on. I'll show you. I need to shave anyway," his uncle replied, grabbing a night satchel and his cane.

The showers in the adult lavatory were much nicer than the children's. Each showerhead had its own stall and curtain, providing a lot of privacy. After he showered and dressed, he watched his uncle finish shaving and splash aftershave on his jaw.

Spencer glanced at him and smiled. "You better brush your teeth." He motioned toward the sink beside him before packing up his razor and toiletries back into his leather pouch. "While your father's gone, I have a couple of ground rules. First, your studies are a priority. I don't want your studies to be neglected and suffer in his absence."

"They won't," he gurgled out past the foamy toothpaste.

His uncle gave him an amused glance. "Well, I'm afraid I'm going to need more reassurance than that, nephew. Your father would skin me alive if I let you slack off. So, after classes each day you are to report back to the chambers to do your homework before dinner. I don't want you saving it to the last minute. Secondly, since your bedtime is precisely at ten o'clock, you are to be back in the royal chambers by no later than nine-thirty. Understand?"

Xavier rinsed his mouth and looked up at his uncle. "Geez, Uncle Mike. Take it easy. Can't I just..."

"This is not a negotiation," his uncle interrupted, meeting his eyes unwaveringly.

"But, I'm not a little kid! I told you my studies wouldn't suffer, and I meant it. My word should be enough."

"No, Xavier. Your word doesn't stand for much when you do things like you did yesterday morning. With that said, this is not a negotiation!" he barked.

"Yes, sir," he mumbled and sulked.

Later at breakfast, Courtney entered the Grand Hall with his mother hovering over him spouting warnings.

"Now Courtney, don't overdo it today. Take it easy. All your teachers know that you're not to participate in any strenuous activities."

"All right, Mom," he groaned dismissively.

"I mean it, Courtney Hardcastle! Do not overexert yourself today, or you'll wish you were in that river again!" she snapped.

"I already do," he muttered.

"What did you say, young man?" his mother asked, grabbing him and spinning him to face her.

"I said okay, Mom! Geez!" he snapped. Annoyed, Court stomped over to Xavier. "Hey, mate! Can I sit with you? No offense to my mother, but I've had about as much of her smothering as I can take. I swear, I think I'm going to blow!"

Xavier chuckled appreciatively and motioned to the chair next to him. "No problem. So, I guess you didn't have water intoxication."

"Nah." He dismissed it with a shrug as he sank a fork into his eggs.

"Good morning, Courtney. How are you feeling?" Lana asked with a smile as she settled into the seat on the other side of Xavier.

"I feel great," he answered. "Though I think my mom has gone barmy."

Lana laughed. "Well, just give her some time. She nearly lost you to that river," she noted quietly.

Court glanced sideways at Xavier and muttered, "Nah. It wasn't that bad."

Xavier's face exploded with heat, and he stared fixedly at his plate and toyed with his food. It had been that bad. Court had died. He had stopped breathing, and Ephraim had to resuscitate him.

Lana's arm slide around his shoulders and gave him a reassuring squeeze. "Don't, sweetheart. Don't do that. It wasn't your fault..."

"You know something?" he whispered before glaring at the woman next to him and growling, "I'm freaking sick of hearing people say that when everyone knows it's a damn lie! It was my fault, Lana. I didn't fall into the river. I *jumped* into it. What if...what if..."

He couldn't finish. He stood abruptly and left the hall.

Spencer rose to go after him, but Lana's hand on his arm stopped him, and she followed Xavier instead. She found him in the Royal Chambers lying face down on his bed, his body shuddering in silent sobs. Her heart ached for this motherless boy who had been thrust into a strange world of fantastic powers and dangerous enemies. He had lived through so much, had seen too much, and was carrying too much guilt. Her mothering instincts surged to life, and she crossed the room and pulled the weeping boy into her arms.

"Shhh. It's okay, baby. Everything will be okay," she soothed, stroking his head, neck, and shoulders.

Lana's warm embrace and gentle words were Xavier's undoing, and the dam holding back his grief, guilt, and fear burst. He slumped against the woman holding him, surrendering. She held him like a mother would hold a son, and it only made him cry harder. What he wouldn't give for Lana to be his new mother. In that moment he wanted it so strongly it hurt. Finally, after several long minutes, his tears began to wane, and he snuggled farther into her arms, hiccupping.

"Feeling better?" she murmured, kissing the top of his head.

He nodded, suddenly feeling embarrassed. "Sorry. I didn't mean to..."

"Oh, sweetie. Don't worry about it," she interrupted, releasing him to wipe the tears from his cheeks. "I know you feel guilty about Court, and I'm not going to try to tell you that you had nothing to do with it. But, I stand by what I said earlier. No one event can ever be the result of just one person. It's too simplistic to think like that. Court chose to go into the restricted areas of the mountain. Beckley encouraged all of you to find the river. Yes, you may have intentionally jumped into that river, but so did Courtney. So, yes you had a hand in what happened that day, but so did all the other boys there. But, sweetie, lingering on what might have been or what could have happened isn't good for you. It doesn't change anything or make things better. It only makes things worse. What you can do is learn from the experience and not repeat the same mistakes."

Xavier nodded. He felt better. Lana hadn't tried to lie to him and insist that he had no fault whatsoever just to make him feel better. Nonetheless, her tone, her words, her warm embrace were comforting.

"Now, I think you should go and wash your face, honey. Your first class starts in ten minutes," she suggested, kissing his forehead.

"Yes, ma'am," he whispered hoarsely before giving her a bashful grin and doing as she suggested.

Chapter 17

The Make Up

Xavier arrived in Latin just as Sir Spencer began the class.

"Good morning, students. I'll be covering King Wells' classes for the next couple of days while he's away from the mountain. So, if you'll open your textbooks to page 276, we'll get started."

"Psst! Xavier!" Beck whispered from the seat diagonally from him. "Got great news. Jon Moore, captain of the Knights, said he could probably round up most of his team for a match. What do you say? Wanna play?"

"Yeah, definitely! When?" he responded.

"Before dinner. At 4:30," he told him.

"Okay, I'll be there!" Xavier grinned.

"Boys!" Spencer barked from the front of the room. "Would you kindly focus on the lesson?"

"Yes, sir. Sorry, Sir Spencer," the boys mumbled together.

Finally, after the last class of the day, Xavier raced out of the gymnasium, nearly knocking Lana over.

"Whoa, Xavier! What's the hurry?" she asked, steadying him.

"Sorry, Lana."

"That's all right, sweetie. Are we still eating together at

dinner?" she asked, stroking a lock of hair from his eyes.

"Yes, ma'am. I'd like that!" he said with a grin.

"Good. I'll see you then."

"Ok. See ya!" he called as he ran down the hall and into the stairway.

He took the steps two at a time and paused uncertainly at the entrance to the garden level. There were two passages at the top of the steps, but judging by the excited voices floating from the passage on the right, the rugby pitch had to be there. He hurried down the hall and out onto a full-size rugby field. The majority of the Knights' team was already there, but only he, Garrett, and Harry were present from his team.

"Hey, Garrett! Harry! Where is everybody? It's almost 4:30!" he asked, jogging over to the two boys.

"Well, when Beck saw Jon really did have most of his team, he took off to recruit the rest of...ah, finally, here he comes!" Garrett exclaimed with a sigh of relief.

Beck and ten other children strolled across the pitch with serious, combative faces.

Xavier grinned at Garrett and Harry. "Well, it looks like we're good to go now!" When he turned back to the approaching group, his eyes locked with Robbie's. A sweet heated sensation rushed through his body, and his stomach fluttered madly. He found himself fidgeting and shifting under her hypnotic stare.

"God, Wilson! My grandmother moves faster than you! Are you ready now?" Jon bellowed impatiently from across the field.

"Keep your panties on, Jon, and give us a bloody minute to organize ourselves," Beck spat at the other boy before turning to Xavier. "Good to see you made it! I figured Spencer would have you locked away in the Royal Chambers practicing telepathy or something kingly like that!"

"Well, I'm supposed to be doing my homework..."

"Hey, guys. Wait! I want to play!" Court bellowed.

"Hardcastle! How in the heck did you get away from your mother?" Garrett demanded as Court joined them.

"I told her I was tired and I was going to lie down for a bit before dinner. She took the hint and left me alone to do her errands and chores," he explained with a wicked grin.

"So, you're completely better now?" Erica asked eying him.

Court looked at her, puzzled. "Ah, yeah. Why?"

Suddenly, she launched herself at him, tackling him to the ground. "You jerk! You...idiot!" she screamed and punched him repeatedly. "If you ever do that again...your parents won't have to worry about a burial because when I'm done with you, there won't be a bit of you big enough left to bury! Don't you ever scare me like that again!"

"Ouch! God, Erica! Ouch! Stop it! Geez, have you gone completely barmy?" Court yelled out in between laughs. The rest of the group chuckled.

"Erica? Could you finish beating him up after the game? We may need him to help pound the Knights into the turf!" Beck interrupted, hauling Erica off of Courtney.

Erica embarrassedly brushed the dirt off her jeans. "Sure, Beck," she answered, trying to sound nonchalant but failing. She glared back at Court. "This isn't over, Courtney Aaron Hardcastle! Not even close!"

Then she stormed across the field to get into position for the start of the game.

Court beamed as he watched her walk away. "She's crazy about me!"

But Xavier hardly heard him for he was captivated by Robbie's broad grin, and when her dark, ebony eyes met his, he was paralyzed to the spot. He couldn't have looked away even if he had wanted to. Finally, it was Beck who pulled his attention back with a firm slug on the arm.

"Ow!" Xavier growled, tearing his gaze from Robbie to look at Beck. "Whatcha' do that for?"

"For the third time, *Your Highness*, get into position so we can start the bloody game before Jon throws a temper tantrum," he snapped as he squared his shoulders and stood inches in front of Xavier. His face flushed with anger, his hands flexed into fists, and his thoughts slammed into Xavier's head like a punch. *"Get your head in the game and off my girl before I beat the shit out of you!"*

"I...I'm sorry...I wasn't...I...sorry." Xavier blushed and shuffled off into position.

The Knights received the ball first and scored almost immediately making it clear to Xavier and his friends that the game was going to be a tough one. The Knights weren't just going to roll over and hand them the ball. After a few encouraging words from Beck that sounded more like a verbal spanking, Xavier's team prepared to receive the kick off. The ball barreled straight at Xavier. He caught it and moved quickly toward the center of the field, dodging players, and spinning out of his opponent's grasp, but halfway down the field, several Knights players surrounded him. He spun and tossed the ball to Garrett just as the group mowed him to the ground. Garrett zigzagged through the remaining Knights' players and scored the try. Cheers and banters erupted from the rest of the team. As Xavier climbed to his feet, he watched everyone thump Garrett on the back, sending him staggering between them like a ping-pong ball. Then, his eyes met Robbie's. She was laughing, and for the first time in a long time, when she looked at him, her smile didn't fade. He was left breathless.

The children ended the game five minutes before dinnertime, and Xavier's team won by just three points. The group celebrated by cheering and boasting about the spectacular game.

"Man! It's too bad we couldn't start up the spring season here. We'd win the Wells Cup for sure!" Garrett boasted.

"You know it!" Beck bellowed, draping an arm possessively around Robbie's shoulders. "Awesome goal, Minnows. I didn't know you could kick like that!" Then, surprising everyone, he kissed her squarely on the lips. Xavier went red and quickly looked away while the rest of the group unmercifully taunted and teased the couple.

Then Court turned to Xavier. "We should see if we could play the other teams! What do you think?"

"Sure," he mumbled not really listening. He was eavesdropping on Beck and Robbie who were now in a quiet, intense conversation.

"Beck, I need to talk to you," Robbie was saying.

"Can't it wait? It's dinner time," Beck responded.

"No, I really need to do this now. I might not have the courage later," she told him quietly.

He gave her a long look before nodding. Then, he looked at the group. "Hey, guys. Robbie and I will catch up with you at dinner."

Garrett's eyes widened mocking innocence. "You want some company?"

Beck grinned devilishly. "Absolutely not! Robbie wants to be alone with me."

The group watched Beck and Robbie leave before bursting into laughter.

"Yeah, sure! I bet they're going off to *just* talk...most likely, they're going off to do some *body* talking," Harry goaded as he mimicked kissing to the rest of the giggling group.

Garrett gave Harry a high five and laughed. "You know it, mate!"

The group burst into laughter, eyeing one another knowingly, but Xavier felt as if he was about to be sick. Watching Robbie leave with Beck's arm around her waist was downright agonizing.

"I'm going down for dinner. See you later," he muttered, trying to sound off-handed and relaxed, but he knew he had failed miserably as he walked off the field and into the corridor.

Moments later, Court, Garrett, and Erica caught up with him. The trio walked beside him in silence for several drawn out seconds.

Finally, Garrett spoke. "Sorry, Xavier. I wasn't thinking. I know you have a *thing* for Robbie, but so does Beck. He really likes her. I mean, whenever we're alone and he's not clowning around, she's all he talks about. And...after you guys fought over her...well, he was really worried. He doesn't want to betray you, but he doesn't want to give up Robbie either." Garrett hesitated as he carefully considered his next words. "Although he figures he's already lost her, especially after that letter Drew read."

"What? What do you mean?" Xavier questioned testily. "If she likes him, a stupid letter wouldn't make a difference! Besides, she *hates* me!"

"That's just it, Xavier," Erica interrupted. "She doesn't hate you! She likes Beck, but she doesn't *like* him. She's always liked..." She stopped suddenly and bit her lip as though she had said more than she was supposed to, and the boys stared at her.

"She likes who?" Court asked.

Erica's chin jutted out stubbornly. "I can't tell you. I

promised."

"It doesn't matter," Xavier mumbled. "It's not me. Even when she was talking to me, we were just friends. Beck is being an idiot if he thinks I could steal Robbie away from him."

"You don't get it; do you?" Court demanded, smacking the palm of his hand to his forehead in exasperation. "X, you still think you're one of us, but you're not! You're much, much more, mate! You're our prince, our future king! One day, you will have absolute power over all of us!"

"But I don't want that...I never..."

"Look, Xavier! It doesn't matter if you want it or not!" Court continued as they stepped out of the stairwell and into the Grand Hall corridor. "You have to see this from Beck's point of view. He's threatened by you! What kind of competition would he be if you decided to try to get Robbie for yourself? He's only a citizen, a...a merchant. What chance would he have against the Prince of Warwood?"

"Oh, please," Xavier sputtered. "Beck isn't threatened by me! He's the most confident person I know, next to Loren."

"Yeah, well, he is around most people, but not when it comes to you, Xavier," Garrett told him.

"Xavier Wells!" a gruff, deep voice bellowed from the Grand Hall's entrance. "I sure hope you've got a damn good reason why I didn't find you in the royal chambers studying after classes today," Spencer spat out, limping over to the approaching children.

"Well...I..."

"Do you have homework, boy?" he repeated.

"Ah...yes, sir," he stammered before quickly adding, "but not a lot!" That was a lie. He had at least two hours worth.

His uncle swelled with anger, and Xavier shuffled under his silent glare. Finally he turned to the other children and barked, "Get yourselves to dinner! Now!"

His friends scrambled into the Grand Hall, abandoning him to an irate uncle.

"What was our agreement about your studies?" Spencer asked quietly, his voice deepening with irritation.

"Agreement? What agreement? It was more like an order," he muttered.

"Xavier," his uncle growled, warningly.

Xavier sighed testily. "You told me to do my homework after classes. Look, Mike, can we speed this up? Lana is expecting me at dinner..."

"Excuse me?" he snapped.

"What does it matter if I do my homework before or after dinner as long as it gets done?" he snapped back before stepping around his uncle, but he didn't get far before Mike grabbed his arm and spun him to face him.

"It matters because you were told to do it before dinner!" he spat.

"Whatever," Xavier groaned, rolling his eyes.

Spencer lost what little control he had over his anger, and he wrenched the boy painfully against his hip and struck his backside with two sharp smacks. Then, he jerked him at arm's length, pinning him with fierce eyes.

"Are you done sassing me?" he hissed.

He nodded, rubbing his bottom.

"Now, you will go to the Royal Chambers and begin your homework. You will not be eating in the Grand Hall this evening. A kitchen volunteer will deliver your dinner to the chamber, and I'll explain to Lana why you were unable to dine with her this evening," Spencer told him.

"Yes, sir," Xavier responded meekly.

"Go on then. I'll be there shortly," his uncle scolded, and Xavier sulked down the hall, down the stairwell, and into the residential corridor. He entered the Royal Chambers feeling thoroughly put out and sullen. He had been looking forward to eating dinner with Lana and staring at Robbie from the head table. Now, he was a prisoner for the remainder of the evening. He threw himself into a chair at the small table with his Latin and Mathematics textbooks. With a disgruntled, aggravated sigh, he opened his Latin book and began studying.

"Xavier?" a small voice whispered from the door.

Robbie stood just inside the doorway looking bashful.

"Robbie," he gasped, jumping to his feet and slamming his knee on the edge of the table. Ignoring the pain, he moved toward her. "Wh...what are you doing here?"

"I need to talk to you," she whispered, fidgeting with the hem of her shirt.

"Okay," he responded awkwardly. Then, remembering his manners and motioning toward the sofa, he blurted, "Would you like to come in and sit down?"

"Yeah, thanks," she replied, moving to the couch.

He joined her there, watching and waiting expectantly. She seemed to be having trouble starting the conversation so he asked, "So...what did you want to talk to me about?"

"Me," she answered, avoiding his eyes. "I wanted to talk to you about me and the way I've been treating you since Dad died." She looked up at him then, tears swelling in her eyes. "I'm so, so sorry, Xavier. You didn't deserve the way I've been treating you. It wasn't your fault." Seeing doubt waver across his face, she continued in an earnest rush. "No, it really wasn't, Xavier! I only said those things to hurt you. None of it was true! You've got to believe me!" She reached out and took his hand.

Xavier nodded, unaware of anything other than her

hand in his.

"Xavier?" she whispered, her smooth lips just inches from his. "You believe me, don't you?"

He stared at her mouth, his heart pounding deafeningly in his ears.

"Xavier?" she began again, but his actions stopped her.

Unable to think clearly, he reached out and felt her lips with his fingertips. They were smooth and soft, and he had a sudden, strong urge to kiss her.

"Excuse me? Miss Minnows? Why are you in the Royal Chambers?" Spencer demanded softly.

Robbie jumped and stood quickly. "Ah, I just came to...ah..."

"Get yourself to dinner and tell the rest of Xavier's friends that he is grounded to the chambers tonight," Spencer commanded, shooing her from the room.

"Yes, sir," she murmured and left the room.

"The last time I checked, the school's curriculum didn't include entertaining and kissing girls. So, do you think you could return to an academic subject, such as Latin or Mathematics?" his uncle asked, hiding a reluctant smile.

For the first time in a long time, the overwhelming guilt pressing in on him lifted, and he couldn't stop the easy grin that Robbie's visit placed on his face.

"Yes, sir," he responded and saluted his uncle with a broad grin.

Spencer groaned exasperatedly and chuckled at his nephew's sudden elated mood. "Get to work, cheeky, little monster!"

Chapter 18

The Kiss

The next morning, Xavier ate breakfast with Lana, but his thoughts and attention wandered repeatedly to Robbie. When she found him watching her, she smiled, flooding Xavier's body with heat.

"It appears Robbie has finally made up with you," Lana whispered in his ear.

He grinned up at her. "Yeah. She did."

"I'm glad. What do you think made her come around?" Lana asked.

He shrugged. He knew perfectly well why, but he didn't want to share his most embarrassing moment, next to being thrown naked into the girls' dormitory, with Lana.

"You know what I think? I think it was your letter," she continued with a smile.

"My letter? You know about that?" he questioned stupidly.

"My dear prince, I think the entire mountain knows about it. When someone reads a very revealing, very heart-felt letter from the prince, word gets around quickly," she told him.

He groaned. "When did you hear about it?"

"The day it happened," she answered.

"Does Dad know about it, too?" he asked.

"Sweetie, your dad is the king and has telepathy. What do you think?"

"He never said anything about it," he muttered thoughtfully.

"Of course he didn't, honey. Whenever anyone mentioned Robbie's name, you'd give this look like someone had killed your puppy. No one wanted to cause you any more pain," she explained, rubbing his back soothingly.

"Oh," he answered simply.

Following breakfast, Xavier and Court made their way out of the Grand Hall when Robbie and Erica caught up with them.

"Don't even think about it, Jefferson," Court growled without looking at Erica.

"What?" she responded innocently.

"Don't hit me. I've had my fill of your little lovey-dovey patty cake game. So if you hit me again, I'll be forced to get physical in return," he explained seriously.

Xavier raised an eyebrow at Court's words. His tone and demeanor reminded him so much of Ephraim that he snickered.

"What!" Erica guffawed. "I'd like to see you..."

But her words died away the moment Court grabbed her and kissed her fully on the lips in front of everybody. Then, he released her and walked away with a grin.

"When did you grow a backbone like that?" Xavier asked as he followed him.

Court ignored the question and asked, "What's she doing?"

Xavier looked back at the girls. "She's just standing there sort of staring off into space. Robbie's laughing at her."

"I knew it! She's crazy about me!" he exclaimed.

"Xavier! Wait a second," Robbie called as she ran to catch up with him.

"Go ahead. I'll see you in class," he told Court and stopped to wait for her.

"Hey," she whispered as she reached him. "I...I was wondering...would you sit with me at lunch today?"

"S...sure. I'd like that," he responded as an enormous grin spread across his face, and when she smiled back at him, it took his breath away and sent his heart racing madly. He floated into Latin class behind Robbie, smiling like a fool.

Morning classes seemed to take twice as long as usual as time crawled closer to lunch. When it finally arrived, Xavier rushed into the Grand Hall and found Robbie already there, sitting at a table waiting for him. She waved at him as he moved toward the buffet line.

He smiled at her and told her telepathically, *"I'll be there in a couple of minutes."*

"Hey, X! Save us a table!" Garrett called from the back of the line.

He didn't know how to answer him so he just pretended he hadn't heard, which was a horrible decision. Soon, the rest of the guys joined in with Garrett singing, "Oh, Prince Xavier! Yoo-hoo!"

Then Beck hollered, "Oi! X, you big git!"

He could no longer ignore them and turned. "Sorry, guys. I—I have other plans today."

Xavier was sure Robbie wouldn't have minded if his friends joined them, but he didn't want to share her with anyone today. After weeks of silence and hateful glares, he wanted her all to himself.

"What? What other plans could you possibly have?" Beck bellowed.

Xavier ignored his dig and continued through the line,

filling his plate with tomato soup, fruit, and a couple of ham sandwiches. Then he made his way over to Robbie and sank into the chair next to her.

"Hey," she greeted with a smile. "I see you survived the evening grounded with Sir Spencer."

"Huh?" he uttered, snapping from the trance that her smile had placed him under. "Ah, yeah, barely, though. I thought Dad was kidding when he said Uncle Mike had a shorter temper than him, but he wasn't."

Robbie laughed. "Geez, Xavier! Didn't having telepathy classes with the man for the past year already tell you that?"

He laughed with her. Lord, it was so good to hear her laugh. It was so good to hear her say his name without resentment or revulsion.

"So, *this* is your *other* plan, Wells?" Beck growled from behind them.

Xavier turned and looked into his friend's enraged face. He knew that look; Beck was about to blow. Slowly, he got to his feet.

"Ah, now, look, Beck…"

"No, Xavier! Answer my question! Was moving in on my girlfriend your other plans?" he shouted, glaring down at him.

"I'm not moving in on her! God, Beck. We're just talking! If you haven't noticed, Robbie and I haven't been doing a lot of that lately!" he responded condescendingly, his voice growing to match Beck's.

"Don't talk down to me, *sire!*" he hissed.

"I wasn't! God, Beck! I was just saying that you know…"

"I know you're in love with her! Everyone knows it thanks to that dopey, girly letter you wrote!" he continued.

"Watch it, Beckley," he growled, stepping aggressively

toward the other boy.

"Oh, stuff it, Wells!" Beck yelled, shoving him to the ground.

Xavier jumped to his feet and lunged at Beck, tackling him to the floor.

"Whoa! Boys! Boys! That's enough!" Loren yelled, hauling the boys off the floor. "What is going on?"

"Nothing, sir," Xavier muttered.

"Beck?" Loren questioned.

"What?" he snapped.

Loren's brow rose, and as Xavier watched a muscle roll across his jaw, he knew the general's temper was close at hand. "Beckley Wilson, I suggest you not make things worse for yourself and mind how you speak to me. Now, what's going on with you two?"

"You know what, Loren? I don't give a damn about what you suggest. It doesn't matter what I say; you'll only take *his* side. So why don't you just butt out?" he bellowed.

Loren didn't say a word. He simply reacted by pulling Beck out of the Grand Hall by the scruff of the neck while every child in King's Mountain watched.

"What happened?" Garrett questioned.

"How should I know? He just went completely insane," Xavier retorted.

"You had to have done something! He's never back-talked an adult like that, ever! And, he sure wouldn't disrespect Loren. He idolizes him," Frankie muttered.

"I'm telling you! I didn't do anything!" Xavier blared.

Then Robbie spoke up. "Well, it might have something to do with the fact that I broke up with him last night."

The boys looked at her with wide, dawning eyes.

"Oh, bloody hell," Court muttered, giving Xavier an "I told you so" look.

Without a word, Xavier strolled to the double oak

doors and exited the Grand Hall. His only thought as he exited the hall was to find Loren and Beck and explain. Loud voices drew him toward the library.

"He stole her right from under me, Loren! How would you have felt if King Wells had done the same thing to you? What if it had been Lucy? If she had a choice between you and the king, would she have chosen you?" Beck demanded, his voice drowning in emotion.

"Beck, I'm sorry for what you're going through, but a girl cannot be *stolen*. Robbie must have feelings for Xavier. You need to be man enough to let her work through those feelings. As for my wife and the king, Lucy did have a choice, and she chose me. Being royalty may give a king absolute power in governance, but it doesn't give him absolute power over a person's heart," Loren told him quietly.

"So, you're saying Robbie likes Xavier more than me?" Beck whispered, hurt unmistakable in his voice.

"I don't know, Beck. Only Robbie can answer that," Loren replied.

Xavier started to open the door, but a hand stopped him. He turned and found Robbie standing so close that he could feel her breath on his face when she spoke.

"Xavier, don't. You'll only make things worse."

"But I've hurt him. He thinks I've stolen you," he whispered.

"No, Xavier. This has nothing to do with you. It's about me. I need to talk to him again. You need to stay out of this. Please, you've got to let me handle it," she pleaded quietly.

He stared at her, contemplating her request. Finally, he nodded. "Okay. I suspect you're right but will you meet me later and tell me how things went?"

"Sure," she agreed with a small smile. Then she

entered the room and closed the door firmly behind her.

Following advanced fencing, Xavier found Robbie waiting for him outside the classroom door.

"Come on," she whispered, pulling him down the hall and into a vacant classroom.

"So? How did it go?" he asked as Robbie closed the door and turned to face him.

"Okay. Well, at least he doesn't blame you now," she muttered.

Xavier sighed and smiled. "Good. Beck is a great friend. It would be hard not having him as a friend anymore."

Robbie's eyes fluttered from his, and she squirmed uncomfortably.

"What? What's wrong?" he asked.

"Well," she moaned, tears filling her eyes, "he doesn't hate you, but he's not so fond of me right now. I guess I deserve this. I only started seeing him after Daddy died to annoy you. I knew that doting over Beck and ignoring you would drive you crazy." Tears streamed down her cheeks, and she moaned miserably.

Xavier felt a stab of pain. God, he hated it when Robbie cried. "Robbie, please don't cry. Beck will get over it."

She leaned against him as guilt and sorrow overwhelmed her, and he awkwardly embraced her. His heart pounded so hard in his chest, he was certain Robbie could feel it, and for no other reason than to fill the uncomfortable silence between them, he whispered huskily, "Besides, who could possibly stay mad at you. You're so..."

She pulled away just enough to look at him and gave him a watery smile. "I'm so what?" she asked softly.

Xavier's breath caught in his throat, and what he said

next came out wispy, airy. "You're so beautiful."

Her smile faded and she blushed. "Really? Do you really think so?"

"Absolutely," he whispered, and then, surprising them both, he kissed her. Never in his twelve, almost thirteen, years of life had he ever experienced anything like this. His heart soared and hammered painfully in his chest, but it was a sweet, addictive kind of pain. Pain he wanted to feel for the rest of his life. His stomach fluttered madly in his gut, and his body felt light and tingly. It felt like he was floating. Robbie's soft giggle pulled him out of this euphoric state, and he opened his eyes. Oh my God! He was floating! He was actually floating! Panicking, he clutched onto Robbie as they drifted gracefully to the floor.

He looked at her with bewilderment and whispered. "Did you do that?"

She laughed. "No, Xavier. You did."

"I did? But...I can't...I've never..."

"Yes, you have. When...you first kissed me...this happened. Only, your landing was much better this time," she snickered.

He smiled and laughed with her. Her enormous smile and purring laughter lured him back to her, and he covered her lips with his. He couldn't help himself.

When he begrudgingly pulled away and looked at her, he smiled. Her eyes were closed, and her lips were still puckered. Then, she opened those large, dark eyes, and his heart drummed excitedly in his chest.

"Still think I kiss like a fish?" he blurted.

"What?" she questioned baffled. Then, she remembered and started giggling again. "No, Xavier. You definitely don't kiss like a fish."

He grinned triumphantly at her before taking her

hand.

"Come on. We better get going. We're late for class."

After walking Robbie to her next class, Xavier was nearly ten minutes late for anima-lingua, but he couldn't bring himself to feel worried. Those few stolen moments with Robbie had been the most amazing moments of his life. He didn't have it in him to be anxious about anything. No matter what Sir Blaire had to say about his tardiness, it was worth it. Robbie liked him. She didn't just like him; she really *liked* him. The kiss wasn't the only indication of this; it was in her thoughts as well. She was in love with him, and if her thoughts were to be believed, she had been since before they ever came to Warwood.

With this thought, he brazenly strolled into class grinning ear to ear.

"Prince Wells! Why are you late?" Sir Blaire barked.

"I was ah...busy with...someone, sir," Xavier replied still grinning.

"Really now? Well, I hope it was worth it, young sire, because you've just earned yourself detention. Report to me after classes," Blaire growled irritably.

"Yes, sir," he chirped, moving toward his seat next to Drew.

Drew grinned at him. "You were *busy* with...someone, huh? Would that someone be a cute little brunette?"

Xavier shrugged, his grin growing.

After he served his grueling detention cleaning animal cages, he barely had enough time to shower before dinner. Lana was waiting for him at the head table and greeted him with a smile as he approached.

"How was your day, sweetie?" she asked as he sat next to her.

"Pretty good," he chirped.

"I'm glad to hear that. So there weren't any problems

today?"

"Nope, not really."

"Really? That's strange because Sir Blaire told me differently. He said that you were late to class and earned detention."

He shrugged. "Yeah, but it wasn't a big deal."

"Well, I'm afraid your uncle doesn't agree, and I doubt your father would either." Xavier stiffened before she added softly with a wink, "But, I convinced Michael to let me chew you out."

He expelled a breath and smiled. "Thanks, Lana. I...I was just talking to Robbie."

"I see. You were *just* talking with her then," she commented with amusement.

Xavier blushed and began playing with his food.

"That's what I thought. Look, sweetie, I'm glad you and Robbie made up, but you need to go slow. Get used to being friends again before you escalate the relationship into something more. Okay?"

He gave her a bashful glance before whispering, "I'll try, but I think I like her more than just as a friend. I think I always have."

Chapter 19

The Break Up

That night, Xavier was awakened by a loud thump in the common room. Hearing hushed voices, he climbed from bed and shuffled toward the partially open door. His father was back. He looked exhausted and appeared to have simply collapsed onto the sofa.

"Dad!" he gasped, running and throwing himself into his father's arms. Jeremiah gave a soft grunt of pain before enclosing the boy in his arms.

"Hello, son. How have you been? Behaving yourself?" he asked with a tired, hoarse voice.

"Yeah, well, I tried to," he replied with a sheepish grin, sitting up and seeing his father's wincing, bruised face. "Are you okay?"

"Yeah," Jeremiah answered with a weak smile. "Just a bit banged up."

"You should go tell Lana your back. She's been really worried about you. I haven't been reading her mind or anything," he reassured his father. "But her thoughts about you are too strong not to hear some of it. I've tried to keep her mind off things, but I don't think I was that good at it. I only seemed to remind her of you."

Jeremiah smiled weakly at him and tussled his hair affectionately. "I appreciate you looking out for her, son."

"Anytime! I think Lana's great! I'm glad you're seeing one another."

His father's smile dropped. "Son, we need..."

"Jeremiah! What happened?" Spencer hissed from the door to the king's bedchambers.

"We ran into a little trouble..." Ephraim answered roughly from the doorway, looking as scuffed up as the king.

"Should I call for a healer?" Spencer asked.

"No!" Jeremiah snapped standing and dislodging Xavier from his lap. Then in a calmer, but nonetheless urgent voice, he explained, "There's too much to be done, Mike. I need you to go and wake Loren."

"Alright, but are you sure you don't need to see..."

"I'm sure. Loren is the only man I need to see right now," Jeremiah interrupted with such force, Mike simply nodded and left the chambers.

"Jer? What about Lana?" Ephraim whispered.

"I'll talk to her in the morning," he answered shortly.

"Are you sure? Are you really going to..."

"Hardcastle!" the king snapped, nodding toward Xavier.

Ephraim understood the silent command and clamped his mouth shut.

"Son, you should go back to bed. It's only three o'clock, and you still have classes tomorrow," his father ordered gently.

"But, Dad! I want to stay up with you..."

"No! I'm too tired to argue with you, boy. Now, go to bed!" he barked.

His father's words stung like he had been slapped with them. His head dropped despondently, and reluctantly he turned toward his room.

"Xavier?" his father called, stopping him. "I'm sorry I

snapped at you. I'm just really tired," he added softly, moving to him, kissing his forehead, and squeezing him close. "I'm very glad to see you. I've missed you."

He smiled and muttered against his father's chest, "Me too, Dad. Night."

Xavier entered the small room but didn't go back to bed. He paused next to the door with his hand on the knob and listened. After a moment, he slowly, silently opened the door and peered out into the common room.

"Ephraim, I'm sure about Lana. We've discussed this. You know what William did to Julia. Do you think he wouldn't do the same to Lana if he discovered...that...that I love her?" Jeremiah didn't wait for the other man to respond as he continued savagely, "You know he'd do the same vile things to her, or worse, as I watched!"

"I understand that, Jer, but the boy won't. It's obvious that he's gotten very close to Lana in the past few days. So when you do this, it isn't just one heart you'll break; it'll be two," Ephraim told him fiercely.

"No, my friend. There's a third heart in all this," he sighed.

But, before Xavier could wonder what this cryptic conversation meant, Loren rushed into the room with Lucy, Spencer, and Lana behind him. Jeremiah tensed as his tired gaze fell on her.

"Lana?" he sighed sadly.

"Jeremiah!" she gasped, running to him and wrapping herself around him.

His arms moved to hold her, but he didn't. Awkwardly, they dropped to his sides, and he stepped out of her embrace.

She looked up at him, bemused. "What's wrong? Are you hurt?" she asked, stroking his bruised jaw.

He went rigid and flinched at her touch.

"What? What is it, Jeremy?" she continued, searching his face.

He turned away and looked heavenward. Then, sighing heavily, he whipped around to her. "I can't do this," he whispered savagely.

She blinked and asked quietly, "Do what?"

"This!" he hissed, gesturing wildly between them.

"What? What are you talking about?" she demanded, her voice growing stouter.

The king growled in frustration and turned his back to her.

"What's going on, Jeremiah? Just spit it out!" Lana ordered, her voice growing harsh.

"I told you!" he roared, and she flinched.

She glared incredulously at the king, her eyes narrowing and darkening in anger. "No! You haven't!" she told him furiously.

"Lord, woman! You're not that dense! Why do I have to spell it out for you?" he spat.

Lana's hand came without warning, and with a loud smack, the king's head snapped to the side.

"Say it! I want to hear you say it!" she shouted, tears streaming down her cheeks.

He avoided her eyes and hissed, "Lana..."

"No! Just say it! Say it. But know this, Jeremiah Wells, if you say it, there's no taking it back! If you do this," her voice drowned in a sob as she fought to continue, "there's...there's no taking *me* back!"

His eyes darted to hers, and his face grew pale and stricken. Then, clenching his jaw, he glared down at her with a rock-hard expression and said quietly, "We're through, Lana. I must focus on regaining Warwood...I don't have time for it all. Damn it, Lana...I don't love you!"

Fresh tears rolled down her cheeks, and he turned

away from her, his face crumpling in pain. After a long, quiet moment, she wiped her face and whispered, "Liar."

He spun and watched as she stomped from the room.

"I cannot believe you!" Lucy hissed. "I never thought you were capable of being that cruel! Shame on you, Jeremiah Wells!" Then, she hurried out of the chamber after Lana.

Xavier felt a sickening lump of despair drop into the pit of his stomach. What had just happened? Why had his father said those things? Why had he hurt Lana?

"Dad? What...why...why did you do that?" he hissed, stepping into the room. "Why? I mean...You love her, right? You told me you did!"

He looked down at his son with surprise. Regret flickered across his face before he answered quietly, "It doesn't concern you, son. Go back to bed." Then, rubbing the angry, red imprint on his cheek, he hissed dryly to Ephraim, "Lord Almighty, that woman can hit!"

"Not my concern?" he spat, stomping further into the room. "Not my concern! She could have been my new mother, and you ruined it...you...you big..."

"Stop right there, boy. Don't you dare finish that sentence!" his father growled.

"No!" he yelled. "You deserved that slap! If I was bigger, I'd punch you myself, you jerk!"

"Whoa!" he bellowed. "Watch the attitude, young man, before you entice a few slaps from me!"

"Fine!" Xavier barked. "You're the one who's wrong, but it's me who's going to get spanked just because you don't have the balls to admit when you're wrong!"

The king lunged at him, but he danced away and raced from the chambers.

"Jer, no! The boy's hurting. Just...let it go," Ephraim told him, grabbing him.

"Let it go? He has no right talking to me like that!" he growled.

"Maybe not," Ephraim commented calmly, "but the boy heard you make a mess of your talk with Lana. He's upset."

"Damn it, Ephraim. You know why I did it! You know what William would do to her if he ever found out about her. I couldn't bear it if I brought her that kind of pain!"

"But Xavier doesn't know or understand your reasons. He only saw his father being a jerk to a woman he began to think of as a mother."

"Is that what this fiasco was all about?" Loren asked quietly. "All of this was in order to protect Lana? God, there had to be a better way, Jer! Why didn't you just tell her all this?"

"Tell her?" he spat. "Lord, Loren! Do you really think that would have worked? That would be like throwing a teaspoon of water on a forest fire! Don't you see? I had to push her away, hard, to keep her from coming back to me and placing herself in danger. There was just no other way!" The king deflated and collapsed onto the sofa, burying his face in his hands.

"Well, you know the old saying, 'Be careful what you wish for.' You just might get it," Loren added.

Xavier ran with no thought as to where to go, but soon he found himself next to the river. He sat for several minutes at the water's edge, simply watching the roiling, roaring water. Then, when he felt a cold draft on the back of his neck, he knew he was no longer alone.

"Hello, Xavier," a deep voice called quietly from behind him.

He turned and saw the handsome, bearded face of the prophet, Abraham Vincent. Once again, he had the distinct feeling of déjà vu. He couldn't shake the feeling that he somehow knew the man. However, as quickly as the feeling came, it was gone, and he gave the man a curt nod before turning back to the river.

The prophet approached and sat next to him.

"Your father ended his relationship with Lana?" he asked quietly.

Xavier nodded, and the prophet sighed.

He looked eagerly up at the man next to him. "Sir? Will they make up? Do they work things out?"

Again, the prophet sighed. "That all depends. It's not clear one way or the other, Xavier, but I will tell you this: Lana Applegate will not come back to your father. She's a stubborn woman. It must be your father who swallows his pride and goes to her."

"Great!" he groaned. "That'll never happen."

The two sat comfortably in silence for several minutes, until finally, Xavier blurted, "What's a time bender?"

"Where did you..." He studied the boy next to him and smiled. "Ah, that's right. You were listening to your father and I talk from inside the tent at Mirror Lake."

Xavier looked away guiltily and nodded.

Abraham Vincent looked out over the water as he carefully chose his words. Finally, he explained, "A time bender has the ability to travel back in time. It's a rare ability, almost as rare as aeronautics, the ability to fly. Most people who develop this ability can only alter time within a few hours or at most a few days. No time bender has ever had the ability or the strength to travel years into the past until me."

"Years? What year are you from?" he asked, intrigued.

"About fifty years into the future," he answered.

"Fifty years? Whoa!" Xavier gasped, trying to wrap his mind around this concept. Then, he asked quietly, "Sir? If you're a prophet and a time bender, why didn't you save my mother? Why didn't you warn Maggie about the illness and to stay away from Catherine?"

Again, the prophet hesitated before answering. "Prince Xavier, there are cosmic rules that govern my abilities. You see...I can only materialize near the Clavis de Rex. I am bound to it. It is an instrument, a catalyst, for my powers. So, I couldn't have possibly warned your mother. As for Maggie, I warned you, but you chose not to heed my warning."

Guilt stabbed deep into Xavier's chest, and he slumped in despair.

"Now, boy! None of that! Wallowing in guilt and feeling sorry for yourself will not change anything," the prophet scolded, nudging him affectionately with his elbow.

The odd pair stared into the roaring river for several long seconds. Once again Xavier was struck by how at ease and comfortable he felt in the old man's presence.

"The mountain's river has always been my place to think things through, too," he whispered softly. "It lulls and relaxes me. I know it's hard to imagine this now, but things will work out."

Xavier believed him. He trusted the prophet more than he trusted just about anybody. He nodded. "Sir? Can you predict my future? Like, can you tell me who I'll marry, when I'll die, and that kind of stuff?"

"Ordinarily, no. Visions don't work like that. I don't have control over what I see, and it's not always easy to determine the right course of action," he told him.

"Well, I imagine being a time bender should help. I mean, if you made a mistake, you can just go back in time..."

The prophet began shaking his head long before Xavier

could finish. "It doesn't work like that, boy. I cannot leap into a period of time prior to another jump."

"Huh?" he muttered.

"Okay, look," the prophet began, turning to squarely face Xavier. "Right now, I'm in this time and place with you. But if something were to happen while I'm here, I can't leap into a time before this point in time. Once I leap, the energy acts as a...well, like a roadblock so that I'm unable to come back or visit time periods before it."

"Oh. Well, that kind of sucks. Then, you couldn't fix a mistake if you made it?"

"No. I couldn't. This is why I only interfere with destinies that must be changed. It may sound harsh to you, Xavier, but I must pick and choose my battles. And I'm never sure that what I've done will truly work out for the best until I leap back home, assess the people and changes there, and allow the altered, new memories to sort of download into my brain," the prophet said.

It all sounded very complicated, and Xavier wasn't sure he truly understood. Instead of seeking an explanation, he changed the subject. "So...what's it like there, your home? Are you married? Do you have a family?"

The prophet smiled surreptitiously. "Yes."

"Am I still alive? Am I king?" he asked.

The prophet went rigid, and Xavier thought he wouldn't answer. But finally, he did, but he did so begrudgingly, as though it was against his better judgment. "Yes. You are a good king."

"Really? Do you know me? Are we friends?" he questioned, straightening with interest.

Abraham Vincent smiled. "Yes to both of your questions, but we're much more than friends, Your Highness."

Before he could ask him what he meant, Abraham

stopped him with a light chuckle. "Please, sire. Don't ask. I can't tell you any more than that. Knowing too much about the future can alter it needlessly."

Xavier nodded, biting back the question, but another question boiled over and before he could stop himself, he blurted out, "Can you jump into the future?"

Abraham looked at him and replied, "Like I said, it's never a good idea for anyone to know too much about the future."

Though he nodded, Xavier didn't understand or agree with the prophet. Surely knowing what was going to happen was a good thing! If it was bad, you could stop it. If it wasn't, then no harm done.

With a jovial clap to Xavier's back, the prophet stood. "Well, I better get going. I need to visit with Loren, Ephraim, and your father. What do you say you warn your father of my visit? He's never thrilled when I appear without warning. I'll see you in the Royal Chambers in a few minutes."

Chapter 20

The Chosen

Xavier returned to the royal chambers and found his father alone, sitting on the sofa with his face buried in his hands. The room rippled with a heavy, depressing energy that sent Xavier ducking behind the large, chestnut wardrobe by the door. Without glancing in his direction, his father rubbed his face, stood, and crossed the short distance to the hearth. He leaned against the mantle and stared at the waving flames for several minutes.

"Come here, son."

Xavier jerked and banged his knee against the wardrobe at the sound of his father's voice. He studied the king's silhouette standing in front of the fiery glow. He hadn't moved. Had he imagined him calling to him? This thought no sooner crossed his mind when his father turned toward him and spoke aloud.

"Yes, son. I called to you. Please come out from behind the wardrobe."

Slowly, Xavier crept out of hiding and approached him. His father's shadowed face was intimidating and hard to read, and he found himself fidgeting as he drew closer and closer to him.

"D...Dad?" he whispered urgently. "I...I'm really sorry. I shouldn't have yelled those things at you. It was disrespectful. I'm sorry."

"Yes, it was disrespectful," Jeremiah responded quietly, "but, I know how it upset you to hear Lana and I fight. You shouldn't have eavesdropped, son. You weren't meant to hear all of that."

He moved out of the shadows and sat on the sofa, motioning Xavier to join him.

"But, why did you do it, Dad? Why did you say those mean things to her? Don't you love her anymore?" he asked quietly.

His father's face flickered briefly from the unwavering, rigid mask he wore. "It's not about love, Xavier. I cannot have Lana associated with me; it would only put her in danger."

"Danger?" he blurted, studying his father's face. "Wait! Did something happen at Warwood, Dad?"

Jeremiah shifted on the sofa next to him.

"Please, Dad! Tell me! I'm not a baby. You don't have to protect me from the truth!" he pleaded.

His father looked at him with eyes brimming in pain. "But I'm your dad. I'm supposed to protect you."

"You can't! You can't protect me from everything! Please Dad, just tell me!"

The king's eyes clamped shut, and he released a frustrated sigh. After rubbing away the tension in his neck, he whispered, "Warwood isn't the only kingdom William invaded. The kingdom of Coasta was attacked as well."

"What? What happened?"

"The pilot I sent to warn them arrived just as over two hundred of LeMasters' men stormed the kingdom in the cloak of night. They never saw it coming." His voice broke, and he paused before continuing. "Many innocent people were killed. The king, his wife, and their three, young daughters were all slaughtered."

Xavier was speechless. He simply stared at his father, waiting for him to continue.

"That is why I ended my relationship with Lana," he concluded hoarsely. "When I go to battle, when I challenge William to take back our land, everyone close to me will be in danger. If he knew about her...he would..."

"Torture and kill her," Xavier finished hollowly, finally understanding why he'd said those harsh things. He thought of Robbie. She was in just as much danger as Lana! LeMasters would love to find out about her and their relationship. It wasn't fair. He finally had a chance with her, but he couldn't continue it. Like Lana, she was in danger if she remained close to him.

"Most of Warwood is in shambles. William has stationed himself in the palace. He's calling himself the King of Warwood. About a hundred loyalists are still there, imprisoned. William has been torturing them, trying to get them to renounce me as their king. If they do not recognize William as their absolute ruler, they are tortured to death. Even those who give in and renounce me are not spared." His father paused, struggling to continue. Finally, with an unsettling look, he whispered, "Xavier, Mrs. Sommers is still there. She didn't make it out."

"Wh...what? Mrs. Sommers?"

"Milton, too," Jeremiah added.

"Dad! We have to go after them! We have to save them!" he exclaimed, jumping to his feet.

"I will, Xavier. That is why I've returned, to organize the guard and plan the attack," he told him, standing. "But there will not be a *WE* in any of that, son."

"But I can help! I know I can!" he whined.

"A twelve-year-old boy has no place on the battlefield!"

his father insisted, his temper rising.

"I'll be thirteen in four weeks, Father! And besides, I'm not just any twelve-year-old! I'm the Prince of Warwood! I have more abilities than most of your men!" he blared.

"That may be so, but your powers are not yet fully developed. You're of no use to me!" he retorted brusquely.

"Gee, thanks a lot!" Xavier grumbled.

"I'm afraid I'll have to disagree with your last statement, Your Highness," a deep voice called from the doorway. Abraham Vincent stood just inside the doorway with Loren, Ephraim, and Spencer.

"Abe? You cannot be serious. You're not suggesting that he be allowed to go into battle!" Jeremiah spat.

Abraham calmly studied the king. "No, I am not. However, sire, it's time. The boy must be told."

"NO! No, Abe. Absolutely not!" Jeremiah shouted, advancing on the man.

"Jeremiah, he must know before..."

"Stop right there, Abe. Do not say another word, damn it!" the king interrupted harshly before turning to Xavier. "Go to your room, boy, and do not come out until I send for you."

He didn't argue. His father's wild eyes were frightening, and he obeyed the order without a peep. As he shut the door, he lingered, and immediately his father's livid voice leaked through the door.

"What in God's name do you think you're doing? How dare you come into my chambers making announcements and decisions concerning my son without discussing it with me first?" he yelled.

"Sire, I apologize, but it's time for the boy to learn the truth about his destiny," the prophet replied sharply.

"Jeremiah, Abraham is right. You know Xavier. If he finds out another way...if one of the children let it slip...his reaction will be unpredictable at best. You've got to tell him," Spencer insisted softly.

"Mike, you know as well as I do the guilt he's been struggling with. If I tell him this...it will only confirm his fears. I'm afraid he'll do something rash!" he implored.

"That's why it's important that YOU tell him, Jer. You need to be there to calm him...to hold him down if necessary. I have no doubt he'll handle the news horribly. How would any of us react if we suddenly discovered that we were the Chosen and responsible for saving the world?" Loren responded.

The men's discussion continued, but Xavier was unable to hear a single word of it. With his heart hammering in his ears, he sank into the darkness of his chamber. Had he heard right? Had Loren said that he, Xavier Wells, was the Chosen? He was the poor bloke who was responsible for saving the world! He shook his head and dropped onto the edge of his bed. The thumping in his ears grew deafening, and he buried his face in his hands. He didn't hear the door open or his father enter the room.

"Xavier?" he whispered.

He slowly lifted his head and eyed his father wildly.

"Son? Take it easy...just calm down. Let's talk about..."

"No," he moaned, shaking his head vigorously. "Is it true? Am I the Chosen? Dad, is it true?"

His father's face was answer enough.

"No, Dad! No! I don't want it!" he screamed, jumping to his feet. "I don't want to be the Chosen. I just want to be a normal kid! I don't want these powers! I never wanted them! Take them back! Take them all back!"

"Xavier, please...it's going to be okay," Jeremiah urged.

"NO! It's never going to be okay! Never! I don't want people sacrificing their lives for me because I...I'm the Chosen. I don't want to be responsible for the survival of the world. I don't want any of it, Dad," he screamed and before the king's fumbling hands could reach him, he teleported out of the chamber.

Chapter 21

Tasks, Visions, and Death

Xavier huddled in the darkness of the fencing classroom, sobbing. It was one of the few chambers in King's Mountain that was protected by lead. Since no empowerment could penetrate the room, this gave him a bit of time to figure out what to do next.

"It's not fair!" he cried, stomping and punching the floor with his fists. Wasn't it enough that he was future king and responsible for an entire kingdom? Why did he have to be responsible for the world, too? "It's not fair! It's not fair! I don't want to be the Chosen! I refuse to be the Chosen. I won't do it!"

Finally, he stopped crying and rubbed the tears from his face. With a shuddering sigh, he stared at the stone floor just beyond his feet and noticed a strange glow reflected in the polish stones.

"What the..."

Slowly, his gaze followed the light across the blackened room to its source: a long, glass case. His problems temporarily forgotten, he stood and moved toward the case. The light was coming from a sword! No, not just a sword. The Sword. The Sword of the Chosen! As he drew closer and closer, the glow grew brighter and brighter.

Then, Henrick's words came back to him. "Well, young

sire, legend states that the sword will emit a fantastic light in the presence of the true Chosen One."

Xavier's throat tightened, and his stomach dropped as his feet stilled. He was the Chosen! The glow confirmed it! Self-pity sank over him, and he turned away from the sword and his destiny. He didn't want it! Then, as if the sword knew his thoughts, it emitted a sudden burst of light that lit up the entire room. He spun back toward the sword. It was made of the brightest, clearest, purest silver known to man. Adorned into its handle was the kingdom's emblem, surrounded with encrusted diamonds and gems. Engraved along the blade's length were the Latin words, *Teneo vestri, victum vestri, sceptrum orbis terrarium.*

"Know thyself... con...conquer thyself, and reign the world," he translated, as his shivering fingers slid along the case, tracing the length of the beautifully crafted sword.

Slowly Xavier lifted the glass and warm air rushed across his face as a burst of indistinct voices swirled out of the case. Convinced that men had entered the chamber, he spun around, searching the blackened room, but saw no one. He turned back to the case. The sword's glow had begun to pulsate and the voices continued to bore into him intermittently. Although he didn't understand a word the voices were hissing at him, he knew without question that they were encouraging him to pick up the sword. Hesitant and with a sense of reverence, he lifted the sword from its case and found it almost hot to the touch.

The instant he touched the weapon, the chorus of voices became lucid and understandable. Seven distinct male voices chanted insistently, "Teneo vestri, victum vestri, sceptrum orbis terrarum."

Then, one by one, each voice spoke to him.

"Know thyself!"

"Ye shall be a great king."

"The sword belongs to thee."

"Ye art the great King of the Light."

"Know thyself!"

"Conquer thyself!"

"Ye shall possess countless powers."

"Ye wilt become the greatest empowered man the world has ever seen or wilt ever see."

"Thy powers must be mastered or ye and thy own wilt perish."

"Conquer thyself!"

Finally, the voices came together and chorused, "Accept. Accept the weapon. Accept it and fulfill thy destiny and reign the world. Take heed, King of Kings. Teneo vestri, victum vestri, sceptrum orbis terrarum."

Suddenly, the voices went silent and the glow and heat from the sword vanished. Xavier stood steadfast, his mind whirling over what had just happened when the door flew open with a bang, flooding him in light.

"There you are!" Loren gushed in relief. "We've been looking everywhere for you. Your father is all roused up, and we both know how impossible he gets when he's agitated. What have you got there?" he finished, his voice wavering when his eyes settled on the sword in his hands. Then, with a wave of his hand, light filled the room, and he strolled toward Xavier, his eyes fixed on the sword.

Xavier snapped from his state of awe with a jerk. "Ah...a sword," he responded stupidly.

The general strained to grin down at him and chuckled weakly. "I can see that, but how did you get it out of the case? That case has been sealed for over a century...no one has been able to open it!"

He didn't know how to respond to that so he simply shrugged.

Loren glanced at him suspiciously and asked, "Xavier, why do you have the sword? Why did you pick it up?"

Again, he shrugged. How could he tell Loren that the sword had beckoned him to pick it up? He couldn't tell him about the voices that proclaimed the sword rightfully belonged to him. He doubted the truth would sound sane. His eyes dropped from the general's as he whispered weakly, "Just curious to see how heavy it was...that's all."

Loren stared down at him with an arched brow. "Really, now?"

But, before the general could probe further, the prophet rushed noisily into the room. His eyes darted from Loren to Xavier before finally settling on the sword. He grinned shrewdly.

"Ah, I see you've found your sword. Good!"

"Ah...Abe, I don't think Jeremiah wanted Xavier to know about the sword just yet. You *know* what he's capable of..."

"Stop talking about me like I'm an idiot kid who doesn't know what's going on, General Jefferson," Xavier snarled, glaring up at the large man.

Then, his father burst into the room with Ephraim and Mike following behind him.

"Xavier! Thank God, I was afraid you..."

"What, Father? You were afraid of what?" he spat, quickly losing his patience with the secretive looks and cryptic words being exchanged by the men.

The group looked anxiously at the king, who stared down at his son intently. This only infuriated him more.

"God!" he yelled, his hand clenching around the sword. "Stop treating me like a little kid! And stop lying to me!"

For several moments, father and son stood transfixed, staring at one another. Finally, Abe broke their silent rivalry.

"King Wells, it's time. Tell him. We are all here to...assist if you need it," he told him quietly.

He looked at the older man, his chin tilted stubbornly, but after a brief glance at the men around him, he sighed with resignation and looked down at the boy.

"Okay, son. Come, I'll tell you all I know," he whispered.

As he led Xavier to one of the tables at the back of the classroom, the other men drifted toward the door to give father and son privacy.

Xavier wasn't sure if the fluttering in his stomach was from uneasiness or eagerness to finally know the truth. His father sat rigidly across from him with his hands stretched out on the table's smooth surface. For several long seconds, he simply sat there staring down at his hands. When he finally looked up, his expression diminished Xavier of any hope that there'd been a mistake. He was the Chosen.

"No. No, please Dad."

"You are the Chosen, son. You will be the downfall of the Dark King. You are destined to be the savior of all mankind," he whispered.

He shook his head long before his father finished, his mind refusing to accept the facts. His control teetered into near hysterics. "No!" he screeched. "No, I don't want this, Dad. God! Isn't it enough that I have to be king? Isn't that enough to deal with? I don't want this...this *destiny*. I refuse to be the Chosen! Do you hear me? I refuse it!"

"I'm sorry, son. I don't want this for you either, but it cannot be changed. Hiding your head in the dirt will not change it or prevent the inevitable from happening. If you persist in denying it, the world will spiral into destruction and doom."

"How do you know for certain it's me? Maybe there's

been a mistake...maybe the prophet is wrong!" he sputtered desperately.

Abraham Vincent spoke softly from across the room. "I'm sorry, young sire, but I did not make a mistake. You are the Chosen. That is why Dublin died for you and why your father..."

"Abe!" Jeremiah interrupted, glaring at the older man.

"What?" Xavier asked, his gaze jumping between the men. When neither man spoke, he blared, "What? What is it? Dad?"

Finally, his father sighed heavily and looked back at him. The grief Xavier saw in his father's face twisted his anger into outright fear. There was more, much more, and what his father was about to tell him would change everything. "Son, during your divination...every person in attendance received visions and tasks in guiding you, in helping you to adjust to your destiny and fulfilling it. One of my tasks was... to choose between my duty as king and my duty as your father, which in the end is one and the same since you're not only the future of Warwood, but of the world. I fulfilled this task when I saved you from the Super Flu. Secondly, I have the task of tutoring and molding you into an honest, respectable man and into a wise and honorable king."

"But what was the prophet talking about, Dad?" he asked, sensing the king was holding back.

Jeremiah looked at Abe before answering slowly. "I foresaw a great battle. I saw us fighting side by side, but an attack came from behind us, and a dark soldier was poised to send his sword through you." He took a slow steadying breath and added quietly, "I...did what I had to do to save you."

"What do you mean; you did what you had to do?"

His father didn't answer, but the answer came to him

nonetheless. "Wait! You'll sacrifice yourself to save me?" he hissed, looking at the prophet. "Is it true? He still dies?"

Abraham gave a slight nod and answered gruffly, "Your father will have a choice. If he chooses to protect you, he will die..."

"Don't give me that, *Abe*!" he shouted. "I'm sick and tired of your riddles and puzzling words! Just tell me! Is my dad still alive in the future or not?"

The prophet shifted uneasily before answering, "No. He's not."

"Then, stop it!" he ordered, jumping to his feet and storming over to him. "You've got to stop it from happening!"

"Xavier, I can't. I've told you the laws of my abilities...I can't stop it. Even if I could, I...I doubt that your father would allow it."

"No!" he cried, lunging at the prophet and grabbing him roughly by his shirt. "Why would you save him once and not do it now? Please! Help him!"

"I can't, young sire. You're the only one who can prevent it," Abe told him regretfully.

"How? Tell me!" he cried, tears rolling down his cheeks as he shook the man in his grip.

Jeremiah intervened, seizing him in his strong arms and lifting him away. "Stop, Xavier. I wouldn't have it any other way. I would rather die than for one hair on your head to be harmed. Please, son, stop crying. I'm not afraid. I don't dread it. I simply embrace it as my destiny."

"No! It's not your destiny, Dad. Your destiny is to be with me. Your destiny is to marry Lana and live to be an old man. Your destiny is NOT to die for me!" he wailed. "I won't let you! I won't!"

Jeremiah sank to the cool stone floor cradling the

despondent boy. "Sh! It's all right, son. Please, don't cry. It'll be okay," he murmured, hugging him.

But Xavier knew in his heart it wouldn't be okay. The prophet was right; only he could stop his father's sacrifice. So as his father soothed and held him close, he vowed silently to save him.

"Abe? Abe, are you all right? What is it? What's wrong?" Loren yelped, hurrying to the old man's side.

The prophet had dropped to his knees in obvious agony. A sudden spasm of pain sent the man to all fours, and he cried out. For several long seconds, he knelt on the cold stone, panting and heaving violently. Then another invisible torment slammed him onto his back and he screamed, clutching his right hip while blood crept to the surface of his trousers.

Loren grabbed Abe and tried to steady his seizing body. "Abe? What's going on?"

The king rushed over and dropped to his knees next to the prophet.

"Hold him still, Loren. I'll apply pressure to the wound and try to stop the bleeding."

Xavier shuffled toward the men, watching his father press his hands against the bloody wound.

The prophet yelped and swore as perspiration beaded on his flushed face.

"Abe, what hap..." Loren's words fell away as the prophet's body pitched and arched against another invisible force. Tremors violently threw his body against the hard, rocky floor.

"Hold him, Loren!" Jeremiah yelled as he struggled to keep pressure on the now profusely bleeding wound.

Abe let out a long, loud scream as some invisible force severed the finger on his left hand, leaving a small bloody stump.

"Oh, God! Oh, God!" Abe hissed as a long ugly scar ripped its way across his jaw. There was one last painful shudder as blood oozed over the front of his cloak, and then his face turned ashen gray.

Rasping for breath, the prophet's eyes bore into Xavier's as he moaned, "Xavier...d...don't... please..." Then, before any of them could ask him what he meant, there was a great blinding silver light, and the prophet disappeared.

"What the hell?" Jeremiah hissed, looking at his general. "Loren, what happened?"

"I don't know, sire, but something has changed the prophet's future," he replied, eyeing Xavier suspiciously.

"What do you mean? How do you know that?" Ephraim questioned, approaching them.

"God, Ephraim! You saw what happened! Did it look like Abe was playing charades to you?" Loren spat sarcastically. "He was dying...or more accurately...he was being murdered. How else do you think those injuries and scars occurred?"

"What do we do, Loren. Can we stop it?" Jeremiah asked.

"I don't know, sire. I just don't know," Loren responded, shaking his head.

The men stared at the pool of blood where the prophet had been just a moment ago.

Only then did Xavier feel the pain in his palms. He looked down and found the Sword of the Chosen still clutched tightly in his hands. With great mental effort, he released the blade and stared at his blood-covered hands.

Chapter 22

Secrets

Breakfast an hour and a half later seemed illusory and dreamlike. The shock of it all still had its dark, sinister claws in him. He knew his father had been candidly truthful in their discussion, but he still couldn't quite believe it. He was the Chosen! The Great White King! Savior of mankind. It was hard to wrap his mind around it. The violent disappearance of Abraham Vincent was a conundrum. It was as if the prophet knew about the budding plan sowing in Xavier's mind, and it somehow hurt him.

He was so preoccupied that his father had led him back to the chambers where he showered and dressed without ever remembering having done it.

Now, sitting in the Grand Hall with pancakes and bacon in front of him this overwhelming mood lingered, and he toyed absent-mindedly with his food. Even Robbie's approach didn't change the funk he was in.

"Hi, Xavier. Oh, what happened to your hands?" Robbie asked.

After a nudge from his father, Xavier snapped his attention to her. "Ah...my hands?" He looked down at his bandaged hands. "Oh...I cut myself. It's nothing."

Robbie gave him a funny look. "Are you all right?

You're acting weird."

"He hasn't had much sleep, Robbie. You'll have to be patient with him today," Jeremiah told her.

"Oh," Robbie noted with a relieved grin. "Well, okay. Will you sit with me at lunch?"

"Ah, sit with you? Sure," Xavier muttered and watched as Robbie returned to her seat. Then, his gaze fell on Lana, sitting at the far end of the first row of tables. Her eyes were puffy and red, and she looked miserable. He glanced at his father to find him studying Lana as well. His face was stoic, but the pain in his eyes was unmistakable, and his control on containing his thoughts was weak. He still loved Lana, and his heart broke at the sight of her. He carried enormous guilt for hurting her and wished things could be different. The brief insight into his father's feelings was short yet informative. In the blink of an eye, the king clamped down on his emotions and regained his control. Then, he stood, raised his hand, and waited as the crowd grew quiet.

With a weak smile, he announced, "Good morning, ladies and gentlemen. As many of you know, General Hardcastle and I returned this morning from our trip to gain intelligence on how best to reclaim our kingdom."

A loud bang from a back table drew the entire hall's attention to Lana, who had jumped from her chair and was storming out. Jeremiah watched her exit the room, slamming the doors behind her, and he winced. The room erupted in heated whispers and gossip.

After a moment, the king cleared his throat and continued, "As I was saying...we've gained enough knowledge to do this. Therefore, all men between the ages of fifteen and fifty and in good fighting condition are asked to train for the imminent invasion to recapture our great kingdom. All men that meet these specifications are to report to the gym after lunch today. Following breakfast tomorrow, we will leave the Mountain to train and prepare at Mirror Lake. You'll need to pack your camping gear. We'll be roughing it for the next couple of weeks, gentlemen. Make no mistake about it; your training will be grueling, exhausting, and painful. Then, we will retake our kingdom! It's time for retribution, my brothers! LeMasters will pay for his crimes!"

The hall exploded in cheers and applause, before the crowd began chanting, "Long live, King Wells! Long live, King Wells! Long live, King Wells!"

The crowd didn't grow quiet until the king humbly raised his hands.

"Thank you. You honor and humble me. A king is only as great as his citizens, and I have to admit, I have the best citizens any king has the right to have. Thank you! Now, boys and girls, starting tomorrow, all empowerment classes will be cancelled for the next few weeks. You will have core classes only from eight to eleven. For the remainder of the day you will help to maintain the facilities of the mountain during the men's absence. You are needed now more than ever. We'll restart Wells Academy with a full schedule as soon as we're back in our homes. So, until then, I appreciate your help and understanding. If anyone has any questions, I will entertain them throughout the day today. Have a good day."

A loud throng of murmurs filled the hall as the crowd dispersed.

"You're going to Mirror Lake for training? What about me? Am I going?" Xavier questioned.

"No. You will not, son," Jeremiah answered.

"Let me guess," he noted acidly, "I'm staying with Uncle Mike?" When his father nodded, he jumped to his feet filled fury. "Great! You obviously don't have time for me! Why don't I just move in with Uncle Mike for good? Maybe I should start calling him Dad! After all, I've seen more of him in the past two months than I have you!" With that said, he stormed from the hall not waiting for his father's rebuttal.

Xavier skipped his morning classes and spent the morning staring into the river. His anger toward his father had ebbed away, and now, he felt...weird. He felt strange, disconnected, like he no longer belonged among the empowered, like he had surpassed them. It was the loneliest feeling in the world.

"Stop feeling sorry for yourself, Xavier!" he hissed out loud. "You know what you have to do. It's probably good that Father will be leaving the mountain tomorrow. He won't be around to complicate things."

It was nearly lunchtime when Xavier finally left the river with a fully formed plan in his mind. The way he figured it, if he was successful, he wouldn't have to worry about being the Chosen anymore. If he was successful, his father and Lana could be together without any worries of what LeMasters might do to them. If he was successful, he was free to see Robbie. If he was successful, no one would have to worry about William LeMasters ever again. IF he was successful!

Xavier, deep in thought with examining his plan for flaws, found himself outside the Grand Hall with no memory of having walked there.

"Hey, X! Where have you been?" Court's voice hammered into his thoughts as the boy jogged toward him and fell into step beside him.

"I didn't feel like going to classes this morning," he mumbled, entering the hall ahead of Court.

"Oh, yeah, I understand, mate. If I'd found out that I

was the Chosen, I'd probably want to hide too," Court whispered.

He stopped and looked at his friend. "How long have you known, Court?"

"Dad told me this morning..."

"No. That's not what I mean," Xavier growled. "When did you *first* know about who...what I was?"

He squirmed under the question. "Ah, well...since your divination ..."

Xavier huffed bitterly and stomped ahead of the other boy to the buffet line. Court scrambled up behind him.

"You're mad, aren't you?" he asked, as they began filling their trays with food.

"No, *Courtney*. Why in the hell would I be mad? After all, one of my best friends has been keeping an enormous secret from me! He's known for months that I was the *Chosen* and didn't say a damn thing about it. Now, why on Earth would that make me mad?"

"I'm sorry, mate. I really wanted to tell you, but if I had, my father would have beaten my butt. As for King Wells, well, I sure didn't want to find out what he would have done to me," Court pleaded.

Erica and Robbie approached the arguing boys with their lunch trays.

"What's going on?" Erica questioned.

"I suppose they know as well?" Xavier asked shortly.

Court simply nodded.

Not even bothering to muffle his string of curses, Xavier stomped toward the table at the very back of the hall.

"Sire Wells!" one of the cooks blared. "Did you just say what I think you said? That kind of language is unbecoming for the Prince of Warwood."

"So?" he spat. "We're not in Warwood, are we?"

"That may be true sire, but you are still our prince. And, as the Prince of Warwood, you should set an example for all the children here, and that kind of language is highly inappropriate," she continued, shaking her finger at him.

He glowered at the woman, his anger swelling. "As the Prince of Warwood, I don't take orders from the kitchen help. You take orders from me! So, shut your mouth and do what you do best. Cook something!"

The woman looked at him, stunned. Then with a scowl, she chastised, "Your father will hear about this!"

"So? What else is new?" Xavier shouted at the top of his lungs. "If I forget to do my homework, someone has to tell my father! When someone reads a letter I wrote in front of every kid in the kingdom, my father is told. God! If I breathe wrong, someone has to tell him. Why wait? Go and tell him now while you've got the chance. Lord knows with this tasteless slop you're trying to pass off as food, you won't be missed!"

The woman rushed from the hall in tears.

"Xavier? I don't care if you didn't sleep well or not, what has gotten into you?" Robbie scolded. "You made her cry!"

He felt a stab of guilt, but quickly pushed it away and shrugged nonchalantly as he continued to the back table and settled himself into a chair. Robbie followed.

"Xavier..."

"Don't spout your holier-than-thou crap at me, Robbie. You're not the perfect, thoughtful, do-gooder you make yourself out to be!" he blared.

"What are you talking about?" she exclaimed.

"You KNOW what I'm talking about!" he hissed under his breath. "Why didn't you tell me that I'm the Chosen?"

"How did you..."

"That doesn't matter! You should have told me!"

"Xavier...I'm sorry...I..."

"Forget it," he grumbled, waving her away. "Just leave me alone! If I don't eat something before Father comes, I won't eat..."

"XAVIER WELLS!" the king's voice boomed. "Come here, NOW!"

"Great! Looks like I won't have lunch today," he grumbled, getting to his feet and making his way across the hall to his father, who stood imposingly in the doorway.

The moment he was within arm's reach, his father's hand shot out, and hauled him out into the hall. The cook stood outside the door with red, watery eyes, and another pang of guilt wrenched at Xavier's insides.

"Son?" Jeremiah hissed expectantly.

His eyes fluttered from the woman to the floor in front of him.

"Xavier Wells!" the king growled, his hand tightening warningly on his arm.

Xavier looked up at the woman again and cleared his throat. "I...I'm sorry, ma'am. I was angry, and I wrongly took it out on you. You didn't deserve it...please, accept my apology..."

When Xavier didn't continue, Jeremiah added stoutly, "And as retribution, Xavier will volunteer to do your cleanup duties this evening so that you can have the night off, Ms. White."

Leave it to his father to make sure his apology exceeded normal standards. Xavier looked up at the woman in front of him and gave her a small encouraging smile. "Yes, ma'am. Of course I'll do that."

The woman smiled. "Thank you, young sire. I should have known you'd come to your senses, and...I'm sorry you're having a bad day. I hope it gets better."

"Thanks," he replied, looking at his large, daunting father standing beside him. "But I have a feeling that my day is only going to get worse."

The woman exchanged an uncomfortable glance between the king and the prince before announcing, "Well, thank you again. I'd better get back to my chores. Good afternoon, sire."

"Good afternoon, Diana," Jeremiah responded, flashing a warm smile.

As soon as the doors closed behind Ms. White, Jeremiah's steely eyes bore into Xavier as he ordered, "Come with me. We'll finish this in the residence."

Then, he turned and strode toward the steps. Xavier released a shaky breath and sluggishly drifted after his father.

Jeremiah didn't look back until he reached the entryway to royal chambers. He opened the door, turned to the slouching, shuffling boy, and commanded, "Inside."

Xavier slipped past his father and into the chamber.

"Sit." Jeremiah ordered shortly, pointing at the sofa.

Xavier sat on the edge of the sofa and timidly glanced at his father, who dragged a chair from the table and settled in front of him.

"Well? What do you have to say for yourself?" he probed.

Xavier squirmed under his father's glare but didn't answer.

"Answer me, son! What happened to make you believe that you have any right to treat an adult that way?"

He tried to meet his father's eyes but faltered under the power and intensity there. He quickly looked away and stared at his feet.

"I...I was angry at my friends," he finally whispered,

shifting uncomfortably on the edge of the sofa.

"I see," Jeremiah noted stiffly. "So being angry with your friends gave you the right to backtalk, disrespect, and act insolently toward an adult?"

"No," he retorted.

"Oh, so being the Prince of Warwood gives you that right, then?"

"No! Jeez, Dad! Stop twisting my words. I'm trying to explain. I was already mad at Court, Erica, and Robbie, and that's why I lost my temper with Ms. White!"

"You do not have the luxury to lose your temper, boy! Not only because you're their prince, but more importantly, you're the Chosen. Losing your temper could result in deadly consequences!"

"Damn it, Dad!" he spat. "I wouldn't hurt anyone!"

"Watch your language with me, boy!" his father barked.

Heat flashed over Xavier's body, and he took a deep breath trying to simmer down his temper. "Then, stop exaggerating! Just because I got mad and I said things I shouldn't have doesn't mean anyone was in danger. I wouldn't kill anyone just because I'm mad!"

"No? Then what exactly happened with Drew? You're still young and your control over your abilities isn't fully developed yet. It's easy to lose control of them. It only takes a millisecond to create disastrous effects."

He opened his mouth to argue that he wouldn't lose control, but then remembered how angry he had been when he attacked Drew. However, when he'd propelled the force at the older boy, he had known it wouldn't kill him, only hurt him a bit. He still believed that the entire incident was Drew's fault. After all, he had thrown him stark naked into the girls' dormitory for God's sake! But, looking into his father's unyielding face, he knew it was futile to explain any of it. He wouldn't see it his way no matter how he tried to explain and justify his actions.

The king looked down at the boy and watched a range of emotions play across his features. He saw guilt and regret flicker to the surface the moment Drew's name was mentioned. Then, stubbornness filled his eyes, and his jaw stiffened, but he didn't argue. This would have been an ideal time to tell the boy about the most unfortunate incident of his own youth. It had nearly cost him everything. But, the boy wasn't quite thirteen yet and was too young to hear such a story. He would prefer to wait a couple of years for when Xavier reached the age he had been when it all happened. In the meantime, Jeremiah would take his silence as a small parental victory.

"Now, can you tell me where you were this morning?" Jeremiah continued.

"Around," Xavier mumbled, slouching back into the sofa.

"What kind of answer is that? Around? Why weren't you in classes, son?"

He shrugged and grumbled, "What's the big deal, Dad? You're canceling half the classes tomorrow anyway."

"The big deal is that you are expected to attend classes and LEARN something!" the king replied stoutly.

"Well, I guess I didn't feel like sitting in a classroom, Father! It seems a bit...pointless knowing that I have...bigger things to worry about than algebraic algorithms," he muttered.

Jeremiah went silent. After a moment, he whispered, "I'm sorry, son. If I could take this burden from you, I would, but Xavier, you must stay the course. I know it's hard for you to accept the burden of being the Chosen, but I promise you that I will do everything I can to help you. Regardless of your destiny, your education is of key importance. Promise me to stick with your studies, son."

A painful knot lodged in Xavier's throat, and he looked up at his father. His eyes stung with unshed tears. "Okay, Dad. I promise, but you have to promise me something too," he whimpered. "Promise me that no matter what happens, you won't sacrifice yourself for me. I could handle this...*prophecy,* my destiny if I knew you'd be okay."

Jeremiah sighed heavily, moved onto the sofa, and pulled the boy into his arms. He held him in silence trying to sooth the despair radiating from him. After a moment, he whispered adamantly, "I'm sorry, son, but I can't do that!" His arms tightened around the boy when he fought to pull away and argue, and he continued in a quiet rush. "It's not the job of the son to watch out for his father. It's the job of the father to watch out for his son. I cannot let anything happen to you, and I would die to protect you, not because you're the Chosen but because you're my son, and I love you. I love you more than my next breath."

A quivering sob erupted from Xavier, and he wrapped his arms more tightly around his father's waist. Biting back sobs, he whimpered against the king's chest, "I was afraid you'd say that."

Chapter 23

Cave-in

Later that afternoon, Xavier wandered onto the children's level looking for a distraction from the feeling of hopelessness, dread, and anger still swirling inside him. And, boy was he angry! He couldn't shake the fury he was feeling toward his father. To Xavier, it felt like his father had already abandoned him, and he wasn't even dead yet. He wasn't even going to try to keep it from happening. It was as if he *wanted* to die! It really ticked Xavier off. As a result, he had a careless, reckless spirit as he entered the boys' dormitory.

"I'm going exploring! Who's in?" he announced the moment he spotted the group lounging around their bunks looking bored.

"Exploring? Are you mad?" Frankie blurted.

"Don't be a git, *Francine*," Beck hissed, sitting up and giving the other boy a playful shove. He looked back at Xavier with a wink. "We're in as long as you and Court promise not to go for any more swims."

The other boys chuckled.

"What are you talking about? We would've made it to that rock if King Wells hadn't come along and *saved* our lives," Court ribbed with a wide grin.

"Oh, yeah. I'm sure it would've been a great

accomplishment to have reached that rock *dead*," Harry retorted sarcastically, and again the group laughed.

"Well?" Xavier interrupted impatiently. "Are you going to sit around here talking about it or are you coming?"

The boys looked at their prince, taken aback by his commanding tone and edginess.

To escape their stares, he turned and strode from the room. The boys hurried out of the dorm behind him.

"Well, I think going exploring is an excellent idea." Garrett announced, trying to calm the static air he felt around the prince.

"Hey, I've got an idea," Beck exclaimed. "Let's go to the crystal cave! I've been dying to check it out! Dad's been working there, harvesting crystals to replace the old ones when they'll no longer reflect and refract sunlight."

"The crystal cave?" the others chimed together.

"What crystals?" Harry asked.

"The crystals that provide the mountain with light and solar energy, you daft prat! How else did you think we're able to have natural sunlight a mile or more beneath a mountain? How do you think crops are able to grow on the upper level?" Beck spat irritably.

Harry opened his mouth to recant but only managed a wistful, "Oh."

"Sounds good to me. Can we invite the girls?" Court asked, eying Erica and Robbie across the hall near the girls' dormitory door.

Beck made a face and glanced darkly at Xavier before answering. "Why? They'll only slow us down!"

"Slow us down? Are you nuts? Have you ever met Erica? We'll be running to keep up with her!" Court laughed.

Beck shrugged in surrender, unable to think of a reason against it without looking like a complete jerk.

"Okay. If you want your little *sweetums* with you, Court, I guess she can come."

"Robbie, too," Xavier whispered.

"Fine! Why not bring the entire girls' dormitory? Find me after you *ladies* have gathered up your girlfriends," Beck growled and stomped down the hall toward the stairs.

Since most of the men were meeting with King Wells to discuss plans for retaking Warwood, the children found it easy to sneak onto the lower level. They traveled past the warning sign without hesitation this time and followed Xavier into a narrow passage, talking loudly and teasing one another. The hottest topic of conversation seemed to be Court and Erica.

"So, Erica? When are you going to give poor Courtney a break and admit what we all know, that you like him?" Garrett taunted.

"Me? Like that ugly jug? Not on your life!" Erica hissed.

"Then why is it you jumped at the chance to go exploring with me today? I didn't tell you anyone else was going, and you were so eager to go that you were blushing," Court retorted unscathed.

"Xavier?" Robbie whispered, falling into step next to him. "Are you still mad at me?"

"No." He sighed, and then, taking her by the hand, he added, "but, you have to tell me something."

She gave him a sideways look before responding suspiciously, "Okay, what?"

"What did you see at my divination? Dad told me that everyone there had visions and were given tasks. What are yours?" he asked, staring hard at her so that she couldn't lie to him.

"Well, my task is to be...I guess I'm your emotional guardian. I'm supposed to help you through the rough times ahead of you. But that's not a big stretch since we've always done that for each other, huh?" she told him.

"That's it?" he interrogated. "You only saw that you were to help me through stuff? That's all you saw?"

Robbie looked away, her face blushing. "No," she whispered.

"What then?"

"Well," she hesitated. "Xavier...it's embarrassing...and personal. It wasn't bad. I promise..."

Xavier's stare intensified, and he found himself working his way into Robbie's thoughts. He saw a brief image of a couple lounging in a bed. The woman was nursing an infant while the man laughed and kissed the woman.

"Xavier! Stop it!" Robbie blared, shoving him hard.

Xavier stumbled and fell firmly on his butt. The group behind them burst into laughter.

"Nice, Wells! Walk much?" Beck teased.

"Jeez, Cousin," Court teased Robbie with mock disappointment. "No one likes a bully."

Xavier jumped to his feet and dusted himself off as Beck led the giggling group farther down the passage.

"Sorry, Xavier," Robbie whispered. "I shouldn't have pushed you."

"Yeah, me too. I should have waited for you to tell me instead of violating your mind like that," he replied softly.

"How much did you see?"

"Not much. Just a couple with a baby. Who are they, Robbie?"

"Us."

"Us?" he asked.

"You know, *US*," she emphasized.

As the implication of the scene he had seen finally registered, he blushed.

Robbie rushed to continue. "It's some time into the future...because we're older...well you saw. You're really tall, almost as tall as your dad," she added with a smile.

He had to smile at that. "Well, it's nice to know I won't be the Prince of Pipsqueaks my entire life," he joked. Then he added seriously, "So, you're like...my wife?"

She nodded, blushing more.

"Robbie, I don't think that your vision is that surprising either. I mean...I've..." Xavier swallowed hard, trying to gain courage to say the rest. Finally, he blurted it out in a rush, "I've always liked you."

She stared at him. "So...the kiss...was real and not just to prove you don't kiss like a fish?"

He smiled and slipped his hand into hers. "Yeah, it was real, all right."

She grinned and squeezed his hand.

"We're here!" Beck called over his shoulder at the group. "Welcome to the Crystal Cave!"

When the group entered the cavern, they gasped. Crystal Cave was enormous! The ceiling was at least a hundred feet high, and its expansive walls were made of the strangest substance they had ever seen. The walls were pale, almost white, and glistened as if wet. Fragments of light danced around the room and over their faces like insistent fireflies.

"Whoa," Garrett muttered, speaking for every child there.

"Are the walls completely crystal?" Mac asked.

"Yeah, at least that's what Dad says. He says this pocket of crystal rock extends for half a mile down, and it's one of only five crystal deposits! There's enough crystal in this mountain to light New York City for thousands of years," Beck explained.

"Double whoa!" Mac exclaimed.

"So this stuff reflects light?" Frankie asked.

"Yeah, but it also intensifies it...I'm not exactly sure how it works so don't ask!" Beck added, strolling farther into the room and spinning around to take in the spectacular sight.

"Cool," Xavier whispered, releasing Robbie's hand to move next to Beck. "If this stuff reflects and strengthens light...I wonder..."

Then, without thinking, he thrust his hand into the air and sent an electro force spiraling toward the lofty ceiling. When the force struck the ceiling, it absorbed the energy momentarily before squirming worms of golden light wiggled across the ceiling. Suddenly, there was a loud crack as the crystal cave repelled the electro force into the air in a fantastic light show.

"WOW!" the children exclaimed.

"It's like fireworks! Let me try!" Garrett whooped, peeling off his sweatshirt, throwing it aside, and rolling up his sleeves. Garrett sent a force to the ceiling, but it only fizzled and gave a small burst of light. The children laughed.

"Give it up, Bracus. You're not the Prince of Warwood; your powers don't have the same intensity as Xavier's," Mac teased. Then turning back to Xavier, he urged, "Go on X. Do it again. Give us a real show!"

"Yeah, come on Xavier!" Frankie and Harry chimed.

Xavier looked around at the other children all eagerly nodding their heads.

"Yeah, Xavier. Please? It was beautiful," Robbie whispered, and he couldn't refuse.

Without another thought, he grinned as he released a powerful electro force toward the crystal ceiling. The effects were even more magnificent than the first, and the children around him exclaimed in awe.

Encouraged by their reactions, he couldn't resist showing off and shot force after force toward the ceiling. Soon, it looked like a grand finale at a pyrotechnic show, and the group shrieked with delight.

"Again! Again!" the children chanted.

They felt the rumble long before they heard it, and their excitement came to an abrupt halt. The cavern began to shake and soon the rumble became a thunderous roar. Suddenly, the floor lurched violently, and the children were thrown to the stone floor as bits of rock, crystal, and earth from the ceiling crumbled on top of them.

"What's happening?" Harry yelled.

"What do you think?" Beck screamed. "It's caving in! Quick! Everybody get out! The place is going to collapse!"

The children scrambled from the chamber and sprinted down the passage. They had gone no more than a few meters when the cavern collapsed behind them with a deafening crash.

"GO! KEEP RUNNING!" Xavier screamed, pushing the others forward as a cloud of dust and debris billowed out of the chamber behind them. Finally, the rumbling stopped. Choking on dust, the group turned and stared back at the settling earth in wide-eyed shock.

"Oh, man! Oh, man! Oh, man! Geez, we're in so much trouble!" Garrett rambled, and the others moaned their agreement.

"Maybe not," Xavier whispered, "unless we stick around long enough to get caught. Come on, guys. Let's get out of here."

The children bolted from the restricted section and didn't stop running until they reached the children's corridor. Only then did they slow to an awkward stroll.

"Man! Did you see that? The whole..."

"Shut up, Garrett!" Xavier bellowed, turning on the smaller boy. "They can't prove we had anything to do with it! For all they know, it was just an accident, and it caved in on its own! So don't talk about it! Don't even think about it! Just...just pretend it never happened. Got it?"

Garrett slowly nodded.

Xavier turned to the rest of the group. "The same goes for all of you. Just forget about it! We were never there! Okay?"

They all nodded dutifully.

"Right. We should shower; we look like ghosts covered in all this dust. See you at dinner," Xavier instructed.

After another nod, the group immediately separated into the girls' and boys' lavatories while Xavier was forced to slip one floor down to the royal chambers to get cleaned up. Just as he reached the fourth level, he heard a thunder of footsteps and urgent voices from the stairwell above.

"There's been a cave-in!"

Xavier recognized Mr. Wilcox's voice and ducked out of sight as a dozen men, his father among them, barreled past, racing to the lower level.

Chapter 24

Busted

As a result of the cave-in, dinner was delayed for nearly an hour. The group of children avoided eye contact with each other and kept their heads down in the hope that no one would discover they were responsible. Just as dinner was being served, most of the men who had been restoring and repairing the damaged chamber entered the hall with the king among them. As Jeremiah reached his seat at the head table, he raised his hand and instantly silenced the fevered whispers.

"Ladies and gentlemen, as many of you know, there's been a major cave-in on the lower level. First, I want to reassure everyone that the uninhabited chamber and surrounding passages have been secured, and there is nothing to worry about. A handful of volunteers chose to stay below to finish up and investigate the cause. As soon as we get word..."

The hall doors slammed open, and two grim, dust-covered men approached the head table. It wasn't until they stopped in front of Jeremiah that Xavier realized with horror that one of the men had a very dirty sweatshirt in his hand. Garrett's sweatshirt! Xavier's panicked gaze darted to Garrett, who stared at the men with an open mouth.

Quickly, he connected with the other boy and told him silently, *"Garrett, stay calm and ignore it! They can't prove anything with just a sweatshirt. Just sit tight and stay calm."*

"But X..."

"Garrett! Stop thinking about it!" Xavier blared before disconnecting with the other boy.

"Sire," one of the men was saying, "the cave-in was not accidental. We found scorched crystals that could only have been caused by fire or an electro force, and we found this in the chamber."

The king took the sweatshirt into his hands and immediately looked at the tag. Then, he glanced darkly down at his son.

Xavier felt a cold sensation as Jeremiah attempted to probe into his mind for answers. He fought his father's penetration with every bit of will power he had and it worked. Finally, Jeremiah withdrew and turned his attention to the crowded hall.

"Ladies and gentlemen, may I have your attention please," he called, which was unnecessary for the entire hall had fallen silent the moment the men entered the room. "This shirt was discovered while sifting through the debris in the cave." He held up the filthy sweatshirt. "It appears to be a boy's shirt with the initials G.B. and belongs to the person sleeping in bunk eighteen," he continued.

Mr. and Mrs. Bracus' heads jerked toward their son, and Mr. Bracus feverishly whispered to Garrett.

"Whoever is responsible for the cave-in, this is your chance to come clean and take responsibility for your actions," the king announced.

A prickling sensation crept up Xavier's spine, and he looked up and met his father's steel, unwavering eyes.

Jeremiah opened his mouth to say something when Mr. Bracus' loud words drew his attention away.

"Garrett! Answer me, boy! Is that your shirt? Did you have something to do with the cave-in today?" Mr. Bracus bellowed heatedly.

Xavier watched Garrett's head drop, and then after a moment, he nodded. Xavier groaned inwardly and closed his eyes with dread.

"Sire?" Mr. Bracus called, standing nervously. "Sire, I'm sorry, but that shirt belongs to my son."

"Is this true, Garrett Bracus?" Jeremiah questioned sternly. "Does this shirt belong to you? Were you on the restricted level in the Crystal Cave?"

Garrett seemed incapable of looking up at the king as he nodded.

"There's no way the boy acted alone. I doubt his empowerments are strong enough to do the kind of damage we saw. Let me talk to the boy and find out what he knows. You need to eat. I'll get back to you as soon as I know something," Loren whispered.

Jeremiah nodded. "All right. Thanks, Loren."

Loren stood and waved Garrett to him, and they left the hall with Mr. Bracus behind them. His appetite suddenly lost, Xavier slouched back into his chair.

"Xavier? Please tell me you had nothing to do with this," his father whispered, staring at him suspiciously.

"Uh, I didn't have anything to do with it," he muttered.

Halfway through dinner, Loren returned and approached the front table with a grimace. "Jer, Garrett refuses to talk. I may need you after all."

Jeremiah shoveled one last spoonful of mashed potatoes into his mouth before gently pushing the plate away from him, wiping his mouth, and standing. "Okay, where is he?"

"The fencing room," Loren answered, leading the king from the head table, past the rows of citizens finishing their meals, and out of the hall.

"Uh oh," Court groaned as he plopped himself in the king's chair. "Garrett must be putting up a good fight if Loren came after the heavy guns...if your father uses telepathy on Garrett, we're all screwed."

Xavier couldn't help but agree with Court. "Damn! We've got to get everybody together and get our story straight! Come on."

The boys stood, and after beckoning the other children to them, they made their way toward the back of the hall. They had trouble finding a table to themselves because even though most of the mountain's population had finished eating, many lingered, visiting with one another.

"What are we going to do, Xavier?" Frankie asked in a panic-stricken voice once the group had settled around a table at the far side of the hall.

"Well..." Xavier began, but the doors opened with a loud bang, and the king stood rigidly in its entrance.

"Xavier Wells! Courtney Hardcastle! Beckley Wilcox! Harry Sims! Franklin MacCorkle! Mackenzie Clarke! Erica Jefferson! And Roberta Minnows! Come here!" he boomed, his voice echoing around the hall.

The children exchanged looks of terror.

"Now!" the king shouted.

Slowly, as though they were walking to their own execution, the group of children shuffled to the doorway as every eye in the hall watched. They followed King Wells down the hallway and into the fencing classroom. Garrett sat at a table with Mr. Bracus, Loren, and Henrick Davies, who was covered head to toe in grime.

"Sit!" Jeremiah barked, pointing at the table.

The children scrambled to oblige. The four men glared

silently down at them, and the children ducked their heads guiltily.

"Children?" Loren questioned, calmly.

Not one child said a word. They simply slumped deeper into their seats.

Xavier quickly connected with his friends and warned, *"Don't say a word. Just keep your minds blank and let me do the talking."*

"Xavier? Don't play games with me, boy!" his father shouted.

"Games? What..."

"Son, you may have been able to block my telepathic advances earlier, but you're not consistent at it." Xavier opened his mouth to protest that he hadn't blocked him, but his father interrupted. "In addition, you do not yet possess the ability to send telepathic messages without those messages being easily intercepted or heard. So you can be assured that I heard every message you sent today. I know you warned Garrett about the sweatshirt. I know you warned these children to let you do the talking and to keep their minds blank. I know you had a major hand in all of this. After all, none of these children have a strong enough electro force to destroy those crystal reserves. So, aside from an adult being responsible, that leaves you, my son."

"Maybe it was an adult," Xavier grumbled. "I...didn't...do it, Father. Really."

Jeremiah grabbed him by the collar, hauled him out of his seat, and held him within inches of his snarling face. "Don't lie to me!"

"Why not? You've lied to me for months, Dad!" he spat back.

Uh, oh! His father had that fiery look in his eye again, and Xavier swallowed anxiously. After a long moment, he whispered, "Fine. You're right. We were there...in the Crystal Cave. We went exploring and we found that...cave, and before any of us knew it, there was this loud rumble and the place began falling apart...so we ran for it."

His father released him but continued to stare astringently down at him. He wasn't buying it. "Really?" he asked sarcastically. "Just like that? It just caved in?"

"Yes, sir..." Xavier began, but faltered under his father's stare. His eyes dropped to his father's boots and muttered, "Although...I might have...fired a few electro forces at the ceiling."

All four men jerked to attention.

"You did what?" Loren hissed incredulously.

"I...I didn't know it would cause a cave-in!" he continued in a rush. "It just...it looked like fireworks...I...I'm sorry!"

"You endangered your life and the lives of your friends!" his father barked. "Not to mention, you've single-handedly destroyed a large crystal reservoir that is invaluable to our survival in the mountain! Those crystals provide our gardens with essential sunlight. Without them, we would have a major food shortage! Sorry just doesn't cut it!" The king's anger wasn't diminishing. If anything, it seemed to be escalating.

"Father, I didn't know...I didn't do it intentionally! Really!" he stammered.

"But, you have been told, REPEATEDLY, that the lower levels are off limits to unauthorized citizens! Why do you think that is, son?" The king didn't wait for a response. "I'll tell you why! Because those passages and chambers are DANGEROUS! None of you had any business being down there!"

"But, sire," Frankie said timidly. "Xavier gave us authorization. He said as king, he could do..."

"HE IS NOT KING! He has absolutely NO authority to do that, Franklin!" Jeremiah boomed, and every child ducked and flinched.

"Easy, Jer," Loren interrupted calmly.

Jeremiah visibly tried to compose himself and after a moment, he looked back at the children. "All right, all of you are grounded to the children's dormitories indefinitely. After studies and chores, you are to be in the dormitories! No visiting the games room. No playing rugby! Nothing but work and confinement! Understand?"

The group nodded solemnly.

"Go on to your dormitories. Loren and I will be down in a few minutes to administer the final touch to your punishments!" Jeremiah growled.

"Final touch, sire?" Robbie questioned meekly.

"He means we're being spanked." Xavier groaned.

The children looked at each other in alarm.

"Did you really think you wouldn't be spanked for this?" Loren asked the children. "You could have been killed. Hell, we're lucky that the crystals didn't intensify the energy created by the cave-in! If it had, it would have caused a disaster of unforeseen proportions. This entire mountain could have exploded!"

"Seriously? That could have happened?" Beck whispered in awe.

"Yes, it could have, Beckley! By the grace of God, it didn't!" the king told him. "Now, all of you go straight to the dorms. We'll be there shortly."

The group slinked out of their seats and quietly left the room.

"Son, I'll be with you as soon as I have dealt with the others. So I want you ready for bed before I get there."

Xavier closed his eyes with dread, and with a nod, he left the room.

Nearly a half an hour later, Xavier was sitting on the couch trying to concentrate on his make-up assignments, when his father entered the chambers. He looked exhausted, but that didn't diminish the look of foreboding and anger on his face. Slowly, Xavier closed his book and set it aside.

"I got word that the Crystal Cave is nearly cleaned up. It's estimated that at least twenty percent of the crystals are damaged beyond use." After rubbing his face wearily, Jeremiah crossed the room, grabbed a chair from the table, and moved it to sit in front of his son. "Xavier, what were you thinking? Why did you and your friends go into the restricted level again?" he questioned.

"I don't know, sir. I...I just wanted to do something fun to get my mind...off...*things*. I really am sorry, Dad. I wouldn't have used electro forces on the ceiling if I'd known..."

"That's not the point, son. You had no business being down there to begin with!" he interrupted as he stood and began pacing to calm his temper.

Xavier sighed miserably. "I know, Dad. I...I'm sorry."

His father stopped to pin him with a stern glare. "You're sorry? You know what, Xavier? Sorry doesn't bring back those destroyed crystals. Sorry doesn't change the fact that you and your friends could have been killed today, son!"

"Yeah, and I bet it pisses you off that it would have ruined your suicide plans," he mumbled.

"What in the hell is that supposed to mean?"

"Just that if I were to die, you wouldn't be able to fulfill your stupid vision of killing yourself for me! You're not even trying to avoid it!" he spat.

"What? Of course I'm going to try to avoid it! My vision has nothing to do with what happened in the Crystal

Caves today."

"Whatever," he spat and started to roll his eyes, but the king had him by the collar before he could.

"Don't roll your eyes at me, *boy!*" his father growled, pulling the boy inches from his face.

Xavier stared obstinately into his eyes.

"Fine," he snapped, propelled the boy across his hip, and pinned him there. Xavier squirmed in his grasp, but his father tightened his grip and proceeded to pummel his backside with several solid, jolting smacks before finally releasing him. Xavier glared up at him with a tear-soaked face as he rubbed his butt with a grimace. For a long moment, father and son stared at one another in strained silence.

Finally, his father whispered, "It's getting late. Go to bed."

Without a word, Xavier turned, stomped into his chamber, and slammed the door behind him.

Chapter 25

The Plan

That night, Xavier had nightmare. He found himself standing outside of Warwood Palace. It was a moonless night and the palace looked dark and uninhabited. He could barely make out the horseshoe-shaped drive and median, which was normally a luscious flowerbed. But, there weren't flowers in the garden now, only barren earth, and something erected in the center. It appeared to be a large altar and something was resting on it.

Slowly, he moved toward the structure, terror mounting in him like a geyser building up for an eruption. The heap on the altar was covered by a dark cloak that seemed to be stained by something wet and sticky. Panting as though he had just run a marathon, Xavier peeled back the cloak, and a scream caught painfully in his throat. His father's lifeless, dismembered body lay on the altar in a pool of blood. With the image of his father's wide, lifeless eyes still haunting him, Xavier jerked awake screaming. Still caught in limbo between the horrific images of the dream and consciousness, he didn't hear his father enter the room nor did he acknowledge the room being flooded in light.

"Xavier?" Jeremiah called, hurrying to his side.

"Xavier, wake up, son!"

"Dad?" he croaked, blinking up at his father. Then, his face fell into anguish. "Dad!" he cried, throwing himself into his father's arms.

"Lord, boy, you're shaking! What on Earth..."

"I saw it, Dad! I saw your death! You had been...sacrificed on an altar like some kind of animal! You weren't even whole...you had...someone...chopped you up!" He clung to his father weeping as he begged, "Dad, please...PLEASE promise me you won't sacrifice yourself for me...PLEASE...I couldn't stand it if...*that* happened to you. I'll kill myself. You hear me? If you die for me, I'll kill myself." Then he broke down, his entire body racking on each howling sob.

"Xavier..." Jeremiah cooed, holding him close. "It's okay, son. Please, stop crying. Look, I promise you I'm looking for every way possible to avoid what I saw. And I did not see myself being sacrificed as you described. What you saw in your dream was just that, a dream, a nightmare. Aw, son. Please, stop crying."

As his crying gradually ebbed away, his father scooped him up into his arms and carried him into his bedchambers, settling into bed next to him.

"Are you okay, now?" his father asked hoarsely, stroking his cheek and jaw.

He nodded and whispered sheepishly, "Thanks."

"No problem, son. Let's get some sleep."

Without a word, he cuddled into his father's warmth and felt himself beginning to relax into a slumber.

The next morning Xavier awoke with a strong urge to pee, but he was pinned beneath his father's arm and leg. His father was still sleeping deeply, and he struggled to free himself. Finally he managed to lift an arm off his chest and set to work on the leg draped across his, but his father moaned and pulled him back into his embrace.

"Dad?" Xavier whined, elbowing him in the ribs.

Jeremiah jolted awake. "What?" he blurted sleepily.

"I've got to go to the bathroom and you're holding me down," he complained.

"What? Oh, sorry about that. Come on," his father muttered before climbing from the bed and pulling Xavier with him. With a wave of his hand, the crystal lamps provided just enough light so they wouldn't walk into things but not so much that it hurt their eyes.

"Dad, I can go by myself. You don't have to hover over me," he told him when Jeremiah followed him into the common room. Though he wouldn't ever admit it, he kind of liked the hovering.

"I'm not hovering. I have to go too," his father retorted.

Xavier knew that it was a lie, but he appreciated it all the same. Father and son walked into the hall and padded down the passage toward the lavatory. "Are you doing okay?" Jeremiah asked.

"Yeah, I'm fine," he answered.

"Are you sure?"

"Yes, Dad. Really, I'm fine. It's just..."

"What, son?"

"It was like some of the dreams I've had before...the ones that came true," Xavier said with a shiver. "I'm afraid...Dad, I don't want you to go with the Royal Guard to get Warwood back."

Jeremiah stopped him. "Son," he began, grasping his shoulders and stooping to eye level with him, "I must go. It's my duty. What kind of king would send his men into battle without fighting alongside them?"

"Okay, then, take me with you. Let me fight with you. I couldn't stand it if I had to remain behind and worry about what was happening. Please!" he begged.

"Absolutely not, Xavier. We've been through this before. I will not take a twelve-year-old boy into battle. A war is no place for a boy," his father stated with such finality that Xavier knew it was useless to argue.

He didn't say another word as they continued into the lavatory, but his mind busily planned what to do next. No one would die to protect him again. He would save his father's life. LeMasters wouldn't threaten anyone ever again. He would make sure of it. Xavier planned to kill William LeMasters.

The next morning following breakfast, the men said farewell to their families before their journey to Mirror Lake. It was a solemn time; many wondered if they would ever see one another again.

"Dad, can I walk out with you?" Xavier asked quietly.

Jeremiah looked down at him hesitantly.

"Please? I promise, I won't make a scene. I just...I just want to walk you out," he pleaded.

Jeremiah nodded. "Okay. Get your cloak. The outer passages are very cold."

"Yes, sir." he grinned and hurried toward the stairwell.

When he reached the fourth level, he sprinted down the hall and into the royal chambers, grabbing his long, blue cloak. Then he ran out of the chambers and started toward the stairwell, but skidded to a stop outside the Jefferson's chambers. As Keeper of the King's Key, Loren would keep the key close to him. It had to be somewhere inside his chambers. It could prove to be extremely useful. He wanted, no, he *needed* the King's Key to accomplish his plans.

Xavier entered the chambers without hesitation for he knew both Loren and Lucy were saying goodbye on the main level with all the other families. However, he had no idea where to look for the key, and his father was expecting him to return to the mountain's entrance at any minute. With a frustrated groan, he frantically peered around the room when a thought occurred to him: his abilities! With a small grin at his stupidity, he closed his eyes and focused on beckoning the key to him. Suddenly, he felt a warm presence and opened his eyes. The key hovered next to his outstretched hand, and he simply grabbed it.

"Whoa!" he muttered, staring down at the key.

But, he had no time to ponder the ease in which the key came to him, and he tucked the King's Key through his belt loop before racing out of the chamber, down the hall, and up to the main level. Instead of going straight to the group waiting by the mountain's entrance, he ducked into the fencing room. He went directly to the glass-encased sword. With a wave of his hand, the case sprung open and the sword flew into his hand. Quickly, he tucked the sword under his cloak next to the key, slipped from the room, and hurried down the corridor toward the group departing the mountain. His father lingered by the door with Michael Spencer.

"Dad, wait! I'm coming!" Xavier called, running awkwardly toward the men.

"Not to worry, son. We were waiting for you. I wouldn't leave you without saying goodbye," Jeremiah reassured him with a smile, clapping him on the back. He turned to the group of women and children lingering nearby. "I know this is hard, but I promise each of you that we will plan the invasion carefully, and I will do everything in my power to ensure that your loved ones return home to you. Until then, take care of each other. See you all soon."

There were murmurs of farewell and good luck as the

king, Xavier, and Michael Spencer walked through the door, shutting it firmly behind them.

The moment Xavier entered the Cavern of Kings, voices from the past kings began drumming into him, and he paused, staring up at the statues with renewed awe.

"Come, Xavier. It's a long walk and I need to get these men to Mirror Lake before nightfall," his father told him softly, extending his hand.

He took his father's hand and was led deeper into the Cavern. The farther they walked, the louder, more intense the voices became until Xavier clamped his hands over his ears and tried to muffle out the noise. It didn't help.

"Xavier? Are you all right?" his father asked.

He tried to smile as he dropped his hands. "Yes, sir."

His father wasn't buying it and asked, "Are the kings speaking to you?"

He nodded. "They're just...really loud."

Jeremiah grabbed Xavier's arm and stopped him. He looked down at him with worried, tired eyes. "What are they saying?"

He shook his head and moaned. "I can't tell. They're all talking at once!"

"Xavier, listen to me. If the kings are trying this hard to speak to you, it must be important. Stop fighting them. Calm down and even out your breathing."

He did as his father instructed, and soon, the voices grew quieter. "King of Light, it will not work. Your reckless plan will only result in your death. Do not go through with it!"

Xavier shook his head.

"What? What did they say?" Jeremiah asked.

"Ah...nothing. They...stopped talking," he lied.

When the king opened his mouth to press the issue, Loren called out jovially, "Excuse me, King Wells? Could you move it along back there? We'd like to get to Mirror Lake while we're all still fairly young!"

Xavier took this distraction to hurry past his father and join the group, exiting through the enormous doors of the cavern. He could feel his father's presence pushing against his consciousness and quickly shifted his thoughts to Robbie. He thought about her vision and what he saw there. His wife! She would be his wife some day! He smiled at the thought as he felt his father's hand drop onto his shoulder, affectionately.

"So you saw Robbie's vision?" he asked.

Xavier looked up, feigning an expression of surprise. "How did you... oh, you were in my thoughts, huh? Well, I only saw a little before she realized I was in her thoughts and knocked me on my butt."

He snickered. "She will make a fine queen someday. Just don't be in a hurry. Ok?"

After ten minutes of walking, the group finally came to a halt in front of an enormous rock wall.

"All right, Jer. It's time to do your thing," Loren called.

The king brushed past the men and moved to stand unobstructed in front of the stone barrier. He raised his hand and the wall began to rumble and creak as it slowly opened. A blinding white light blasted into the passage from the snow-coated landscape, forcing the group to blink and shield their eyes.

After a moment, Jeremiah announced, "Well, men, let's head on down the mountain." He turned to Xavier. "This is where we say goodbye, son. Behave yourself and mind your uncle," he whispered, enveloping the boy in his arms.

Suddenly, the king went rigid. "What the..." He pushed Xavier at arm's length, pulled back his cloak, and saw the Sword of the Chosen and the King's Key strapped to his waist. "Why in the hell do you have the key and that...that sword?"

He twisted out of his father's hands. "I have to do it, Father. I can't let anyone else die for me. I can't let him kill anyone else. I can't let you die!"

"Xavier..." Jeremiah began, but the boy pushed past him and out into the bright light. "Stop him! Loren! Grab Xavier! Don't let him teleport!"

But, Loren didn't reach him in time. Just as his hand closed over the prince's arm, he was gone, and the king gave a great bellow of despair.

Chapter 26

Child Soldiers

Moments later, Xavier slammed against something wet and cool. The spiraling sensation of teleporting still had his head spinning, and he felt dangerously close to throwing up. He opened his clamped eyes and found himself on his hands and knees in some kind of forest. Slowly he got to his feet and peered around. He knew this area! He had teleported the entire distance to Warwood! He stood in the Wood next to the lake. It was still daylight and by his calculations, it had to be about two o'clock in the afternoon. He had a long time to wait before he could sneak into the palace and kill William LeMasters. In the meantime, he would use his time wisely and scout out the security around the palace.

He withdrew his sword and held it at the ready as he crept through the dense foliage, careful to stay off paths and out of sight. He didn't want any accidental encounters. His mission was too important to risk. Everything depended on it. Soon, he came to the immense field adjacent to the academy and the coliseum. Half a dozen men wearing black uniforms and cloaks and armed with swords were standing in a huddled group in the middle of the field. The men looked completely relaxed, as though they were confident that no one would dare try to overtake them. They were perfectly at home. Anger soared into Xavier, and any fear he had initially felt was shoved to the back of his mind. Maybe their confident attitudes could be used against them. Maybe they would be so confident in their strength that they wouldn't see a twelve-year-old boy as a threat. His eyes traveled to the academy. A string of children dressed identically to their adult counterparts marched in single file lines as adults barked orders.

"Damn it, Mr. Calhoun! That's the second time you've dropped your free hand!" a voice boomed a few meters from the edge of the woods.

Xavier immediately dropped to the ground.

"S...sorry, sir," Ken Calhoun's voice trembled. "I f...forgot."

"FORGOT! FORGOT!" bellowed the voice, which was followed by a flickering light and Ken's screams.

Xavier crawled through the brush toward the commotion. Ken was sprawled on the muddy ground panting, while a man with short, blond hair stood menacingly above him.

"Maybe now you'll remember, Mr. Calhoun, because if you forget again, this punishment will tickle in comparison to what you'll receive," the man hissed. "Now, get to your feet boy, and do it again."

Ken scrambled to his feet and joined the two lines of children facing one another with swords.

"All right, soldiers! En guarde!" the man shouted, and instantly the group erupted in a series of lunges, feints, and parries. Several minutes later, somewhere within the academy, a loud horn blared.

"Now, you are to practice for an hour this evening, except for you Mr. Calhoun. You will practice for two hours tonight. I'll see you in my chambers at seven o'clock. You're dismissed to your next lesson," the man order roughly before turning to a small boy at the end of the line. "Mr. Fine? After you gather all the equipment and take it to the storage shed, you can go to the nurse's station and have that wound healed."

"Yes, Commander," the boy squeaked, saluting.

The commander turned and marched toward the academy behind his students, leaving the smaller boy behind to pick up spare swords and sabers. Once everyone was out of sight and the boy was alone, Xavier took a deep breath, stood, and stepped out of the woods.

"Hey, mate. How's it going?" he called softly, trying not to scare the kid.

The boy looked up quickly, his eyes large and anxious. "Sorry, sir. I didn't hear you walk up. I was just picking up like the Commander ordered. I...I won't be long."

"Need a hand?" Xavier asked, nodding to the boy's overflowing arms and dozen swords still lying on the ground.

"Ah...no, sir. I can manage. I can pull my own weight, sir. Don't worry."

"Why are you calling me sir?" Xavier asked.

The boy looked at him suspiciously. "Well, sir. You are a lord, of course," he responded, nodding at the royal blue cloak Xavier was wearing. "I recognize the royal colors of course, sir."

Xavier looked over his own appearance, but as he did so, the hood of his cloak slipped, exposing his white hair. The boy's gray eyes grew enormous. "Oh, my God! You're Prince Wells! What are you doing here, sire?" the boy squeaked, dropping to his knees and sending the swords in his arms clattering to the ground. "Are you here to save us?"

Xavier dropped to his knees in front of the boy. "How

do you know me? Are you a citizen of Warwood?"

"No, sire. I'm not from Warwood. Master has your picture posted all over the kingdom. We are supposed to be on constant vigilance for you and King Wells. Master has soldiers actively searching for you guys. He says that his men are close to finding you, but I think he's lying. I don't think they have a clue where you are." The boy smiled.

"How did you end up with LeMasters?" Xavier asked.

The boy shrugged. "I don't remember much before I was brought to live with Master," the boy replied, shaking his head and sending his long dark hair spinning around his head. "I remember my mother a little. She was always smiling, and she loved to hug me. She did it all the time," the boy ended, his face becoming melancholy.

"Look...ah, what's your name?" he asked.

The boy's grin was back. "Daniel. Daniel Fine, sire."

"Okay, look Daniel, I am here to stop William LeMasters. When I'm done, everyone being held captive will be freed, but I need your help. Can you get me a disguise so I won't stand out? Could you get me one of your uniforms, and something to color my hair with?" he asked.

"Yes, sire. I can do that! I'll meet you back here in ten minutes," Daniel agreed, jumping to his feet and lifting the swords into his arms.

"Wait," he called, noticing the deep cut on the smaller boy's arm. "Hold still." After a brief white glow, the wound stopped bleeding and closed into a thin, pink scar.

Daniel looked down at the wound. "Whoa! Thanks! I didn't know anyone...well, as young as you could heal like that!" Then, with another enormous, genuine grin, he raced toward the academy.

Xavier slid back into the cover of the wood's vegetation

and waited. Within ten minutes, little Daniel was jogging back from the academy with a bulge under his black cloak. As he drew near the Wood, he slowed, scanning the wood's edge.

"Sire? Sire?" he called softly.

"Here," Xavier whispered.

Daniel slipped into the woods to where he stood behind a bush leafing in young foliage.

"Here you are, sire," he announced with delight as he dumped a black uniform and cloak onto the ground between them. "And, for your hair...I got this." He pulled out a bottle of liquid shoe polish.

"Shoe polish?" Xavier laughed.

"Yes, sire. It'll work; won't it?" Daniel asked timidly.

He looked at the boy beside him and smiled. "Yeah, it's perfect! Thanks, Daniel. You did great. Come on. Let's go to the lake so I have water to rinse this stuff off."

The boy beamed up at him.

After Xavier colored his hair, he was sporting grungy, dirt-brown locks. It looked horrible, but at least his hair wasn't white anymore. Then he pulled on the black uniform and turned to Daniel, who sat on a rock watching his transformation.

"Well, how do I look?" he asked.

"Great, sire! No one would know it was you!" he declared in wonder.

"Good. Daniel, from now on, you can't call me sire or sir. Got it? Call me...Adam, okay?"

"Yes, Si...I mean, Adam."

"Come on. Show me around and tell me everything you know about the security to the palace," he instructed, draping an arm around Daniel and leading him out of the Wood.

Daniel, as it turned out, knew quite a lot about the

security of Warwood. LeMasters' men had discovered only five of the eight secret passages into the castle and stationed a man at each entrance. The palace guards always changed shifts at one in the afternoon and one in the morning. LeMasters had claimed the king's bedroom with his wife, Veronica. Their son, Fox, slept in Xavier's room.

"Wait! Did you say...his wife?" he interrupted, stopping Daniel. "Dr. Angelo is his wife?"

"Yeah, well, I think so. I mean Fox is *their* son. They would have to be married, right?" he asked.

"Ah, yeah, I guess so," Xavier replied as they entered the academy.

"Come on, we need to hurry. General Stephens said that if I was late for electro force training again, he'd cane me!" Daniel blurted, rushing ahead.

"No, he won't, Daniel," he retorted firmly. "I won't let him."

When the boys entered the gym, Xavier saw a dozen children standing at attention facing a large, imposing man. "Now, electro forces can be used to render your enemy helpless and reeling in pain while you impale him with your sword. May I have a volunteer from the group to assist me in demonstrating?"

A sudden terror rippled down the line of children, and every child's eye avoided the general's.

"Calhoun? What about you?" General Stephens questioned.

Ken hesitantly stepped forward and seemed to be fighting back tears. Xavier truly felt sorry for him and without thinking, he announced, "General Stephens? I'd like to volunteer."

The man whipped around in surprise. "And who are you, soldier?"

"I am a loyal servant of Master," he replied haughtily, trying not to gag on the words.

A sneer of respect spread across the general's face. "Good answer, soldier. Now, what is your name?"

"Adam. Adam... Jones, sir."

"All right, Soldier Jones. Step forward," the man announced, motioning Xavier to him.

He went without hesitation and stood staring blatantly up at the man. General Stephens turned to the group where Daniel had managed to slip inconspicuously in line with the others. Ken Calhoun fell back into line, keeping his head low and meek.

"Now, watch as I demonstrate how to use an electro force to immobilize my opponent so I can easily take him out," the general boasted before turning back to Xavier.

But, before General Stephens could raise his hand to conjure the force, Xavier's hand shot up and sent a stream of electricity into the man. Within seconds, the general collapsed to the floor, and Xavier withdrew his sword and held it inches from the man's throat. Only then did he release the electro force from the man. Soaked in his own sweat and still trembling from the empowerment he had endured, General Stephens gaped up at Xavier with fear and then hatred.

"Something like that, *sir*?" he hissed condescendingly down at him.

The general gave a nervous chuckle as he gingerly moved the tip of Xavier's sword away from his throat and stood. "Nicely, done, soldier! Nicely done." Though everything in the man's tone and demeanor said he thought the act was far from being nicely done.

"I'm a fast learner, sir," he replied.

He fell into line with the rest of the group as the other children's silent cheers and supportive thoughts burst into his mind. He was surprised by their mutinous feelings, but then, he realized that these child-soldiers were just as much prisoners as the loyal citizens who had been unable to escape the kingdom during the invasion. They held no loyalty to William LeMasters or his thugs; they simply feared them and knew of no other way.

"Pair up!" the general barked.

As the group paired up, Ken stepped up next to Xavier and whispered shakily, "Thanks for that. Stephens has been giving me a hard time ever since I started military training. Most of these guys have been in training for months or even years. So, I'm far behind everyone else...and, well, thanks."

He gave the other boy a quick nod before muttering, "No problem."

Chapter 27

Captured

Electro force was the last lesson of the day, and Xavier followed Daniel into the halls of the academy. The smaller boy led him into a wing of the school where classrooms had been converted into dormitories.

"You *live* here?" he gasped.

Daniel glanced timidly at him and nodded. "Yes, S...I mean...Yeah. All soldiers still in training live at the school. The bed next to mine is free if you want to sleep there tonight."

"Sorry, Daniel, but I won't be staying. I need to find a way into the palace," he whispered.

"Oh." He looked disappointed as he settled on a bare mattress on the floor, frowning. "I could get you in. I'm a kitchen helper at the palace for most evening meals. Sometimes, I bring one of the other boys with me to help. You could come with me tonight."

"Great, Daniel! That would be perfect!" he exclaimed, and the smaller boy beamed up at him.

The children staying in the academy dormitories were eerily silent. Most simply lay on their moth-eaten, stained mattresses staring at the ceiling. A handful of children were silently playing with a deck of dirty, crumbling cards. Only a sniffle or an occasional cough could be heard.

"Is it always like...this in here?" he whispered.

Daniel looked around at the other boys in the room before looking back at him with wide, sorrowful eyes. "Yeah, it is. If we appear to be having fun, if we laugh or talk at all, the academy warden *punishes* us. That's why I volunteered to be a kitchen helper. It's hard and sweaty work, but at least it gets me out of here and away from the warden."

"Who's..."

"Private Fine!" a steely voice snapped from the dorm's entrance and several boys cowered.

Daniel jumped to his feet and saluted before responding, "Yes, Warden LeMasters, sir!"

Xavier felt his heart jerk painfully as he whipped around and found Danson LeMasters strolling into the room. The man seemed to thoroughly enjoy the swell of terror he created in his wake and gleamed malevolently down at the children as he approached Daniel, who was fighting to stand straight and still. When Danson's eyes bore into Xavier, he met them with unwavering defiance. The man's glee slipped as he stepped past Daniel and stopped in front of Xavier.

For several long seconds, the two simply glared at one another in a silent battle, with Danson trying desperately to collapse Xavier's mental defenses and Xavier effortlessly keeping the man at bay with a small smile. Danson held no power over him anymore. It was in this moment that he realized that his abilities had surpassed Danson's. He was now the stronger telepathist, and his smile broadened.

"What are you grinning at, boy?" Danson blared testily before drawing back and slapping him across the jaw.

He stumbled and fell, slamming his head on the concrete floor.

"You dare to mock me, boy?" Danson roared as he withdrew a leather strap coiled at his waist. "No one, ABSOLUTELY NO ONE mocks me, especially a flea like you!"

A faint whistling noise was the only warning Xavier had before the strap struck him. He rolled onto his side and tucked his exposed flesh under his cloak. Although the cloak shielded him from the worst of the beating, he knew he would have welts when Danson was through with him.

"Sir! Sir, please!" Daniel cried. "Please forgive my friend, Adam. He's not accustomed to his place here. He's new. Please, sir. Please!"

"Oh, shut up Daniel!" Danson spat, and there was another whistle, but this time the strap didn't strike Xavier. It struck Daniel, and the small boy cried out.

Xavier leaped to his feet and found Danson drawing back to hit Daniel again. The strap never made contact with its target for he propelled a powerful electro force at the man, sending him hurling across the room. Danson smashed against the wall and fell heavily to the floor. He didn't move and didn't get up.

The room erupted into thunderous cheers. Suddenly, Xavier found himself surrounded by the other children.

"Well done!" one boy exclaimed, thumping his back.

"Yeah, I've been wanting to do that ever since he did this," another boy shouted gleefully, gesturing to the black eye patch he wore on his left eye.

"What's going on in here?" a strangely calm voice asked, and instantly the boys quieted and spun toward the doorway.

No one answered.

"Children? I asked a question. What happened to my brother?" Xavier felt a shudder pass through him as

William LeMasters' deep grating voice continued, "Who's responsible for this?"

The children remained silent, but Xavier knew that as inept as Danson was at telepathy, William LeMasters was not.

"I did," he announced, stepping out from behind the group. "He was beating up Daniel so I gave him a little zap."

When William LeMasters' eyes met his, he immediately felt the familiar sensation of infiltration, and he fought to block the advances. LeMasters' eyes narrowed on him, and for an instant, he thought he saw recognition in their depths.

Finally, William ordered, "Come closer, boy."

He moved awkwardly toward the man he feared above all others, fighting the urge to run from the room screaming. Then he thought of Mr. Minnows and his fear twisted into intense hatred. With a deep breath, he straightened his shoulders and met the man's black, bottomless eyes.

William smiled. "My, my, you're an insolent one. If looks could kill, I think you'd have me hung, dismembered, and electrocuted to death simultaneously if that were possible." He laughed. Then, as though someone had flipped a switch, his face grew wildly ominous. "Well, *Prince* Wells? Do it! If you think you're *man* enough, draw your sword and strike me down."

Driven by fear more than anything, he fumbled in his cloak for his sword, but before he could dislodge it from his belt, a sword pressed against his neck, and he froze.

William smiled triumphantly down at him. "Really, now! You need to be quicker than that, Prince Wells." At that moment, Danson groaned, and his attention left Xavier briefly to glance over at his brother.

Xavier took that briefest of moments to release an electro blast that sent LeMasters staggering backwards. Then, he quickly drew his sword and swung with all his might at the evil man, but LeMasters had regained his balance and parried his attack with a laugh.

"My, my, my! Well done, boy. Fight dirty! It doesn't matter how you win as long as you do! It's a shame I'll eventually have to kill you. You would have made a nice addition to my army," he taunted as he attacked and struck Xavier's blade to the side with his own sword.

Xavier backpedaled, trying to keep the attacking sword away from his body, but LeMasters barreled down on him and swung, narrowly missing his chest. He lashed out desperately, but the dark man blocked his attack lazily and countered with a complex move that jarred Xavier's weapon from his hand and knocked him to the floor. With a sadistic grin, LeMasters positioned his foot over his neck and applied enough pressure that he had to gasp for breath. Then, with brutal patience, LeMasters slowly impaled his hip with his sword. Xavier's screams only made his smile widen.

"That's it, Prince Wells, scream! Scream and call out to Daddy to save you," he goaded, twisting the sword lodged in his side.

Xavier screamed himself hoarse.

"That's a good boy." The evil man laughed. Then, after withdrawing his sword and foot, he barked, "Get to your feet!"

Xavier was close to passing out, and his attempt to sit up made the room spin and go dangerously dark.

"Come on, come on! Get up, boy!" William ordered impatiently. "Calhoun! Fine! Help the prince to his feet!"

Each boy grabbed an arm and hauled him, screaming, to his feet. He swayed and nearly collapsed, and Ken and

Daniel had to hold him upright.

William laughed darkly. "Take a good look, lads! *This* is the great light hope meant to save the world from the dark king! What a disgrace! How can *he* save all of mankind when he can't even save those closest to him? His mother? Dublin Minnows? That sweet little girl, what was her name? Maggie?"

Anger soared through his body, and he glared at the evil man in front of him. Adrenaline coursed through his veins, clearing his vision and deadening his pain. All he could see was William's sneering face.

"Did she know she was second best, Prince Wells? Did she know she wasn't as important to you as Dublin Minnows' daughter... that wildcat of a girl, Robbie! I can see it all in your head..." LeMasters paused and studied the boy. "She's to be your queen? My!" He laughed. "Like father, like son. The pair of you seem to like your females *feisty*. As I remember, Julia Wells was quite spirited too. I can see why Jeremiah went for her. Personally, I find those filthy *Neos* loathsome and unworthy of my time, but I made an exception for that wonderful morsel of a woman. Your mother was quite...feisty indeed."

His mother's name slipping so cheaply from William's mouth was Xavier's undoing, and he simply reacted. He summoned his sword to his hand, shrugged the other boys' hands off him, and lunged at LeMasters. The sudden attack caught him by surprise, and he was unable to lift his sword into an effective parry before Xavier's blade sliced into his free arm. William gave a gasp of shock before swatting the sword away from his body. However, Xavier's success was short-lived and precarious. He had only managed to enrage the man, and he felt a shiver of fear as LeMasters pinned him with murderous eyes.

"You will pay for that, boy," he snarled.

LeMasters lunged at him, swinging his weapon mightily. Xavier lifted his sword and struggled to block the violent blow. No sooner had steel clanged against steel than LeMasters swept into another attack. He barely managed to counter the attack, but LeMasters continued to bludgeon at his sword until it finally clattered to the floor. He froze as a sword pressed painfully against his chest, poised for the kill.

"You're lucky I need you alive," William LeMasters hissed. Then, he struck the boy on the temple with the hilt of his sword. Xavier was unconscious long before he hit the floor.

Chapter 28

Sacrifices

When Xavier woke up, he found himself stripped down to his boxers, and shackled to a stone wall in a damp, cold cell. A healer had obviously tended to the wound on his hip for a vivid pink scar now branded his skin. There was a barred window to his left, and he surmised that he was being held in one of the prison cells in the basement of the Governing Hall for he had a clear view of the palace and the horseshoe-shaped drive. As his eyes settled on the long, stained altar erected in the muddy median of the drive, a deathly cold chill raced down his spine. Oh, God! It truly existed! His father's horrific death wasn't just a dream. It was a vision! His father would come for him and when he did, LeMasters would be ready, and the King of Warwood would be captured and slaughtered.

He didn't have time to fret over the vision and the fate of his father for the door squealed open, and Danson with two armed guards stepped into the cell. Danson grinned fiendishly at the sight of Xavier chained to the wall.

"Well, well, well. You don't look so smug now! Do you, *boy*?" he hissed wickedly.

Xavier didn't answer. He simply glared at the man pacing like a predator teasing its prey.

"William has requested that you be...*broken*. Of course, I eagerly volunteered for the job. Do you recognize the metal your chains are made from, *boy*? Lead. You will not be able to summon your powers now!" Danson snarled vindictively as he moved within inches of Xavier. He nodded toward the sour-looking men behind him. "My companions are quite talented. They are hypno-illusionists. They can trap a man in a dream-like state indefinitely if they choose. They can also make him relive his worst memories, fears, and pain. If you try anything funny, I'll give them the order to alter your mind into madness." He sneered venomously as the boy glanced fearfully at the men behind him. "Now, brace yourself, boy. I can only hope that this will be painful."

When the force came, Xavier's entire body went rigid, and the chains binding his arms and legs snapped taut. As the electric pulsated through his body, his muscles quivered and strained. He clamped his eyes shut and waited for the pain to end.

After several long seconds, Danson paused in his torture to cackle down at him. "Damn, this is fun! Are you ready for some more?"

Not waiting for an answer, he delivered another long, agonizing electro force into Xavier's body as he taunted, "Go ahead, Prince Wells! Scream for me! William says that you screamed like a little girl for him. I want to hear it. Go on, boy. Scream!"

Humiliated and angry, Xavier knew he was moments away from giving Danson exactly what he wanted. The pain was intensely nauseating, and he bit his lip to keep from crying out. Again, Danson ended the force, and he went limp. If it weren't for the shackles pinning him upright, he would have collapsed to the floor. Every muscle in his body throbbed and refused to obey the simplest of commands. Xavier welcomed the darkness when it came, but Danson wouldn't allow it. His cool hands roughly grabbed his face and jerked his head until Xavier's eyes met his.

"Now, now, Prince Wells, don't pass out! How would it look if the Prince of Warwood, *the Chosen*, passed out after only two bouts of torture? Besides, I haven't heard you scream, yet," he hissed softly, spraying the stench from his sour breath into Xavier's face.

"You will... never...hear me...scream!" he choked out weakly.

"You don't think so?" Danson questioned, straightening and glaring down at him challengingly. "Let's see, shall we?"

Then, the real pain began, and Xavier did scream. He screamed louder than he ever thought possible.

When he awoke, it was nearly sunset, and the sky outside the window seemed to be on fire. Staring into nature's own light show had a calming effect on him, and he closed his eyes and thought of Robbie. He should have said goodbye. He'd probably never see or kiss her again. The memory of their first *real* kiss filled his mind, and he smiled. He wasn't sure which he enjoyed more, the kiss or her face afterwards. He took that back; he definitely enjoyed the kiss more!

The squealing cell door jolted him from his thoughts, and he opened his eyes as William LeMasters strolled into the room with two guards, Danson, and a tall, gangly teenage boy. In the months since their first meeting, Fox LeMasters had grown considerably and stood nearly as tall as his father.

"See here, Fox? He may be the Chosen, but he's no longer a threat. He's nothing more than a small child. He's nowhere near as powerful as you," William chided softly. "Now, go ahead, boy. Interrogate him." William nudged Fox toward Xavier.

Fox looked anxiously back at his father before facing Xavier with a smug expression. "Prince Wells, we want to know the exact location of your refuge. Tell us, and we'll spare you from a painful death." His voice had deepened an octave, and he sounded eerily like his father.

Xavier glared up at the older boy with more confidence than he felt. "Everyone in this room knows that's a lie!" he spat, his voice surprisingly strong considering the terror that was coursing through him. "I know your plans for me. I know just how you plan to kill me." He nodded toward the barred window. "I will be killed slowly, chopped bit by bit while everyone in this kingdom watches. I know this to be true because your weakling uncle is drooling and can't stop thinking about it. The moron is easier to read than a picture book!"

Silence filled the cell as the three LeMasters glared at him before William laughed. It wasn't a cruel or vindictive. It was an honest, throaty laugh.

"Brother, I believe young Wells just belittled your telepathic abilities," William snickered.

"Maybe we should nail a lead shackle into his skull," Danson hissed irritably, turning crimson at his brother's ridicule.

William turned toward Fox, the levity fading from his face as quickly as it had appeared. "He just insulted your uncle. Are you going to let a vile *Neo-mix* talk about your family like that, boy?"

The boy turned to Xavier and pointed menacingly at him. "Shut your mouth..."

"Fox, a Neo-mix doesn't understand words. He only understands actions. Now, punish the boy!" William growled impatiently.

Fox jutted out his hand and hit Xavier with a quick yet powerful force that lacerated his skin. He cried out with surprise.

William and Danson chuckled.

"Don't talk about my family again, or you'll get worse!" Fox spat. "Now, answer my question! Where is King Wells' refuge?"

"Forget it! I'm not saying a thing!" he insisted.

With a quick swipe of Fox's hand, the flesh across Xavier's abdomen sliced open. "Tell me!" the older boy screamed.

Panting and biting back the pain from the latest assault, Xavier met his eyes boldly and growled, "Haven't you been listening? I won't tell you a damn thing! You can torture me and threaten to kill me, but I will NEVER TELL YOU!"

Fox's face turned livid and in that moment, he greatly resembled his father. He charged at Xavier and punched him repeatedly until his arms felt like jelly and dropped to his sides. William and Danson simply watched, chuckling.

"Have you had your fill of brutality, son?" William asked as Fox stopped and backed away from Xavier, wheezing.

"Yes, sir. He's all yours," he snarled.

"Good. Danson, heal the boy's face enough so that his eyes don't swell shut. I want him to be able to see tonight's festivities," he remarked.

Danson healed the cuts around Xavier's eyes only and quickly moved away to allow his brother to approach the prince.

"Prince Wells? I'm a bit concerned. Your father hasn't turned up. I had expected him to appear almost immediately after your distressful screams, but..." He motioned around the room, to point out the absence of King Wells. "So I think it's safe to move on to my original purpose for you." As he spoke, William reached inside his cloak and withdrew the King's Key. "Endow me. Give me all the powers the key possesses."

"Never," he growled.

"I was afraid you'd say that, and I'm sure your father's assistant will be sorry to learn of your answer as well. Well, if that's your final answer, I have no choice but to do what I'm about to do," William responded indifferently. Then, to Xavier's surprise, they left the cell, leaving him alone.

It wasn't long before Xavier learned what William LeMasters had meant. Outside his window, a large group had gathered around the altar and burst into cheers when William stepped onto an elevated platform near the palace.

"Hello, my faithful followers!" his voice rang out above the shouts and applause. "I have great news. I've captured the Prince of Warwood, and it won't be long before I have King Wells himself! Our moment of glory and eternal dominion over the Earth is close at hand!"

There was a loud cheer from the crowd, and William looked around at them with a smile. "Yes, yes, it's all so very good, but the young prince needs proof that I'm the rightful ruler of this kingdom. So, today, we will have a sacrifice in Prince Wells' honor. Bring forth the traitor."

There was another loud applause as two soldiers shouldered their way through the crowd, escorting a tall, lean, older man. Milton! Milton walked proud and straight as he was led to the altar. His face was stoic and impassive and remained that way as the soldiers pushed him onto the altar and strapped him down. He wasn't going to allow these people the satisfaction of seeing the fear that was mounting inside him, but Xavier could feel the terror radiating off the older man.

"*No!*" Xavier thought desperately. "*No! Don't, please! Not Milton!*"

"*Then, endow me, Prince Wells, and I'll make his suffering short,*" William encouraged.

"*I...I can't! I won't!*"

"*So be it. You'll have his excruciatingly slow death on your hands.*"

William directed his attention back to the eagerly awaiting crowd and announced, "This man has been charged with treason! He willingly aided and supported Jeremiah Wells." There were loud hisses and boos. "Milton Bailey, if you publicly denounce Jeremiah Wells as your lord and commander and accept me as your king, I can make this punishment swift and painless."

To Milton's credit, he didn't flinch or hesitate in answering with a sturdy, stout voice. "Never! I'll never betray my king."

William didn't reply. He simply nodded to the hooded guard who stepped forward and withdrew an ax from his waistband. Milton's jaw clenched, and his breathing became laborious. The guard paused next to Milton as another guard held his right hand in place on the stone altar. Then, the hooded guard lifted the ax and chopped off Milton's thumb. Milton writhed wildly on the altar, but didn't utter a word.

"NO! No, please, stop!" Xavier screamed, but it was apparent that no one could hear his shouts except William, who seemed to be monitoring his thoughts.

"*It will all end quickly for Milton if you choose to endow me with the powers. If you refuse, then I will take Milton's life, one piece at a time,*" he jeered.

"*I...I can't!*" Xavier pleaded. "*Please...don't. Don't*

butcher him!"

"You know my deal. If you won't accept it, then Milton will simply have to endure his fate," he told him before announcing to the crowd, "Mr. Bailey, the thumb was a precursor of what's to come. I'll give you one more chance to save yourself but only one! Will you denounce Jeremiah Wells and take me as your king? Consider this carefully. If you choose not to recognize me as your rightful ruler, you will die slowly and painfully."

Surprisingly, Milton released a loud, bellowing laugh. The crowd stared down at the bound man as though he was insane. William shifted uneasily on the platform.

"I don't think you appreciate the position you're in," LeMasters spat, glaring down at Milton.

"Oh, I know exactly what my position is LeMasters, but you must think I'm an imbecile! You're not an honest man. You're not even a merciful man. I know I will die here today, and there is no way in hell I'd ever betray King Wells!"

"So be it," William snarled and nodded at the hooded man again.

"No! No!" Xavier screamed as the guard approached the altar and severed Milton's entire left hand.

Milton's control over his pain was lost. He simply screamed, and Xavier found himself screaming along with him.

"No! William...please...please!" Xavier sobbed.

The hooded guard approached Milton again and raised his ax. There was a solid thud as the ax sliced through Milton's arm at the shoulder. Milton's screams seemed to echo in Xavier's cell. The massacre continued until Milton was so badly dismembered, he was barely recognizable. Xavier had never heard anyone scream and sob the way Milton did as the guard took him apart, bit by bit.

"Milton? Milton, only you can end your suffering. Just say the words and the suffering will end," William cooed wickedly.

Then, Xavier heard Milton's weak voice. "Sire? Why? Why have you forsaken me?"

With tears streaming down his cheeks, Xavier's mind reached out to the morbidly injured man. *"Milton? Milton, don't be afraid. You're not alone."*

"Xavier? Dear God, what are you doing here?" Milton asked as renewed terror filled his thoughts.

"Don't worry about me, sir. I just...I wish I could help you somehow," he thought desperately.

Milton released a long, moaning sob. *"You can, Prince Wells. Don't let me betray your father. Please...the pain is too much...I'm afraid."*

"What do you want me to do?"

"Kill me, Master Wells. Please! I'm going to die, anyway. Let me die with honor!" Milton pleaded.

"I...can't...I...I don't think I can do that, Milton," he stammered.

"Please, Xavier. God, please," Milton begged.

"B...but...I don't know how."

"Just use your telekinesis to stop my heart," he instructed.

"Milton...I...I don't think I can do it," Xavier sobbed.

"Please, boy. I'm begging you! Don't let me suffer anymore."

Xavier sobbed, *'God, Milton. Okay...okay...I...I'll t...try."*

'Thank you, young sire! You are a compassionate and great prince. It was an honor and privilege to know and serve you. And, Xavier? Please, t...tell your father that he..." Milton's voice quavered as he forced himself to continue, *"that he is a better king than his father ever*

was, and I wouldn't have this any other way. Tell him...tell him that I've always thought of him as a son...tell him...I'm so very proud of him."

Xavier began sobbing, but he managed to reply. *"Yes, sir. I'll tell him."*

"All right, then, do your thing, Prince Wells. Farewell and Godspeed."

"B...bye, Milton," Xavier moaned and then set to work on trying to stop Milton's heart. It was easier to do than he thought it would be. He started by concentrating on Milton, picturing his face, his eyes. Within seconds, he could hear his raspy breath and slow, weak heartbeat. Not quite sure how to do it, he simply imagined Milton's heart stopping, and after a moment the soft thudding of his heartbeat ended.

Xavier opened his eyes and stared at the fiery, dusky sky. The crowd's bloodthirsty jeers faded as his mind sank into the thick numbness overwhelming all other thoughts and feelings. Then, he sighed deeply and sagged against his shackles as the ramifications of what he'd just done sank in and threatened to drown him in despair and guilt.

"NOOOOOO! No! NO! Nooo!" he screamed savagely as he violently thrashed against the shackles, tearing the skin around his wrists and ankles until he finally broke down into racking sobs. He had just killed someone! He'd murdered a living, breathing human being! He'd killed Milton! Xavier vomited.

Chapter 29

The Dark King

A few minutes later, William LeMasters slammed into the room, brutally grabbed Xavier by the neck, and squeezed.

"What did you do?" he spat.

"I eased his suffering!" Xavier gasped through the choke hold.

"That wasn't your place, boy! He chose his path, as did you!" William spat, slamming him against the wall.

His head hit the stone surface with a crack, and his vision dimmed. Then, William punched him, and his face exploded in pain. The sweet, salty taste of blood filled his mouth, and he gagged.

"How dare you defy me!" LeMasters yelled before turning to the guards. "Where's the key for his shackles? I want him unbound, now!"

"But, Master, his powers..."

"If I wanted your opinion on this, I would ask. Unbind him, NOW!"

The guards jumped into action, and Xavier's chains were loosened.

"Turn him around!" he growled, unbuckling his belt and pulling it from his waist.

The men spun him around and held the chains from

either end.

"I wonder if Jeremiah has ever whipped his precious son. Spare the rod, spoil the child was my father's motto," he hissed, wrapping the belt around his hand. "You, young sire, are about to get the whipping of your life."

Then, the beating began. With the first lash, Xavier felt a rib crack as the belt buckle snapped against his side. He endured lash after lash until LeMasters' anger subsided, and he stood panting behind him. Xavier slid to the floor with a whimper.

"Shackle him back up," he ordered roughly as he slid his belt back around his waist.

The guards complied immediately, and Xavier cried out from the sudden, rough movement. His back felt wet and sticky and burned like it was on fire. At least two ribs were broken, and he wondered if one had punctured a lung. He could hardly breathe!

Once the guards secured the locks on his chains, William LeMasters grabbed him by the throat and lifted him to meet his dark, dangerous eyes. "Now, listen closely, boy! I will be back tomorrow morning. If you chose to defy me again, if you will not endow me with powers, your loving governess will be next on the chopping block. Understand?" he thundered.

Xavier nodded weakly, and LeMasters released him and left the room.

Needless to say, Xavier didn't sleep that night. The stabbing pain he felt with each breath didn't subside during the night; it got worse. He quickly learned that taking small, shallow breaths hurt less. But, as a result of his shallow breathing and being shackled upright all night, his muscles began to seize and cramp. Near dawn, severe muscle spasms assaulted his body. They shook him with such force that he screamed in agony and wondered if the spasms were breaking what was left of the bones in his body.

It was during one of these spasms when William LeMasters returned. He grinned broadly as Xavier sobbed and cried from the rippling pain assaulting his body. Finally, the tremors ended, and he went limp, close to passing out.

"Oh, no you don't, Prince Wells! I need you conscious!" he growled, sending an electro force into Xavier and jolting him awake. He smirked at the exhausted boy. "So, tell me, *Prince Wells*. Have you reconsidered my offer, or do I need to *persuade* you?"

"I...I...I can't!" he moaned weakly.

"Well, maybe if I cut you, you'll come to your senses!" LeMasters whispered, pulling a hatchet from his waist. When the boy didn't respond, William grabbed his hand and separated his thumb from the rest of his fingers.

He began bawling long before the blade pressed against his skin. With the slightest pressure, the sharp edge sank deep into his thumb and lodged itself against the bone there. Xavier screamed.

William paused and looked at the prince, his eyes gleaming. "Well?"

Heaving and panting, he bit back the pain, looked defiantly up at William, and spat in his face. "Go to hell! I will never give you the power to kill millions of innocent people. Never!"

William gave a great shout of fury and thrust the hatchet completely through his thumb, and he shrieked out in agony.

"You little fool! You pompous, arrogant, little..." William paced manically around the cell for several long minutes. Finally, he stopped in front of Xavier and declared, "Your sweet governess will pay for your insolence, boy! She will die slowly while you watch."

Xavier groaned. He should have never come. What made him think he could stop William LeMasters? He might have been able to take on Danson, but William LeMasters was more powerful and definitely beyond Xavier's abilities. This was a suicide mission! No, worse than that, it was a suicide mission and a series of sacrifices! If he hadn't come, Milton would probably still be alive. If he hadn't come, Mrs. Sommers wouldn't be at risk now! Where was his father? Why hadn't he come? Surely, his father knew he was in danger...that William was torturing him...would kill him!

Xavier cried, "All right! All right! I'll do it! I'll do it...just...don't hurt Mrs. Sommers! Please...don't kill her!"

He froze and looked down at Xavier hungrily. "You'll empower me with ALL the powers?"

"Yes..." Xavier groaned. "But...you can't hurt Mrs. Sommers!"

"I promise you. I will not lay a finger on your precious Mrs. Sommers," he told him eagerly as he motioned to the guards to free Xavier from his binds and withdrew the King's Key from beneath his cloak.

Free of his chains, Xavier simply collapsed to the stone floor. The impact jarred his battered body, and he cried out.

"Help the boy to his feet!" LeMasters barked.

The guards grabbed him and hauled him painfully to his feet.

William moved toward him, carrying the key in his hands as though he thought it might break if he handled it too roughly. "All right, boy. Do it. Do it now!" he hissed excitedly.

With a feeling of dread, Xavier reached out to take the

key from LeMasters but dropped it.

"Come on, come on! Pick it up. Do it, boy! Do it!" William growled impatiently.

He quickly picked up the King's Key with his uninjured hand, praying desperately for a way out of this mess. Then he had an idea, and his courage returned. He straightened and met William LeMasters' eyes boldly.

"Father! Father! King Wells and his men are here! They already have control of the kingdom, and they're breaking through the palace gates! What should I tell the men?" Fox bellowed after he burst into the cell.

"Tell them to fight, for God's sake! In a few minutes it won't matter if Jeremiah's here or not!" William spat and turned back to Xavier. "Now, boy! Do it now!"

He hesitated. Even if he didn't do what he was about to do, there was no way he could stall long enough for his father to save him. He had to go through with it. Finally, he whispered, "Okay. I...I need to...touch you for this to work...I think."

William hurried toward him and took his hand.

"No, I think you should kneel," he suggested. At LeMasters' livid face, he explained quickly, "The powers will transfer more completely if I have contact with your head." He wasn't sure how he knew this to be true, but he was certain without a doubt that it was the best way to give or, as in this case, take powers from an empowered person.

William studied him, and Xavier fought to keep his thoughts innocent. Doubt and greed for power battled across LeMasters' hard features. Finally, greed won out, and he turned to the guards standing silently behind him. "If he tries anything funny, kill him."

"Yes, sire. It would be an absolute pleasure," one guard answered with a wicked grin.

William gave a hesitant, almost fearful look at Xavier before slowly kneeling at his feet.

Xavier tentatively placed his hand on the man's black crown. Then he closed his eyes and concentrated, not on providing powers but on eliminating them. The key suddenly went hot in his grasp as he summoned its power. He heard William gasp and give a long, low moan of pain. Then, the guards shouted as they became aware that something was wrong.

"Hey! Hey, boy! Stop!" one guard yelled from behind him.

The guards grabbed him and tried to yank him away from William LeMasters. But, the instant their hands clamped around his arms, a powerful electro force rose in his body and propelled the men across the room, slamming them into the stone wall. They were unconscious before they hit the floor.

"Father!" a voice screamed.

Xavier's eyes snapped open. Fox stood tensely inside the doorway with wide, fearful eyes. He raced to William, who had grown extremely pale and frail-looking. The moment Fox grabbed his father Xavier felt a strange jerk in the key's power. Both boys were knocked off their feet as a surge of energy exploded from the key, and the connection between Xavier and William LeMasters was lost.

This was the final assault Xavier's body could bear, and he lay motionless on the cold stone floor, looking at William crumpled a few feet from him, staring blankly at the ceiling.

"Father? Father?" Fox cried, crawling to him and shaking him. He looked at Xavier with tear-soaked cheeks, his dark eyes full of animosity. "What did you do to him?"

"I did what I had to do in order to stop him...I took his

powers! He's no longer empowered. He's no longer a threat to anyone!" he replied hoarsely.

"You *killed* him!" the boy screamed.

"N...no, I took his powers!" he insisted weakly.

"You idiot! Don't you know anything about the King's Key? If you take a man's powers that quickly, all at once...you can kill him!" he spat.

No, he hadn't known that. "W...well, he deserves it! He killed my mom, my best friend's dad, my dad's assistant, and he would have killed me if he had the chance. I just beat him to the punch. That's all!" Xavier blurted callously.

"Fox? Oh, my God! William!" Veronica Angelo cried, scurrying into the room and dropping to the floor next to William. "What happened?" she asked Fox.

"*He* took his powers, Mother. He drained Father of his life force," he muttered, nodding to Xavier.

"What?" she screeched. "NO! Oh, William! William! Oh, God!" Then, she collapsed, sobbing over William's body. Her gaze shot up at Xavier. "Look what you've done! Look what you've done, you little heathen!" Then, she turned to Fox. "What are you going to do about this, Fox? This ingrate murdered your father! Are you just going to allow him to get away with it?"

He looked at his mother with sudden anxiety.

"Fox!" she screeched. "Don't be a coward! Your father would be ashamed of you! Now, get up and take care of it like a LeMasters!" She pushed Fox to his feet.

He met Xavier's eyes, animosity building in their dark depths. A strange shudder ran down Xavier, and suddenly, he knew that his enemy had never been William LeMasters. His true enemy...the dark king... was standing in front of him now, and he was going to kill him.

As Fox drew his sword, Xavier fought to get to his feet,

but the lack of sleep and the severity of his injuries had dwindled his strength and powers. He wasn't sure he could even stand, let alone conjure an electro force to protect himself. He stood on wobbly legs as Fox swung his sword. Xavier did his best to dodge the attack, but he just wasn't agile enough. The sword raked across his body, and warmth immediately spread over his chest as his shirt became saturated with blood. He staggered and fell to the floor. Quickly, Fox advanced on him again and swung his sword, this time nicking his cheek.

"Fox! Stop playing around and finish him!" Dr. Angelo shouted.

Suddenly, there was a loud crash, and the entire building shook.

"William, Veronica, we need to go! The Royal Guard is inside..." Danson yelled, rushing through the door, but his words choked at the sight of his dead brother. A resounding concussion shook the building and jerked Danson back into action. "We must leave. Now! King Wells is coming this way!"

Fox lowered his sword and after one last vengeful glare at Xavier, he turned and followed his mother and uncle out of the cell.

Xavier collapsed.

Chapter 30

Reconstruction

When Xavier awoke, he was greeted by bright sunlight pouring through a window in what appeared to be a hospital room. His entire body felt like one giant bruise, but at least he could breathe without pain. He examined his wounds and found pale pink scars had replaced the open wounds. His left hand was wrapped in an ace bandage, and his thumb had been reattached.

"How do you feel?" a voice called softly.

His head whipped toward the door and found his father leaning on the doorframe. "Dad!" he gasped as relief and despair flooded over him.

Jeremiah was at his side in an instant, pulling him gently into his arms. The movement twinged a bit, but the warmth and safety he felt in his father's embrace soothed him in every way: physically, mentally, and emotionally. He wrapped his arms around his father and held on tightly, never wanting to let go.

"Xavier, dear God, don't ever do that to me again," his father mumbled, his voice faltering. "God, boy! When I found you in that cell, covered in blood, and d...dead still..." He couldn't continue.

After a moment, father and son separated, and Xavier suddenly found that he couldn't look at his father. He had failed! He had come to Warwood to prevent the war between the dark and the light, but he had only managed to ensure its inevitability. He had seen Fox grow from a timid kid reluctantly following his father's commands into the beginnings of the evil, dark king who could someday destroy the world. However, he couldn't tell his father this...at least, not yet.

"Son? Are you okay?" Jeremiah asked, lifting Xavier's chin so he had no choice but to meet his intense gray eyes.

"N...no!" Xavier cried, hugging him. "I'm not okay. Dad, I...I killed Milton. He's dead because of me!"

"Xavier, Milton's death was not your fault!" he reassured him.

"Yes, it was, Dad!" Xavier insisted, pulling away from his father and meeting his gaze with watery, fierce eyes. "It was! William tortured him because I wouldn't do what he wanted!"

"Xavier..."

"No, Dad, listen to me! He butchered Milton alive! He chopped him up! Milton was afraid he'd betray you! He...he begged me to...he...he asked me...I...I killed him! I stopped his heart and killed him!"

Jeremiah looked down at him, shocked. Finally, he pulled the boy close and kissed him. "Oh, God. Oh, son, I'm so, so sorry you were put in that position...that you had to do that. But, Xavier...what you did was extremely brave! Milton was dying and there was no way you could have prevented that. Stopping his agony and suffering took enormous courage. It was the right thing to do, son."

Crying, Xavier spluttered out between sobs, "He...he wanted me to tell you...that...he...he was proud of you. He...he wanted...me to tell you...that ...you are a better king...than your dad ever was."

His father's face crumpled at these words, and his eyes

filled with tears. "He said that?" he whispered.

Xavier nodded. "Yeah, he said he always thought of you as a son and he was proud of how you turned out."

Jeremiah was speechless. He simply held his son tightly and cried.

Xavier slept a lot the next few days, nearly missing a visit from Lana. His father was sprawled out on a lounge chair next to the bed watching a news program on TV when the door opened. Lana entered with a wide smile, carrying a small present and balloons. As her eyes trailed from the sleeping boy to the man next to him, her smile wavered.

Jeremiah jumped to his feet at the sight of her. "Lana?"

Her name pulled Xavier from his light slumber, but he remained motionless and listened.

"Thanks for coming..."

"I didn't come for you! I came to see Xavier!" Lana hissed coldly.

"I understand," Jeremiah muttered. "I don't blame you for hating me...but you can see now why I did what I did."

Xavier opened his eyes and looked at Lana. She stood rigidly at the foot of his bed, glaring contemptuously at his father.

"Is that your idea of an apology, *sire*?" she spat. When the king didn't answer, she set the package on the bedside cart with a huff and added, "Tell Xavier I'm sorry I couldn't stay."

Then, she stormed from the room, leaving a befuddled, speechless king.

It was several days before Xavier was able to leave the infirmary. His wounds were all nearly healed, but his ribs were still tender and the healers said it would be weeks before he regained the use of his thumb. When he finally left the hospital, he was amazed at how different Warwood looked in just two weeks.

"The palace...the kingdom looks almost as good as new!" Xavier muttered as they exited the infirmary.

"Well, the palace grounds are in order, but the residential area isn't. Much of Wellington is still in shambles actually. We're still getting our citizens back from King's Mountain, and once we have a larger number of telekentic citizens, we'll be able to get everything back to normal more quickly," Jeremiah explained, taking his hand and leading him across the horseshoe-shaped drive and flowering gardens. The sacrificing altar was gone.

"How...how did the flowers grow here so quickly? It was nothing more than a mud pit before."

Jeremiah snickered. "Son, we are an empowered society. Our gardeners have the ability to accelerate the growth cycle of plants."

He nodded and examined his bandaged left hand. He couldn't move his thumb more than a wiggle, and it felt a bit numb.

"How's the thumb?" Jeremiah asked.

"Numb," Xavier replied, dropping his hand to his side again. "Dad? What happened to the child-soldiers at the academy?"

"Well, many of them fled the kingdom when the Royal Guard invaded. However, about twenty or thirty remained behind."

"What's going to happen to them?" he asked.

"Well, son, that's a difficult question. Some of those children killed members of my guard during the invasion. They must be punished," his father responded solemnly.

"But, Dad, they were forced to! They were prisoners themselves! If they didn't follow orders, they were beaten or worse! It's not their fault!" he pleaded.

"Xavier, I know this may sound harsh, but no one can be forced into doing anything. Ultimately it's a decision. Sometimes it's a very difficult decision, but it's still a decision," he noted evenly.

Xavier's shoulders slumped. "So, what will happen to them?"

"That will be decided on an individual basis. We will hold trials for each child. Their crime, if any, will be determined and then, I will determine the appropriate punishment," he answered.

"When do the trials start?"

"Next week," his father answered.

Xavier nodded as they entered the palace and continued in silence down the long corridor and up the grand staircase. Ephraim was on duty outside the entrance to the royal residence and grinned at the sight of him.

"Hello, Xavier! You look a lot better than you did a couple of weeks ago. How are you feeling?" he asked.

"Better, sir. Where's Court? I haven't seen him since we regained Warwood," Xavier asked.

"Well, he's been very busy running errands and transporting goods from supply areas to areas still being rebuilt. Until the kingdom is rebuilt, I'm afraid no one will have much free time. But I'll try to get him to stop by and say hello in the next day or two," Ephraim told him.

He nodded, trying not to feel disappointed.

"Come on, son. Mrs. Sommers is anxious to dote over you. Let's get inside and settle in for the evening," his father ordered gently, placing a hand on his shoulder and directing him into the residence.

As soon as the door opened and Xavier stepped over the threshold, a loud collection of voices yelled, "Happy

Birthday!"

He froze on the spot and looked around at the sea of smiling faces, the balloons and streamers, and the long banner sprawled across the windows that read, "Happy 13th birthday, Xavier!"

"I know it's a bit late, son, but you were still unconscious on your birthday," his father commented after seeing the stunned look on the boy's face.

Xavier looked up at him. "It's not that...I...just...I forgot all about my birthday!"

The king laughed and clapped him on the back.

"Xavier!" Robbie called, fighting through the crowd to reach him.

"Robbie!" He gasped, hurrying to meet her.

"Oh, Xavier!" she cried out again, throwing her arms around him and kissing him fully on the lips.

Xavier savored the kiss, even though the people around them were beginning to snicker. Finally, she pulled away, tears running down her cheeks.

"Why, Xavier? Why did you run away? Why did you leave without telling me? You could've been killed...you *were* nearly killed...you...you...jerk!" she cried.

"I'm sorry, Rob. I'm really sorry...I just thought...I didn't want anyone else to die because of me. I wanted to end it. I thought I could end it all. I'm sorry," he muttered.

"But, X! You did end it! William LeMasters is dead!" Beck told him with an enormous grin.

He hesitated, and his eyes darted to his father, who was watching him closely. Finally, he grinned and answered lightly, "Yeah. I guess so."

There was a loud cheer to this news, and Xavier found himself being knocked around by congratulatory pats and thumps.

It was probably the best birthday he had ever had. His

father had gone all out! There was an enormous seven-tiered cake, a small pile of presents, music, dancing, and pizza! It had been months since Xavier had a pizza. It was heavenly! The majority of his presents replaced his damaged and missing toys and games. He received a new game system, a laptop, radio-controlled car, a new stereo, and all kinds of rugby equipment including a new leather ball from Garrett and a Wales jersey from Courtney.

"Xavier?" Robbie whispered. "I...I'd like to give you my gift in private."

"In *private*, eh? You're a lucky man, Xavier!" Mac snickered.

The rest of the boys began chirping, "Robbie and Xavier sitting in a tree, K. I. S. S. I. N. G..."

"Oh, really!" she hissed at the boys, blushing deeply at the attention she and Xavier were getting from the adults around them. "You guys are such idiots!"

The boys burst out laughing as Robbie grabbed Xavier by the arm and pulled him through the mass of people toward the library. The boys' catcalls and hoots were finally muffled when she pulled him into the library and closed the door behind them.

"I...I didn't want you opening it in front of everybody. It's kind of personal...and a bit embarrassing...oh, here! Just open it!" she rambled as she thrust a small package at him.

Xavier peeled away the paper and opened the small cardboard box. He lifted a Celtic medallion, about the size of a half dollar, by its leather-braided cord from the box. On one side of the gold medallion a tree branched out in every direction, and at the base of the tree was a ruby carved into the shape of an apple. Encircling the image were the words, "Tugaim mo chroí' duit go deo." Then, on the opposite side, there was a pentacle entangled with a

Celtic love knot.

"Wow! It's fantastic, Robbie! Where did you get it?" he whispered.

Her blush deepened. "It's been in my family for years and years."

"Really? Well, are you sure you want to give it to me? Shouldn't you keep it and give it to your kids someday?" he asked.

"I'm very sure, Xavier. Please accept it. It will protect you and bring you luck," she told him.

"What do the words around the edge of the coin mean?" he asked.

Again, Robbie's face deepened in color. "Ah, it says, 'I give my heart to you, forever'."

Xavier stared at her as he realized exactly what she was giving him. Finally, he straightened, and pulled the necklace over his head. "Thanks, Robbie. It's the best present I've ever gotten," he whispered and kissed her.

At that moment, his father opened the library door.

"All right, you two, that's enough of that. It's time to get back to the party. People are starting to ask where the guest of honor went off to," he told them with a chuckle.

"Yes, sir," Xavier responded with a broad grin.

He led Robbie back to the party where most of the guests had ventured into the ballroom to dance. As they joined the rest of the guests, Xavier tried desperately to forget that he hadn't avoided anything in killing William LeMasters. The Dark King would still rise. He would rise and seek vengeance. He hadn't stopped the War of Kings. His father would still sacrifice his life to save him. He would still die, and for the life of him, Xavier didn't know how to stop it.

The Prince of Warwood
and

The Rise of
the Chosen

Coming 2014!

www.ingramcontent.com/pod-product-compliance
Lightning Source LLC
Chambersburg PA
CBHW061553170626
46811CB00001B/192